3·95

CW00524936

The Day We
Got Drunk on Cake

and Other Stories

WILLIAM TREVOR

THE BODLEY HEAD
LONDON SYDNEY
TORONTO

ACKNOWLEDGMENTS

'The Table' and 'The Day We Got Drunk on
Cake' first appeared in *Town*, 'The General's
Day' in the *London Magazine*, 'In at the Birth',
'A Meeting in Middle Age' and 'The Hotel of the
Idle Moon' in the *Transatlantic Review*, 'A
School Story' in the *Listener* and 'The Intro-
spections of J.P. Powers' in *Voices 2*, published
by Michael Joseph.

ISBN 0 370 00623 2
© William Trevor 1967
Printed in Great Britain for
The Bodley Head Ltd
9 Bow Street, London WC2E 7AL
by Redwood Burn Limited
Trowbridge and Esher
Set in Linotype Plantin
First published 1967
Second impression 1980

CONTENTS

I

The Table

IN A PUBLIC library, looking through the appropriate columns in a businesslike way, Mr Jeffs came across the Hammonds' advertisement in *The Times*. It contained a telephone number which he noted down on a scrap of paper and which he telephoned later that same day.

'Yes,' said Mrs Hammond vaguely, 'I think this table is still for sale. Let me just go and look.'

Mr Jeffs saw her in his mind's eye going to look. He visualised a fattish, middle-aged woman with light-blue hair, and shapely legs coming out of narrow shoes.

'It is my husband's affair, really,' explained Mrs Hammond. 'Or I suppose it is. Although strictly speaking the table is my property. Left to me by my grandmother. Yes, it's still there. No one, I'm sure, has yet made an offer for this table.'

'In that case—' said Mr Jeffs.

'It was foolish of me to imagine that my husband might have had an offer, or that he might have sold it. He would naturally not have done so without consultation between us. It being my table, really. Although he worded the advertisement and saw to putting it in the paper. I have a daughter at the toddling stage, Mr Jeffs. I'm often too exhausted to think about the composition of advertisements.'

'A little daughter. Well, that is nice,' said Mr Jeffs, looking at the ceiling and not smiling. 'You're kept busy, eh?'

'Why not come round if the table interests? It's completely genuine and is often commented upon.'

'I will do that,' announced Mr Jeffs, naming an hour.

Replacing the receiver, Mr Jeffs, a small man, a dealer in furniture, considered the voice of Mrs Hammond. He won-

dered if the voice belonged to a woman who knew her p's
and q's where antique furniture was concerned. He had
been wrong, quite clearly, to have seen her as middle-aged
and plumpish. She was younger if she had a toddling child,
and because she had spoken of exhaustion he visualised her
again, this time in soft slippers, with a strand of hair across
her forehead. 'It's a cultured voice,' said Mr Jeffs to himself,
and went on to believe that there was money in the Hammond house, and probably a maid or two, in spite of the
protest about exhaustion. Mr Jeffs, who had made his small
fortune through his attention to such nagging details, walked
on the bare boards of his Victorian house, sniffing the air
and considering afresh. All about him furniture was stacked,
just purchased, waiting to be sold again.

Mrs Hammond forgot about Mr Jeffs almost as soon as
his voice ceased to echo in her consciousness. Nothing about
Mr Jeffs remained with her because as she had conversed
with him no image had formed in her mind, as one had in
his. She thought of Mr Jeffs as a shop person, as a voice
that might interrupt a grocery order or a voice in the
jewellery department of Liberty's. When her *au pair* girl announced the presence of Mr Jeffs at the appointed hour,
Mrs Hammond frowned and said: 'My dear Ursula, you've
certainly got this name wrong.' But the girl insisted. She
stood with firmness in front of her mistress repeating that a
Mr Jeffs had called by appointment. 'Heavens!' cried Mrs
Hammond eventually. 'How extraordinarily stupid of me!
This is the new man for the windows. Tell him to go at them
immediately. The kitchen ones first so that he gets them over
with while he's still mellow. They're as black as your
boot.'

So it was that Mr Jeffs was led into the Hammonds' kitchen by a girl from central Switzerland and told abruptly,
though not intentionally so, to clean the windows.

'What?' said Mr Jeffs.

'Start with the kitchen, Mrs Hammond says, since they
have most filth on them. There is hot water in the tap.'

'No,' said Mr Jeffs. 'I've come to see a table.'

'I myself have scrubbed the table. You may stand on it if you place a newspaper underneath your feet.'

Ursula left Mr Jeffs at this juncture, although he had already begun to speak again. She felt she could not stand there talking to window-cleaners, since she was not employed in the house to do that.

'He is a funny man,' she reported to Mrs Hammond. 'He wanted to wash the table too.'

'My name is Jeffs,' said Mr Jeffs, standing at the door, holding his stiff black hat. 'I have come about the console table.'

'How odd!' murmured Mrs Hammond, and was about to add that here indeed was a coincidence since at that very moment a man called Jeffs was cleaning her kitchen windows. 'Oh my God!' she cried instead. 'Oh, Mr Jeffs, what a terrible thing!'

It was this confusion, this silly error that Mrs Hammond quite admitted was all her fault, that persuaded her to let Mr Jeffs have the table. Mr Jeffs, standing with his hat, had recognised a certain psychological advantage and had pressed it imperceptibly home. He saw that Mrs Hammond, beneath the exterior of her manner, was concerned lest he might have felt himself slighted. She is a nice woman, he thought, in the way in which a person buying meat decides that a piece is succulent. She is a nice person, he assured himself, and will therefore be the easier and the quicker to deal with. He was correct in his surmise. There was a prick of guilt in Mrs Hammond's face: he saw it arrive there as the explanation dawned on her and as she registered that he was a dealer in antiques, one with the features and the accents of a London Jew. She is afraid I am thinking her anti-Semitic, thought Mr Jeffs, well pleased with himself. He named a low price which was immediately accepted.

'I've been clever,' said Mrs Hammond to her husband. 'I have sold the console table to a little man called Mr Jeffs whom Ursula and I at first mistook for a window-cleaner.'

Mr Jeffs put a chalk mark on the table and made a note of it in a notebook. He sat in the kitchen of his large house, eating kippers that he had cooked in a plastic bag. His jaws moved slowly and slightly, pulping the fish as a machine might. He didn't pay much attention to the taste in his mouth: he was thinking that if he sold the table to Sir Andrew Charles he could probably rely on a hundred per cent profit, or even more.

'An everyday story of country folk,' said a voice on Mr Jeffs' old wireless, and Mr Jeffs rose and carried the plate from which he had eaten to the sink. He wiped his hands on a tea-cloth and climbed the stairs to the telephone.

Sir Andrew was in Africa, a woman said, and might not be back for a month. It was far from certain when he would return, but it would be a month at least. Mr Jeffs said nothing more. He nodded to himself, but the woman in Sir Andrew Charles' house, unaware of this confirmation, reflected that the man was ill-mannered not to acknowledge what she was saying.

Mr Jeffs made a further note in his notebook, a reminder to telephone Sir Andrew in six weeks' time. As it happened, however, this note was unnecessary, because three days later Mr Jeffs received a telephone call from Mrs Hammond's husband, who asked him if he still had the table. Mr Jeffs made a pretence of looking, and replied after a moment that he rather thought he had.

'In that case,' said Mrs Hammond's husband, 'I rather think I would like to buy it back.'

Mr Hammond announced his intention of coming round. He contradicted himself by saying that it was really a friend of his who wanted the table and that he would bring his friend round too, if that was all right with Mr Jeffs.

'Bring whomsoever you wish,' said Mr Jeffs. He felt awkward in advance: he would have to say to Mr Hammond or to Mr Hammond's friend that the price of the table had doubled itself in three days. He could not put it like that, but Mr Hammond would recognise that that was what it amounted to.

Mr Jeffs was in the kitchen, drinking tea, when they called. He blew at the mug of tea, not wishing to leave it there, for he disapproved of waste. He drank most of it and wiped his lips with the tea-cloth. The door-bell sounded again and Mr Jeffs hastened to answer it.

'I am the nigger in the woodpile,' said a Mrs Youghal who was standing with Hammond. 'It is I who cause all this nonsense over a table.'

'Mrs Youghal hasn't ever seen it,' Hammond explained. 'She, too, answered our advertisement, but you, alas, had snaffled the treasure up.'

'Come into the house,' said Mr Jeffs, leading the way to the room with the table in it. He turned to Mrs Youghal, pointing with one hand. 'There it is, Mrs Youghal. You are quite at liberty to purchase it, though I had earmarked it for another, a client in Africa who has been looking for that very thing and who would pay an exceedingly handsome price. I am just warning you of that. It seems only fair.'

But when Mr Jeffs named the figure he had in mind neither Mrs Youghal nor Hammond turned a hair. Hammond drew out a cheque-book and at once inscribed a cheque. 'Can you deliver it?' he asked.

'Oh yes,' said Mr Jeffs, 'provided it is not too far away. There will be a small delivery charge to cover everything, insurance in transit, et cetera. Four pounds four.'

Mr Jeffs drove his Austin van to the address that Hammond had given him. On the way, he reckoned what his profit on this journey would be: a quarter of a gallon of petrol would come to one and three; subtracting that from four guineas, he was left with four pounds two and ninepence. Mr Jeffs did not count his time: he considered it of little value. He would have spent three-quarters of an hour standing about in his large house, or moving himself to keep his circulation going. It was not a bad profit, he decided, and he began to think of Mrs Youghal and Hammond, and of Mrs Hammond who had mistaken him for a window-cleaner. He guessed that Hammond and Mrs Youghal were up to something, but it was a funny way in which to be up to something, buying antique tables and having them delivered.

'They are conducting an affair,' said Mr Jeffs to himself. 'They met because the table was up for sale and are now romantic over it.' He saw the scene clearly: the beautiful Mrs Youghal arriving at the Hammonds' house, explaining that she had come about the table. Perhaps she had made a bit of a scene, reminding the Hammonds that she had previously telephoned and had been told to come. 'And now I find the table is already disposed of,' said Mrs Youghal in Mr Jeff's imagination. 'You should have telephoned me back, for God's sake. I am a busy creature.'

'Come straight in, Mrs Youghal, and have a glass of brandy,' cried Hammond in Mr Jeffs' mind. 'How can we make amends?'

'It is all my fault,' explained Mrs Hammond. 'I've been quite hopelessly scatty, placing our beautiful table in the hands of a Jewish trader. A Mr Jeffs whom Ursula in her foreign ignorance ordered to wash down the kitchen windows.'

'The table has brought nothing but embarrassment,' said Hammond, pouring out a fair quantity of brandy. 'Have this, Mrs Youghal. And have a nut or two. Do.'

'I had quite set my heart on that table,' said Mrs Youghal in Mr Jeffs' mind. 'I am disappointed unto tears.'

'A table for Mrs Youghal,' said Mr Jeffs to a woman with a shopping basket who was leaving the blocks of flats.

'Oh yes?' said the woman.

'Which floor, please? I have been given this address.'

'No one of that name at all,' said the woman. 'I never heard of no Youghal.'

'She may be new here. Is there an empty flat? It tells you nothing on these bells.'

'I'm not at liberty,' said the woman, her voice striking a high pitch. 'I'm not at liberty to give out information about the tenants in these flats. Not to a man in a closed van. I don't know you from Adam.'

Mr Jeffs recognised the woman as a charwoman and thereafter ignored her, although she stood on the steps, close to him, watching his movements. He rang one of the bells and a middle-aged woman opened the door and said, when Mr Jeffs had inquired, that everyone was new in the flats, the flats themselves being new. She advised him quite pleasantly to ring the top bell, the one that connected apparently with two small attic rooms.

'Ah, Mr Jeffs,' said the beautiful Mrs Youghal a moment later. 'So you got here.'

Mr Jeffs unloaded the table from the van and carried it up the steps. The charwoman was still about. She was saying to Mrs Youghal that she would clean out the place for six shillings an hour whenever it was suitable or desired.

Mr Jeffs placed the table in the smaller of the two attic rooms. The room was empty except for some rolled-up carpeting and a standard lamp. The door of the second room was closed: he imagined it contained a bed and a wardrobe and two brandy glasses on a bedside table. In time, Mr Jeffs imagined, the whole place would be extremely luxurious. 'A love-nest,' he said to himself.

'Well, thank you, Mr Jeffs,' said Mrs Youghal.

'I must charge you an extra pound. You are probably unaware, Mrs Youghal, that it is obligatory and according to the antique dealers' association to charge one pound when goods have to be moved up a staircase. I could be struck off if I did not make this small charge.'

'A pound? I thought Mr Hammond had—'

'It is to do with the stairs. I must honour the rules of the antique dealers' association. For myself, I would easily waive it, but I have, you understand, my biennial returns to make.'

Mrs Youghal found her handbag and handed him a five-pound note. He gave her back three pounds and sixteen shillings, all the change he claimed to have.

'Imagine it!' exclaimed Mrs Youghal. 'I thought that cleaning woman must be your wife come to help you carry the thing. I couldn't understand why she was suddenly talking about six shillings an hour. She's just what I'm looking for.'

Mr Jeffs thought that it was rather like Mrs Hammond's *au pair* girl making the mistake about the window-cleaner. He thought that but he did not say it. He imagined Mrs Youghal recounting the details of the episode at some later hour, recounting them to Hammond as they lay in the other room, smoking cigarettes or involved with one another's flesh. 'I thought she was the little Jew's wife. I thought it was a family business, the way these people often have. I was surprised beyond measure when she mentioned about cleaning.'

Naturally enough, Mr Jeffs thought that he had seen the end of the matter. A Louis Seize console table, once the property of Mrs Hammond's grandmother, was now the property of her husband's mistress, or the joint property of husband and mistress, Mr Jeffs was not sure. It was all quite interesting, Mr Jeffs supposed, but he had other matters to concern him : he had further furniture to accumulate and to sell at the right moment; he had a living to make, he assured himself.

But a day or two after the day on which he had delivered the table to Mrs Youghal he received a telephone call from Mrs Hammond.

'Am I speaking to Mr Jeffs?' said Mrs Hammond.

'Yes, this is he. Jeffs here.'

'This is Mrs Hammond. I wonder if you remember, I sold you a table.'

'I remember you perfectly, Mrs Hammond. We were amused at an error.' Mr Jeffs made a noise that he trusted would sound like laughter. He was looking at the ceiling, without smiling.

'The thing is,' said Mrs Hammond, 'are you by any chance still in possession of that table? Because if you are I think perhaps I had better come round and see you.'

There rushed into Mr Jeffs' mind the vision of further attic rooms, of Mrs Hammond furnishing them with the table and anything else she could lay her hands on. He saw

Mrs Hammond walking down a street, looking at beds and carpets in shop windows, her elbow grasped by a man who was not her husband.

'Hullo, Mr Jeffs,' said Mrs Hammond. 'Are you there?'

'Yes, I am here,' said Mr Jeffs. 'I am standing here listening to you, madam.'

'Well?' said Mrs Hammond.

'I'm sorry to disappoint you about the table.'

'You mean it's sold? Already?'

'I'm afraid that is the case.'

'Oh God in heaven!'

'I have other tables here. In excellent condition and keenly priced. You might not find a visit here a waste of time.'

'No, no.'

'I do not as a rule conduct my business in that way: customers coming into my house and that. But in your case, since we are known to one another—'

'It wouldn't do. I mean, it's only the table I sold you I am possibly interested in. Mr Jeffs, can you quickly give me the name and address of the person who bought it?'

This question caught Mr Jeffs off his guard, so he at once replaced the telephone receiver. Mrs Hammond came through again a moment or so later, after he had had time to think. He said:

'We were cut off, Mrs Hammond. There is something the matter with the line. Sir Andrew Charles was twice cut off this morning, phoning from Nigeria. I do apologise.'

'I was saying, Mr Jeffs, that I would like to have the name and address of the person who bought the table.'

'I cannot divulge that, Mrs Hammond. I'm afraid divulgences of that nature are very much against the rules of the antique dealers' association. I could be struck off for such a misdemeanour.

'Oh dear. Oh dear, Mr Jeffs. Then what am I to do? Whatever is the answer?'

'Is this important? There are ways and means. I could, for instance, act as your agent. I could approach the owner of the table in that guise and attempt to do my best.'

'Would you, Mr Jeffs? That is most kind.'

'I would have to charge the customary agent's fee. I am sorry about that, Mrs Hammond, but the association does not permit otherwise.'

'Yes, yes, of course.'

'Shall I tell you about that fee, how it's worked out and what it may amount to? It's not much, a percentage.'

'We can fix that up afterwards.'

'Well, fine,' said Mr Jeffs, who meant when he spoke of a percentage thirty-three and a third.

'Please go up to twice the price you paid me. If it seems to be going higher I'd be grateful if you'd telephone for instructions.'

'That's the usual thing, Mrs Hammond.'

'But do please try and keep the price down. Naturally.'

'I'll be in touch, Mrs Hammond.'

Walking about his house, shaking his body to keep his circulation in trim, Mr Jeffs wondered if tables nowadays had a part to play in lovers' fantasies. It was in his interest to find out, he decided, since he could accumulate tables of the correct kind and advertise them astutely. He thought for a while longer and then entered his van. He drove it to Mrs Youghal's attic room, taking a chance on finding her there.

'Why, Mr Jeffs,' said Mrs Youghal.

'Yes,' said Mr Jeffs.

She led him upstairs, trailing her curiosity behind her. She is thinking, he thought, that I have come to sell her another thing or two, but she does not care to order me out in case she is wrong, in case I have come to blackmail her.

'Well, Mr Jeffs, what can I do for you?'

'I have had a handsome offer for the Louis Seize table. Or a fairly handsome offer. Or an offer that might be turned into an exceedingly handsome offer. Do you take my meaning?'

'But the table is mine. Are you telling me you wish to buy it back?'

'I am saying something of the kind. I received hint of

this offer and thought I should let you know at once. "I will act as Mrs Youghal's agent," I said to myself, "in case she is at all tempted to dispose of the article at one and a half times what she paid for it." '

'Oh, but no, Mr Jeffs.'

'You are not interested?'

'Not at all, I'm afraid.'

'Suppose my client goes up to twice the price? How would you feel about that? Or how would Mr Hammond feel about that?'

'Mr Hammond?'

'Well, I am not quite certain who owns the article. That is why I mention the gentleman. Perhaps I should have contacted him. It was Mr Hammond who gave me the cheque.'

'The table is mine. A gift. I would rather you didn't contact Mr Hammond.'

'Well, that is that, then. But since I have acted in your interest in this matter, Mrs Youghal, thinking that I should report the offer to you without delay and involving myself in travelling expenses et cetera, I'm afraid I shall have to charge you the usual agent's fee. It is the ruling of the antique dealers' association that a fee be charged on such occasions. I feel you understand?'

Mrs Youghal said she did understand. She gave him some money, and Mr Jeffs took his leave.

In his house Mr Jeffs considered for a further hour. Eventually he thought it wise to telephone Mrs Hammond and ascertain her husband's office telephone number. He went out on to the street with a piece of paper in his hand which stated that he was deaf and dumb and wished urgently to have a telephone call made for him. He handed this to an elderly woman, pointing to a telephone booth.

'May I know your husband's office telephone number?' said the woman to Mrs Hammond. 'It's a matter of urgency.'

'But who are you?'

'I am a Mrs Lacey, and I am phoning you on behalf of Sir Andrew Charles of Africa.'

'I've heard that name before,' said Mrs Hammond, and gave the telephone number of her husband's office.

'You say you have been to see Mrs Youghal,' said Hammond. 'And what did she say?'

'I don't believe she fully understood what was at stake. I don't think she got the message.'

'The table was a gift from me to Mrs Youghal. I can hardly ask for it back.'

'This is an excellent offer, Mr Hammond.'

'Oh, I don't dispute that.'

'I was wondering if you could use your influence with Mrs Youghal, that's all. If you happen to be seeing her, that is.'

'I'll ring you back, Mr Jeffs.'

Mr Jeffs said thank-you and then telephoned Mrs Hammond. 'Negotiations are under way,' he said.

But two days later negotiations broke down. Hammond telephoned Mr Jeffs to say that the table was to remain the property of Mrs Youghal. Mr Jeffs, sorrowfully, decided to drive round to tell Mrs Hammond, so that he could collect what little was owing him. He would tell her, he decided, and that would surely now be the end of the matter.

'I'm afraid I have come up against a stone wall,' he reported. 'I'm sorry, Mrs Hammond, about that, and I would trouble you now only for what is owing.'

He mentioned the sum, but Mrs Hammond seemed not to hear clearly. Tears rolled down her cheeks and left marks on the powder on her face. She took no notice of Mr Jeffs. She sobbed and shook, and further tears dropped from her eyes.

In the end Mrs Hammond left the room. Mr Jeffs remained because he had, of course, to wait for the money owing to him. He sat there examining the furniture and thinking it odd of Mrs Hammond to have cried so passionately and for so long. The *au pair* girl came in with a tray of tea for him, blushing as she arranged it, remembering, he imagined, the orders she had given him as regards the windows. He poured himself some tea and ate two pieces of shortbread. It was very quiet in the room, as though a funeral had taken place.

'Whoever are you?' said a child, a small girl of five.

Mr Jeffs looked at her and endeavoured to smile, forcing his lips back from his teeth.

'My name is Mr Jeffs. What is your name?'

'My name is Emma Hammond. Why are you having tea in our house?'

'Because it was kindly brought to me.'

'What is the matter with your mouth?'

'That is how my mouth is made. Are you a good little girl?'

'But why are you waiting here?'

'Because I have to collect something that your mother has arranged to give me. A little money.'

'A little money? Are you poor?'

'It is money owing to me.'

'Run along, Emma,' said Mrs Hammond from the door, and when the child had gone she said:

'I apologise, Mr Jeffs.'

She wrote him a cheque. He watched her, thinking of Hammond and Mrs Youghal and the table, all together in the attic rooms at the top of the big block of flats. He wondered what was going to happen. He supposed Mrs Hammond would be left with the child. Perhaps Mrs Youghal would marry Hammond then; perhaps they would come to this house and bring the table back with them, since Mrs Youghal was so attached to it, and perhaps they would take on the same *au pair* girl, and perhaps Mrs Hammond and the child would go to live in the attic rooms. They were all of a kind, Mr Jeffs decided: even the child seemed tarred with her elders' sophistication. But if sides were to be taken, he liked Mrs Hammond best. He had heard of women going berserk in such circumstances, taking their lives even. He hoped Mrs Hammond would not do that.

'Let me tell you, Mr Jeffs,' said Mrs Hammond.

'Oh now, it doesn't matter.'

'The table belonged to my grandmother, who died and left it to me in her will.'

'Do not fret, Mrs Hammond. It's all perfectly all right.'

'We thought it ugly, my husband and I, so we decided to be rid of it.'

'Your husband thought it was ugly?'

'Well, yes. But I more than he. He doesn't notice things so much.'

Mr Jeffs thought that he had noticed Mrs Youghal all right when Mrs Youghal had walked into this house. Mrs Hammond was lying her head off, he said to himself, because she was trying to save face: she knew quite well where the table was, she had known all along. She had wept because she could not bear the thought of it, her grandmother's ugly table in the abode of sin.

'So we put in an advertisement. We had only two replies. You and a woman.'

Mr Jeffs stood up, preparatory to going.

'You see,' said Mrs Hammond, 'we don't have room in a place like this for a table like that. It doesn't fit in. Well, you can see for yourself.'

Mr Jeffs looked hard at her, not into her eyes or even at her face: he looked hard and seriously at the green wool of her dress. The woman said:

'But almost as soon as it had gone I regretted everything. I remember the table all my life. My grandmother had left it to me as an act of affection as well as generosity.'

Mr Jeffs reckoned that the table had stood in the grandmother's hall. He reckoned that Mrs Hammond as a child had been banished from rooms and had been bidden to stand by the table in the hall, crying and moaning. The table had mocked her childhood and it was mocking her again, with silent watching in an attic room. He could see the two of them, Mrs Youghal and Hammond, placing their big bulbous brandy glasses on the table and marching toward one another for a slick kiss.

'Once I had sold it to you I couldn't get it out of my mind. I remembered that my grandmother had always promised it to me. She was the only one who was kind to me as a child, Mr Jeffs. I felt that truly I had thrown all her love back at her. Every night since I sold it to you I've had wretched dreams. So you see why I was so very upset.'

The grandmother was cruel, thought Mr Jeffs. The grandmother punished the child every hour of the day, and left the table as a reminder of her autocratic soul. Why could not Mrs Hammond speak the truth? Why could she not say that the spirit of the old dead grandmother had passed into the table and that the spirit and the table were laughing their heads off in Mrs Youghal's room? Imagine, thought Mr Jeffs, a woman going to such lengths, and a woman whom he had passingly respected.

'I'm sorry I've burdened you with all this, Mr Jeffs. I'm sorry it's been such a bother. You have a kindly face.'

'I am a Jewish dealer, madam. I have a Jewish nose; I am not handsome; I cannot smile.'

He was angry because he thought that she was patronising him. She was lying still, and all of a sudden she was including him in her lies. She was insulting him with her talk of his face. Did she know his faults, his weaknesses? How dare she speak so?

'The table should have passed from me to my daughter. It should have stayed in the family. I didn't think.'

Mr Jeffs allowed himself to close his eyes. She can sit there telling those lies, he thought, one after another, while her own child plays innocently in the next room. The child will become a liar too. The child in her time will grow to be a woman who must cover up the humiliations she has suffered, who must put a face on things, and make the situation respectable with falsehoods.

With his eyes closed and his voice speaking in his mind, Mr Jeffs saw the figure of himself standing alone in his large Victorian house. Nothing was permanent in the house, not a stick of furniture remained there month by month. He sold and bought again. He laid no carpets, nor would he ever. He owned but the old wireless set because someone once had told him it was worthless.

'Why are you telling me lies?' shouted Mr Jeffs. 'Why can't you say the truth?'

He heard his voice shouting those words at Mrs Hammond and he saw the image of himself, standing quietly on the bare boards of his house. It was not his way to go shouting at people, or becoming involved, or wishing for lies to cease. These people were a law unto themselves; they did not concern him. He cooked his own food; he did not bother people.

'Your grandmother is dead and buried,' said Mr Jeffs to his amazement. 'It is Mrs Youghal who is alive. She takes her clothes off, Mrs Hammond, and in comes your husband and takes off his. And the table sees. The table you have always known. Your childhood table sees it all and you cannot bear it. Why not be honest, Mrs Hammond? Why not say straight out to me: "Jew man, bargain with this Mrs Youghal and let me have my childhood table back." I understand you, Mrs Hammond. I understand all that. I will trade anything on God's earth, Mrs Hammond, but I understand that.'

There was a silence again in the room, and in it Mr Jeffs moved his eyes around until their gaze alighted on the face of Mrs Hammond. He saw the face sway, gently, from side to side, for Mrs Hammond was shaking her head. 'I did not know any of that,' Mrs Hammond was saying. Her head ceased to shake: she seemed like a statue.

Mr Jeffs rose and walked through the deep silence to the door. He turned then, and walked back again, for he had left behind him Mrs Hammond's cheque. She seemed not to notice his movements and he considered it wiser in the circumstances not to utter the sounds of farewell. He left the house and started up the engine of his Austin van.

He saw the scene differently as he drove away: Mrs Hammond hanging her head and he himself saying that the lies were understandable. He might have brought Mrs Hammond a crumb of comfort, a word or two, a subtle shrug of the shoulder. Instead, in his clumsiness, he had brought her a shock that had struck her a blow. She would sit there, he imagined, just as he had left her, her face white, her body crouched over her sorrow; she would sit like that until her husband breezily arrived. And she would look at him in his breeziness and say: 'The Jewish dealer has been and gone. He was there in that chair and he told me that Mrs Youghal has opened up a love-nest for you.'

Mr Jeffs drove on, aware of a sadness but aware as well that his mind was slowly emptying itself of Mrs Hammond and her husband and the beautiful Mrs Youghal. 'I cook my own food,' said Mr Jeffs aloud. 'I am a good trader, and I do not bother anyone.' He had no right to hope that he might have offered comfort. He had no business to take such things upon himself, to imagine that a passage of sympathy might have developed between himself and Mrs Hammond.

'I cook my own food,' said Mr Jeffs again. 'I do not bother anyone.' He drove in silence after that, thinking of nothing at all. The chill of sadness had left him, and the mistake he had made appeared to him as a fact that could not be remedied. He noticed that dusk was falling; and he returned to the house where he had never lit a fire, where the furniture loomed and did not smile at him, where nobody wept and nobody told a lie.

II

The General's Day

GENERAL SUFFOLK PULLED on two grey knitted socks and
stood upright. Humming a marching air, he walked to the
bathroom, intent upon his morning shave. The grey socks
were his only apparel and he noticed as he passed the mirror
of his wardrobe the white spare body of an elderly man reflected without flattery. He voiced no comment nor did he
ponder, even in passing, upon this pictured nakedness. He
was used to the sight; and had, over the years, accepted the
changes as they came. Still humming, he half filled the wash-
basin with water. It felt keenly warm on his fingers, a circumstance he inwardly congratulated himself on.

With deft strokes the General cleared his face of lather
and whisker, savouring the crisp rasp of razor upon flesh.
He used a cut-throat article and when shorn to his satisfaction wiped it on a small absorbent pad, one of a series he
had collected from the bedrooms of foreign hotels. He
washed, dressed, set his moustache as he liked to sport it,
and descended to his kitchen.

The General's breakfast was simple: an egg poached
lightly, two slices of toast and a pot of tea. It took him ten
minutes to prepare and ten to consume. As he finished he
heard the footsteps of the woman who daily came to work
for him. They were slow, dragging footsteps implying the
bulk they gracelessly shifted. The latch of the door rose and
fell and Mrs Hinch, string bags and hairnet, cigarette
cocked from the corner of her mouth, stood grinning before
him. 'Hullo,' this woman said, adding as she often did, 'my
dear.'

'Good morning, Mrs Hinch.'

Mrs Hinch stripped herself of bags, coat and cigarette

with a single complicated gesture. She grinned again at the General, replaced her cigarette and set to clearing the table.

'I shall walk to the village this morning,' General Suffolk informed her. 'It seems a pleasant morning to dawdle through. I shall take coffee at the brown café and try my luck at picking up some suitable matron.'

Mrs Hinch was accustomed to her employer's turn of speech. She laughed shrilly at this sally, pleased that the man would be away for the morning. 'Ah, General, you'll be the death of us,' she cried; and planned for his absence a number of trunk calls on his telephone, a leisurely bath and the imbibing of as much South African sherry as she considered discreet.

'It is Saturday if I am not mistaken,' the General went on. 'A good morning for my plans. Is it not a fact that there are stout matrons in and out of the brown café by the score on a Saturday morning?'

'Why, sure, General,' said Mrs Hinch, anxious to place no barrier in his way. 'Why, half the county goes to the brown café of a Saturday morning. You are certain to be successful this time.'

'Cheering words, Mrs Hinch, cheering words. It is one thing to walk through the cowparsleyed lanes on a June morning, but quite another to do so with an objective one is sanguine of achieving.'

'This is your day, General. I feel it in my bones. I said it to Hobson as I left. "This is a day for the General," I said. "The General will do well today," I said.'

'And Hobson, Mrs Hinch? Hobson replied?'

Again Mrs Hinch, like a child's toy designed for the purpose, shrilled her merriment.

'General, General, Hobson's my little bird.'

The General, rising from the table, frowned. 'Do you imagine I am unaware of that? Since for six years you have daily informed me of the fact. And why, pray, since the bird is a parrot, should the powers of speech be beyond it? It is not so with other parrots.'

'Hobson's silent, General. You know Hobson's silent.'

'Due to your lethargy, Mrs Hinch. No bird of his nature need be silent: God does not intend it. He has taken some pains to equip the parrot with the instruments of speech. It is up to you to pursue the matter in a practical way by training the animal. A child, Mrs Hinch, does not remain ignorant of self-expression. Nor of the ability to feed and clean itself. The mother teaches, Mrs Hinch. It is part of nature. So with your parrot.'

Enthusiastic in her own defence, Mrs Hinch said: 'I have brought up seven children. Four girls and three boys.'

'Maybe. Maybe. I am in no position to question this. But indubitably with your parrot you are flying in the face of nature.'

'Oh, General, never. Hobson's silent and that's that.'

The General regarded his adversary closely. 'You miss my point,' he said drily; and repeating the remark twice he left the room.

In his time General Suffolk had been a man of more than ordinary importance. As a leader and a strategist in two great wars he had risen rapidly to the heights implied by the title he bore. He had held in his hands the lives of many thousands of men; his decisions had more than once set the boundaries of nations. Steely intelligence and physical prowess had led him, in their different ways, to glories that few experience at Roeux and Monchy-le-Preux he had come close to death. Besides all that, there was about the General a quality that is rare in the ultimate leaders of his army: he was to the last a rake, and for this humanity a popular figure. He had cared for women, for money, for alcohol of every sort; but in the end he had found himself with none of these commodities. In his modest cottage he was an elderly man with a violent past; with neither wife nor riches nor cellar to help him on his way.

Mrs Hinch had said he would thrive today. That the day should be agreeable was all he asked. He did not seek merriness or reality or some moment of truth. He had lived for long enough to forgo excitement; he had had his share; he wished only that the day, and his life in it, should go the way he wished.

In the kitchen Mrs Hinch scoured the dishes briskly. She was not one to do things by halves; hot water and detergent in generous quantities was her way.

'Careful with the cup handles,' the General admonished her. 'Adhesive for the repair of such a fracture has apparently not yet been perfected. And the cups themselves are valuable.'

'Oh they're flimsy, General. So flimsy you can't watch them. Declare to God, I shall be glad to see the last of them!'

'But not I, Mrs Hinch. I like those cups. Tea tastes better from fine china. I would take it kindly if you washed and dried with care.'

'Hoity-toity, General! Your beauties are safe with me. I treat them as babies.'

'Babies? Hardly a happy analogy, Mrs Hinch—since five of the set are lost for ever.'

'Six,' said Mrs Hinch, snapping beneath the water the handle from the cup. 'You are better without the bother of them. I shall bring you a coronation mug.'

'You fat old bitch,' shouted the General. 'Six makes the set. It was my last remaining link with the gracious life.'

Mrs Hinch, understanding and wishing to spite the General further, laughed. 'Cheery-bye, General,' she called as she heard him rattling among his walking sticks. He banged the front door and stepped out into the heat of the day. Mrs Hinch turned on the wireless.

'*I walked entranced,*' intoned the General, '*through a land of morn. The sun in wondrous excess of light . . .*' He was seventy-eight: his memory faltered over the quotation. His stick, weapon of his irritation, thrashed through the cow-parsley, covering the road with broken blooms. Grasshoppers clicked; bees darted, paused, humming in flight, silent in labour. The road was brown with dust, dry and hot in the sunlight. It was a day, thought the General, to be successfully in love; and he mourned that the ecstasy of love on a hot summer's day was so far behind him. Not that he

27

had gone without it; which gave him his yardstick and saddened him the more.

Early in his retirement General Suffolk had tried his hand
in many directions. He had been, to start with, the secre-
tary of a golf club; though in a matter of months his temper
relieved him of the task. He was given to disagreement and
did not bandy words. He strode away from the golf club,
red in the face, the air behind him stinging with insults. He
lent his talents to the business world and to a military aca-
demy: both were dull and in both he failed. He bought his
cottage, agreeing with himself that retirement was retirement and meant what it suggested. Only once since moving
to the country had he involved himself with salaried work:
as a tennis coach in a girls' school. Despite his age he was
active still on his legs and managed well enough. Too well,
his grim and beady-eyed headmistress avowed, objecting
to his method of instructing her virgins in the various stances
by which they might achieve success with the serve. The
General paused only to level at the headmistress a battery
of expressions well known to him but new to her. He went
on his way, his cheque in his wallet, his pockets bulging
with small articles from her study. The girls he had taught
pursued him, pressing upon him packets of cheap cigarettes,
sweets and flowers.

The General walked on, his thoughts rambling. He
thought of the past; of specific days, of moments of shame
or pride in his life. The past was his hunting ground; from
it came his pleasure and a good deal of everything else. Yet
he was not proof against the moment he lived in. The present could snarl at him; could drown his memories so completely that when they surfaced again they were like the
burnt tips of matches floating on a puddle, finished and
done with. He walked through the summery day, puzzled
that all this should be so.

The brown café, called 'The Cuppa', was, as General
Suffolk and Mrs Hinch had anticipated, bustling with mid-
morning traffic. Old men and their wives sat listening to the
talk about them, exchanging by the way a hard comment on

their fellows. Middle-aged women, outsize in linen dresses, were huddled three or four to a table, their great legs battling for room in inadequate space, their feet hot and unhappy in unwise shoes. Mothers passed unsuitable edibles towards the searching mouths of their young. Men with girls sipped at the pale creamy coffee, thinking only of the girls. Crumbs were everywhere; and the babel buzzed like a clockwork wind.

The General entered, surveyed the scene with distaste, and sat at a table already occupied by a youth engrossed in a weekly magazine. The youth, a fat bespotted lad, looked up and immediately grinned. General Suffolk replied in kind, stretching the flesh of his face to display his teeth in a smile designed to promote goodwill between them, for the pair were old friends.

'Good morning, Basil. And how is youth and vigour today?'

'Oh well, not so bad, General. My mum is in the family way again.'

'A cause for joy,' murmured General Suffolk, ordering coffee with Devonshire cream and the fruit pie he favoured. 'Your mother is a great one for babies, is she not?'

'My dad says the same. He don't understand it neither. Worried, is Dad. Anyone can see that.'

'I see.'

'Well, it is a bit fishy, General. Dad's not the man to be careless. It's just about as fishy as hell.'

'Basil, your mother needs all the support she can get at a time like this. Talk about fishiness is scarcely going to help her in her ordeal.'

'Mum's had five. Drops 'em like hot bricks so she says. Thing is, if this one's fishy what about the others?'

The General placed a portion of pie in his mouth. Crumbs of pastry and other matter lingered on his moustache. 'You are thinking of yourself, Basil.'

'Wouldn't you? I mean to say.'

'I would attach no importance to such a doubt, I do assure you. Basil, what do you say we spend this afternoon at some local fête? It is just an afternoon for a fête. I will stand you lunch.'

The plumpness of Basil's face sharpened into suspicion. He moved his large hams uneasily on his chair and avoided his companion's gaze. 'It's Mum really, General. I've got to tend her a bit, like you say it's a hard time for her. And with Dad so snappish and the kids all over the place I don't think she'd take it kindly if I was to go going off to fêtes and that. Not at a time like this like.'

'Ah, filial duty. I trust your mother appreciates your sacrifices.'

But Basil, not anxious to prolong the conversation in this direction, was on his feet, his right hand hovering for the General's grasp. And then, the handshake completed, he moved himself clumsily between the tables and passed through the open doorway.

General Suffolk stirred sugar into his coffee and looked about him. A lanky schoolmistress from the school he had taught tennis at sat alone at a corner table. She was a woman of forty or so, the General imagined; and he recalled having seen her by chance once, through an open window, in her underclothes. Since then he had often considered her in terms of sex, though now when he might have explored the possibility he found himself unable to remember her name. He watched her, trying to catch her glance, but either she did not recognise him or did not wish to associate with so reprobate a character. He dismissed her mentally and surveyed the room again. There was no one with whom he could fall into casual conversation, except perhaps a certain Mrs Consitine, known in her youth as Jumbo Consitine because of her size, and whose freakish appearance repelled him always to the point of physical sickness. He dodged the lady's predatory stare and left the café.

It was a quarter to twelve. If the General walked through the village he would be just in time for a morning drink with Frobisher. Frobisher always drank—sometimes considerably—before lunch. On a day like this a drink was emphatically in order.

Mrs Hinch, the General reflected, would be settling down to his South African sherry about now. 'You thieving old bitch,' he said aloud. 'Fifty years in Their Majesties' service and I end up with Mrs bloody Hinch.' A man carrying a coil of garden hose tripped and fell across his path. This man, a week-end visitor to the district, known to the General by sight and disliked by him, uttered as he dropped to the ground a series of expletives of a blasphemous and violent nature. The General, since the man's weight lay on his shoes, stooped to assist him. 'Oh, buzz off,' ordered the man, his face close to the General's. So the General left him, conscious not so much of his dismisal as of the form of words it had taken. The sun warmed his forehead and drops of sweat glistened on his nose and chin.

The Frobishers' house was small and vaguely Georgian. From the outside it had the feeling of a town house placed by some error in the country. There were pillars on either side of the front door, which was itself dressed in a grey and white canvas cover as a protection against the sun. Door and cover swung inwards and Mrs Frobisher, squat and old, spoke from the hall.

'It's General Suffolk,' she said.

'Yes,' said the General. 'That old soldier.'

'You've come to see Frob. Come in a minute and I'll fetch him. What a lovely day.'

The General stepped into the hall. It was cool and smelt rather pleasantly of floor polish. Daggers, swords, Eastern rugs, knick-knacks and novelties hung in profusion everywhere. 'Frob! Frob!' Mrs Frobisher called, climbing the stairs. There had been a day, a terrible sultry day in India all of fifty years ago, when the General—though then not yet a general—had fought a duel with a certain Major Service. They had walked together quietly to a selected spot, their seconds, carrying a pair of *kukris*, trailing behind them. It had been a quarrel that involved, surprisingly, neither man's honour. In retrospect General Suffok could scarcely remember the cause: some insult directed against some woman, though by whom and in what manner completely escaped him. He had struck Major Service on the left fore-arm drawing a considerable quantity of blood, and the duel was reckoned complete. An excuse was made for the wound sustained by the Major and the affair was successfully hushed up. It was the nearest that General Suffolk had ever come to being court-martialled. He was put in mind of the occasion by the presence of a *kukri* on the Frobishers' wall. A nasty weapon, he reflected, and considered it odd that he should once have wielded one so casually. After all, Major Service might easily have lost his arm or, come to that, his life.

'Frob! Frob! Where are you?' cried Mrs Frobisher. 'General Suffolk's here to see you.'

'Suffolk?' Frobisher's voice called from another direction. 'Oh my dear, can't you tell him I'm out?'

The General, hearing the words, left the house.

In the saloon bar of the public house General Suffolk asked the barman about the local fêtes.

'Don't think so, sir. Not today. Not that I've heard of.'

'There's a fête at Marmount,' a man at the bar said. 'Conservative fête, same Saturday every year.'

'Ah certainly,' said the barman, 'but Marmount's fifteen miles away. General Suffolk means a *local* fête. The General doesn't have a car.'

'Of course, of course,' said the man. 'Marmount's not an easy spot to reach. Even if you did have a car, sir.'

'I will have a sandwich, Jock,' said General Suffolk. 'Chop me a cheese sandwich like a good man.' He was beginning to feel low; the day was not good; the day was getting out of control. Fear filled his mind and the tepid beer was little comfort. He began to pray inwardly, but he had little faith now in this communication. 'Never mind,' he said aloud. 'It is just that it seems like a day for a fête. I won a half guinea at a summer fête last year. One never knows one's luck.' He caught sight of a card advertising the weekly films at the cinema of the near-by town.

'Have you seen *The Guns of Navarone*?' he questioned the barman.

'I have, sir, and very good it is.'

The General nodded. 'A powerful epic by the sound of it.'

'That's the word, General. As the saying goes, it had me riveted.'

'Well, hurry the sandwiches then. I can catch the one-ten bus and achieve the first performance.'

'Funny thing, sir,' said the barman. 'I can never take the cinema of an afternoon. Not that it isn't a time that suits me, the hours being what they are. No, I go generally on my night off. Can't seem to settle down in the afternoon or something. Specially in the good weather. To me, sir, it seems unnatural.'

'That is an interesting point of view, Jock. It is indeed. And may well be shared by many—for I have noticed that the cinemas are often almost empty in the afternoon.'

'I like to be outside on a good afternoon. Taking a stroll by a trout stream or in a copse.'

'A change is as good as a cure, or whatever the adage is. After all, you are inside a good deal in your work. To be alone must be quite delightful after the idle chatter you have to endure.'

'If you don't mind my saying it, General, I don't know how you do it. It would kill me to sit at the pictures on an afternoon like this. I would feel—as it were, sir—guilty.'

'Guilty, Jock?'

'Looking the Great Gift Horse in the mouth, sir.'

'The—? Are you referring to the Deity, Jock?'

'Surely, sir. I would feel it like an unclean action.'

'Maybe, Jock. Though I doubt that God would care to hear you describe Him as a horse.'

'Oh but, General—'

'You mean no disrespect. It is taken as read, Jock. But you cannot be too careful.'

'Guilt is my problem, sir.'

'I am sorry to hear it. Guilt can often be quite a burden.'

33

'I am never free of it, sir. If it's not one thing it's another.'

'I know too well, Jock.'

'It was not presumptuous of me to mention that thing about the cinema? I was casting no stone at you, sir?'

'Quite, quite. It may even be that I would prefer to attend an evening house. But beggars, you know, cannot be choosers.'

'I would not like to offend you, General.'

'Good boy, Jock. In any case I am not offended. I enjoy a chat.'

'Thank you, sir.'

'Not at all. But now I must be on my way. Consider your problem closely: you may discover some simple solution. There are unchartered regions in the human mind.'

'Sir?'

'You are a good fellow, Jock. We old soldiers must stick together.'

'Ha, ha,' said Jock, taking the remark as a joke, since he was in the first place a young man still, and had never been in the Army.

'Well, cheerio then.'

'Cheerio, sir.'

How extraordinary, thought the General, that the man should feel like that: guilty about daytime cinema attendance. As Mrs Hinch would have it, it takes all sorts.

The thought of Mrs Hinch depressed the General further and drove him straight to a telephone booth. He often telephoned his cottage at this time of day as a check on her timekeeping. She was due to remain at work for a further hour, but generally the telephone rang unanswered. Today he got the engaged signal. As he boarded his bus, he wondered how much it was costing him.

Taurus. April 21st to May 20th. Financial affairs straighten themselves out. Do not make decisions this afternoon: your judgement is not at its best.

The General peeped around the edge of the newspaper at the woman who shared his table. She was a thin, middle-aged person with a face like a faded photograph. Her hair was inadequately dyed a shade of brown, her face touched briefly with lipstick and powder. She wore a cream-coloured blouse and a small string of green beads which the General assumed, correctly, to be jade. Her skirt, which the General could not see, was of fine tweed.

'How thoughtless of me,' said the General. 'I have picked up your paper. It was on the chair and I did it quite automatically. I am so sorry.'

He knew the newspaper was not hers. No one places a newspaper on the other chair at a restaurant table when the other chair is so well out of reach. Unless, that is, one wishes to reserve the place, which the lady, since she made no protest at his occupying it, was clearly not interested in doing. He made the pretence of offering the paper across the tea-table, leaning forward and sideways to catch a glimpse of her legs.

'Oh but,' said the lady, 'it is not my newspaper at all.'

Beautiful legs. Really beautiful legs. Shimmering in silk or nylon, with fine firm knees and intoxicating calves.

'Are you sure? In that case it must have been left by the last people. I was reading the stars. I am to have an indecisive afternoon.' She belongs to the upper classes, General Suffolk said to himself; the upper classes are still well-bred in the leg.

The lady tinkled with laughter. I am away, the General thought. 'When is your birthday?' he asked daringly. 'And I will tell you what to expect for the rest of today.'

'Oh, I'm Libra, I think.'

'It is a good moment for fresh associations,' lied the General, pretending to read from the paper. 'A new regime is on its way.'

'You can't believe a thing they say.'

'Fighting words,' said the General and they laughed and changed the subject of conversation.

In the interval at the cinema, when the lights had gone

up and the girls with ice cream began their sales stroll, the General had seen, two or three rows from the screen, the fat unhealthy figure of his friend Basil. The youth was accompanied by a girl, and it distressed General Suffolk that Basil should have made so feeble an excuse when earlier he had proposed an excursion to a fête. The explanation that Basil wished to indulge in carnal pleasures in the gloom of a picture house would naturally have touched the General's sympathy. Basil was an untrustworthy lad. It was odd, the General reflected, that some people are like that: so addicted to the lie that to avoid one, when the truth is in order, seems almost a sin.

'General Suffolk,' explained the General. 'Retired, of course.'

'We live in Bradoak,' said the lady. 'My name actually is Mrs Hope-Kingley.'

'Retired?'

'Ha, ha. Though in a way it's true. My husband is not alive now.'

'Ah,' said the General, delighted. 'I'm sorry.'

'I am quite over it, thank you. It is all of fifteen years since last I saw him. We had been divorced some time befor his death.'

'Divorce and death, divorce and death. You hear it all the time. May I be personal now and say I am surprised you did not remarry?'

'Oh, General Suffolk, Mr Right never came along!'

'*Attention! Les étoiles!*'

'Ha, ha.' And to her own surprise, Mrs Hope-Kingley proceeded to reveal to this elderly stranger the story of her marriage.

As he listened, General Suffolk considered how best to play his cards. It was a situation he had found himself in many times before, but as always the game must vary in detail. He felt mentally a little tired as he thought about it; and the fear that, in this, as in almost everything else, age had taken too great a toll struck at him with familiar ruthlessness. In his thirties he had played superbly, as good at love as he was at tennis. Now arrogant, now innocent, he had swooped and struck, captured and killed; and smiled over many a breakfast at the beauty that had been his prize.

They finished their tea. 'I am slipping along to the County for a drink,' said the General. 'Do join me for a quick one.'

'How kind of you. I must not delay though. My sister will expect me.' And they climbed into Mrs Hope-Kingley's small car and drove to the hotel. Over their gins the General spoke of his early days in the Army and touched upon his present life, naming Mrs Hinch.

'What a frightful woman! You must sack her.'

'But who would do for me? I need my bed made and the place kept clean. Women are not easy to find in the country.'

'I know a Mrs Gall who lives in your district. She has the reputation of being particularly reliable. My friends the Boddingtons use her.'

'Well, that is certainly a thought. D'you know, I had become quite reconciled to Hinch. I never thought to change her really. What a breath of life you are!'

After three double gins Mrs Hope-Kingley was slightly drunk. Her face flushed with pleasure. Compliments do not come your way too often these days, thought the General; and he ambled off to the bar to clinch the matter with a further drink. How absurd to be upset by the passing details of the day! What did it all matter now that he had found this promising lady? The day and its people, so directed against him, were balanced surely by this meeting? With her there was strength; from her side he might look out on the world with power and with confidence. In a panic of enthusiasm he almost suggested marriage. His hands were shaking and he felt again a surge of the old arrogance. There is life in the old dog yet, he thought. Handing her her drink, he smiled and winked.

'After this I must go,' the lady said.

'Come, come, the night is younger than we are. It is not every day I can pick up a bundle of charms in a teashop.'

'Ha, ha, ha.' Mrs Hope-Kingley purred, thinking that for once her sister would simply have to wait, and wondering if she should dare to tell her that she had been drinking with an elderly soldier.

They were sitting at a small table in a corner. Now and again, it could have been accident, the General's knee touched hers. He watched the level of gin lower in her glass. 'You are a pretty lady,' murmured the General, and beneath the table his hand stroked her stockinged knee and ventured a little beyond it.

'My God!' said Mrs Hope-Kingley, her face like a beetroot. The General lowered his head. He heard her snatch her handbag from the seat beside him. When he looked up she was gone.

'When were you born?' General Suffolk asked the man in the bus.

The man seemed startled. 'Well,' he said, 'nineteen-oh-three actually.'

'No, no, no. What month? When does your birthday fall?'

'Well, October the twenty-first actually.'

'Libra by a day,' the General informed him, consulting his newspaper as he spoke. 'For tomorrow, there are to be perfect conditions for enjoying yourself; though it may be a little expensive. Don't gamble.'

'I see,' said the man, glancing in embarrassment through the window.

'Patrelli is usually reliable.'

The man nodded, thinking: The old fellow is drunk. He was right: the General was drunk.

'I do not read the stars every day,' General Suffolk explained. 'It is only when I happen upon an evening paper. I must say I find Patrelli the finest augur of the lot. Do you not agree?'

The man made an effort to smile, muttering something incomprehensible.

'What's that, what's that? I cannot hear you.'

'I don't know at all. I don't know about such matters.'

'You are not interested in the stars?'

The man shook his head.

'In that case, I have been boring you.'

'No, no—'

'If you were not interested in my conversation you should have said so. It is quite simple to say it. I cannot understand you.'

'I'm sorry—'

'I do not like to offend people. I do not like to be a nuisance. You should have stopped me, sir.'

The man made a gesture vague in its meaning.

'You have taken advantage of an old warrior.'

'I cannot see—'

'You should have halted me. It costs nothing to speak.'

'I'm sorry.'

'Think nothing of it. Think nothing of it at all. Here is my village. If you are dismounting, would you care to join me in a drink?'

'Thank you, no. I am—'

'I swear not to speak of the stars.'

'I go on a bit. This is not my stop.'

The General shook his head, as though doubting this statement. The bus stopped and, aided by the conductor, he left it.

'Did you see *The Guns*, General?' Jock shouted across the bar.

Not hearing, but understanding that the barman was addressing him, General Suffolk waved breezily. 'A large whisky, Jock. And a drop of beer for yourself.'

'Did you see *The Guns* then?'

'The guns?'

'The pictures, General. *The Guns of Navarone.*'

'That is very kind of you, Jock. But we must make it some other time. I saw that very film this afternoon.'

'General, did you like it?'

'Certainly, Jock. Certainly I liked it. It was very well done. I thought it was done very well indeed.'

'Two gins and split a bottle of tonic,' a man called out.

'I beg your pardon,' said the General, 'I think I am in your way.'

'Two gins and a split tonic,' repeated Jock.

'And something for our friend,' the man added, indicating the General.

'That is kind of you. Everyone is kind tonight. Jock here has just invited me to accompany him to the pictures. Unfortunately I have seen the film. But there will be other occasions. We shall go together again. May I ask you when you were born, the month I mean?'

The man, whose attention was taken up with the purchasing and transportation of his drinks, said: 'Some time in May, I think.'

'But exactly? When is your birthday, for instance?' But the man had returned to a small table against the wall, where a girl and several packets of unopened crisps awaited him.

'Jock, do you follow the stars?'

'D'you mean telescopes and that?'

'No, no, my boy.' The General swayed, catching at the bar to balance himself. He had had very little to eat all day: the old, he maintained, did not need it. 'No, no, I mean the augurs. Capricorn, Scorpio, Gemini, you know what I mean.'

'Lord Luck in the *Daily Express*?'

'That's it. That's the kind of thing. D'you take an interest at all?'

'Well, General, now, I don't.'

'When's your birthday, Jock?'

'August the fifteenth.'

'A Leo, by Harry! It is quite something to be a Leo, Jock. I would never have guessed it.'

Jock laughed loudly. 'After all, General, it is not my doing.'

'Fill up our glasses. Let me see what tomorrow holds for you.' But examining the paper, he found it difficult to focus. 'Here Jock, read it yourself.' And Jock read aloud:

'You will gain a lot by mingling with friends old and new. Late evening particularly favours entry into new social circles.'

'Hark at that then! Remember the words, my friend. Patrelli is rarely wrong. The best augur of the bunch.' The General had become dishevelled. His face was flushed and his eyelids drooped intermittently and uncontrollably. He fidgeted with his clothes, as though nervous about the positioning of his hands. 'A final whisky, Jock boy; and a half bottle to carry home.'

On the road from the village to his cottage the General felt very drunk indeed. He lurched from one grass verge to the other, grasping his half bottle of whisky and singing gently under his breath. He knocked on the Frobishers' door with his stick, and scarcely waiting for a reply knocked loudly again.

'For God's sake, man,' Frobisher demanded, 'what's the matter with you?'

'A little drink,' explained General Suffolk. 'You and me and Mrs Frob, a little drink together. I have brought some with me. In case you had run out.'

Frobisher glared at him. 'You're drunk, Suffolk. You're bloody well drunk.'

General Suffolk loosed a peal of laughter. 'Ha, ha, the old man's drunk. Let me in, Frob, and so shall you be.'

Frobisher attempted to close the door, but the General inserted his stick.

He laughed again, and then was silent. When he spoke his voice was pleading.

'One drink, Frob. Just one for you and me. Frob, when were you born?'

Frobisher began to snort with anger: he was a short-tempered man, he saw no reason to humour this unwelcome guest. He kicked sharply at the General's stick, then opening the door widely he shouted into his face: 'Get the hell off my premises, you bloody old fool! Go on, Suffolk, hop it!'

The General did not appear to understand. He smiled at Frobisher. 'Tell me the month of your birth and I shall tell you in return what the morrow holds—'

'God damn it, Suffolk—'

41

'One little drink, and we'll consult the stars together. They may well be of interest to Mrs—'

'Get off my premises, you fool! You've damaged my door with your damned stick. You'll pay for that, Suffolk. You'll hear from my solicitors. I promise you, if you don't go immediately I won't hesitate to call for the police.'

'One drink, Frob. Look, I'm a little lonely—'

Frobisher banged the door. 'Frob, Frob,' General Suffolk called, striking the door with his stick. 'A nightcap, my old friend. Don't refuse a drink now.' But the door remained closed against him. He spoke for a while to himself, then made his way unsteadily homewards.

'General Suffolk, are you ill?'

The General narrowed his eyes, focusing on the couple who stood before him; he did not recognise them; he was aware of feeling guilty because of it.

'We are returning home from a game of cards,' the woman of the two told him. 'It is a balmy evening for a stroll.'

The General tried to smile. Since leaving the Frobishers' house he had drunk most of the whisky. The people danced a bit before him, like outsize puppets. They moved up and down, and from side to side. They walked rapidly, silently, backwards. 'Ha, ha, ha,' laughed the General. 'What can I do for you?'

'Are you ill? You don't seem yourself.'

The General smiled at some little joke. 'I have not been myself for many years. Today is just another day.'

The people were moving away. He could hear them murmuring to each other.

'You have not asked me about the stars,' he shouted after them. 'I could tell you if you asked.' But they were already gone, and uncorking the bottle he drained the remains and threw it into a ditch.

As he passed Mrs Hinch's cottage he decided to call on her. He had it on his mind to play some joke on the woman, to say that she need not again attend to his household needs. He banged powerfully on the door and in a moment Mrs

Hinch's head, rich in curling pins, appeared at a window to his right.

'Why, General dear,' said Mrs Hinch, recognising immediately his condition. 'You've been on the razzle.'

'Mrs Hinch, when is your birthday?'

'Why, my dear? Have you a present for little Hinchie?'

'Give me the information and I will let you know what tomorrow brings.'

'April the twenty-first. I was born at two o'clock in the morning.'

But in his walk he had somewhere mislaid the newspaper and could tell her nothing. He gripped the doorstep and seemed about to fall.

'Steady now,' said Mrs Hinch. 'I'll dress myself and help you home.' The head was withdrawn and the General waited for the company of his unreliable servant.

She, in the room, slipped out of her nightdress and buttoned about her her everyday clothes. This would last her for months. 'Ho ho, my dear,' she would say, 'remember that night? Worse for wear you were. Whatever would you have done without your little Hinchie?' Chortling and crowing, she hitched up her skirts and paraded forth to meet him.

'Oh General, you're naughty! You shouldn't be allowed out.'

The General laughed. Clumsily he slapped her broad buttocks. She screamed shrilly, enjoying again the position she now held over him. 'Dirty old General! Hinchie won't carry her beauty home unless he's a good boy tonight.' She laughed her cackling laugh and the General joined in it. He dawdled a bit, and losing her patience Mrs Hinch pushed him roughly in front of her. He fell, and in picking him up she came upon his wallet and skilfully extracted two pounds ten. 'General would fancy his Hinchie tonight,' she said, shrieking merrily at the thought. But the General was silent now, seeming almost asleep as he walked. His face was gaunt and thin, with little patches of red. 'I could live for twenty years,' he whispered. 'My God Almighty, I could live for twenty years.' Tears spread on his cheeks. 'Lor' love a duck!' cried Mrs Hinch; and leaning on the arm of this stout woman the hero of Roeux and Monchy-le-Preux stumbled the last few yards to his cottage.

III

The Penthouse Apartment

'FLOWERS?' SAID MR RUNCA into his pale blue telephone receiver. 'Shall we order flowers? What's the procedure?' He stared intently at his wife as he spoke, and his wife, eating her breakfast grape-fruit, thought that it would seem to be her husband's intention to avoid having to pay for flowers. She had become used to this element in her husband; it hardly ever embarrassed her.

'The procedure's quite simple,' said a soft voice in Mr Runca's ear. 'The magazine naturally supplies the flowers. If we can just agree between us what the flowers should be.'

'Indeed,' said Mr Runca. 'It's to be remembered that not all blooms will go with the apartment. Our fabrics must be allowed to speak for themselves, you know. Well, you've seen. You know what I mean.'

'Indeed I do, Mr Runca—'

'They came from Thailand, in fact. You might like to mention that.'

'So you said, Mr Runca. The fabrics are most beautiful.'

Mr Runca, hearing this statement, nodded. He said, because he was used to saying it when the apartment was discussed:

'It's the best-dressed apartment in London.'

'I'll come myself at three,' said the woman on the magazine. 'Will someone be there at half-past two, say, so that the photographers can set up all their gear and test the light?'

'We have an Italian servant,' said Mr Runca, 'who opened the door to you before and who'll do the same thing for the photographers.'

'Till this afternoon then,' said the woman on the magazine, speaking lightly and gaily, since that was her manner.

45

Mr Runca carefully replaced the telephone receiver. His wife, a woman who ran a boutique, drank some coffee and heard her husband say that the magazine would pay for the flowers and would presumably not remove them from the flat after the photography had taken place. Mrs Runca nodded. The magazine was going to devote six pages to the Runcas' flat: a display in full colour of its subtleties and charm, with an article about how the Runcas had between them planned all the décor.

'I'd like to arrange the flowers myself,' said Mrs Runca. 'Are they being sent round?'

Mr Runca shook his head. The flowers, he explained, were to be brought to the house by the woman from the magazine at three o'clock, the photographers having already had time to deploy their materials in the manner they favoured.

'But how ridiculous!' cried Mrs Runca. 'It's completely hopeless, that arrangement. The photographers with their camera poised for three o'clock and the woman arriving then with the flowers. How long does the female imagine it'll take to arrange them? Does she think it can be done in a matter of minutes?'

Mr Runca picked up the telephone and dialled the number of the magazine. He mentioned the name of the woman he had recently been speaking to. He spoke to her again. He said:

'My wife points out that the arrangement is not satisfactory. The flowers will take time to arrange, naturally. What point is there in keeping your photographers waiting? And I myself haven't got all day.'

'It shouldn't take long to arrange the flowers.'

Mrs Runca lit her first cigarette of the day, imagining that the woman on the magazine was saying something like that. She had a long, rather thin face and pale grey hair that had the glow of aluminium. Her hands were long also, hands that had grown elegant in childhood, with finger-nails that now were of a fashionable length, metallically painted, a reflection of her hair. Ten years ago, on money borrowed from her husband, she had opened her boutique. She had called it St Catherine, and had watched it growing into a flourishing business with a staff of five women and a girl messenger.

'Very well then,' said the woman on the magazine, having listened further to Mr Runca. 'I'll have the flowers sent round this morning.'

'They're coming round this morning,' reported Mr Runca to his wife.

'I have to be at St Catherine at twelve,' she said, 'absolutely without fail.'

'My wife has to be at her business at midday,' said Mr Runca, and the woman on the magazine cursed silently. She promised that the flowers would be in the Runcas' penthouse apartment within three-quarters of an hour.

Mr Runca rose to his feet and stood silently for a minute. He was a rich, heavily-jowled man, the owner of three publications that appealed to those involved in the clothing trade. He was successful in much the same way as his wife was, and he felt, as she did, that efficiency and a stern outlook were good weapons in the business of accumulating wealth. Once upon a time they had both been poor and had recognised certain similar qualities in one another, and had seen the future as a more luxurious time, as in fact it had become. They were proud that once again their penthouse apartment was to be honoured by photographs and a journalist. It was the symbol of all their toil; and in a small way it had made them famous.

Mr Runca walked from the spacious room that had one side made entirely of glass, and his feet caused no sound as he crossed a white carpet of Afghanistan wool. He paused in the hall to place a hat on his head and gloves on his hands before departing for a morning's business.

At ten to ten the flowers arrived and by a quarter past eleven Mrs Runca had arranged them to her satisfaction. The Runcas' Italian maid, called Bianca, cleaned the flat most carefully, seeking dust in an expert way, working with method and a conscience, which was why the Runcas employed her. Mrs Runca warned her to be in at half-past two

47

because the photographers were coming then. 'I must go out now then,' replied Bianca, 'for shopping. I will make these photographers coffee, I suppose?' Mrs Runca said to give the men coffee in the kitchen, or tea, if they preferred it. 'Don't let them walk about the place with cups in their hands,' she said, and went away.

In another part of the block of flats lived Miss Winton with her Cairn terrier. Her flat was different from the Runcas'; it contained many ornaments that had little artistic value, was in need of redecoration, and had a beige linoleum on the floor of the bathroom. Miss Winton did not notice her surroundings much; she considered the flat pretty in its way, and comfortable to live in. She was prepared to leave it at that.

'Well,' remarked Miss Winton to her dog in the same moment that Mrs Runca was stepping into a taxi-cab, 'what shall we do?'

The dog made no reply beyond wagging its tail. 'I have eggs to buy,' said Miss Winton, 'and honey, and butter. Shall we go and do all that?'

Miss Winton had lived in the block of flats for fifteen years. She had seen many tenants come and go. She had heard about the Runcas and the model place they had made of the penthouse. It was the talk of London, Miss Winton had been told by Mrs Neck, who kept a grocer's shop near by; the Runcas were full of taste, apparently. Miss Winton thought it odd that London should talk about a penthouse flat, but did not ever mention that to Mrs Neck, who didn't seem to think it odd at all. To Miss Winton the Runcas were like many others who had come to live in the same building: people she saw and did not know. There were no children in the building, that being a rule; but animals, within reason, were permitted.

Miss Winton left her flat and walked with her dog to Mrs Neck's shop. 'Fresh buns,' said Mrs Neck before Miss Winton had made a request. 'Just in, dear.' But Miss Winton shook her head and asked for eggs and honey and butter. 'Seven and ten,' said Mrs Neck, reckoning the cost before reaching a hand out for the articles. She said it was shocking that food should cost so much, but Miss Winton replied that in her opinion two shillings wasn't exorbitant for half a pound of butter. 'I remember it ninepence,' said Mrs Neck, 'and twice the stuff it was. I'd sooner a smear of Stork than what they're turning out today.' Miss Winton smiled, and agreed that the quality of everything had gone down a bit.

Afterwards, for very many years, Miss Winton remembered this conversation with Mrs Neck. She remembered Mrs Neck saying: 'I'd sooner a smear of Stork than what they're turning out today,' and she remembered the rather small, dark-haired girl who entered Mrs Neck's shop at that moment, who smiled at both of them in an innocent way. 'Is that so?' said the Runcas' maid, Bianca. 'Quality has gone down?'

'Lord love you, Miss Winton knows what she's talking about,' said Mrs Neck. 'Quality's gone to pieces.'

Miss Winton might have left the shop then, for her purchasing was over, but the dark-haired young girl had leaned down and was patting the head of Miss Winton's dog. She smiled while doing that. Mrs Neck said:

'Miss Winton's in the flats too.'

'Ah, yes?'

'This young lady,' explained Mrs Neck to Miss Winton, 'works for the Runcas in the penthouse we hear so much about.'

'Today they are coming to photograph,' said Bianca. 'People from a magazine. And they will write down other things about it.'

'Again?' said Mrs Neck, shaking her head in wonderment. 'What can I do for you?'

Bianca asked for coffee beans and a sliced loaf, still stroking the head of the dog.

Miss Winton smiled. 'He has taken to you,' she said to

Bianca, speaking timidly because she felt shy of people, especially foreigners. 'He's very good company.'

'Pretty little dog,' said Bianca.

Miss Winton walked with Bianca back to the block of flats, and when they arrived in the large hallway Bianca said:

'Miss Winton, would you like to see the penthouse with all its fresh flowers and fruits about the place? It is at its best in the morning sunlight as Mr Runca was remarking earlier. It is ready for all the photographers.'

Miss Winton, touched that the Italian girl should display such thoughtfulness towards an elderly spinster, said that it would be a pleasure to look at the penthouse flat but added that the Runcas might not care to have her walking about their property.

'No, no,' said Bianca, who had not been long in the Runcas' employ. 'Mrs Runca would love you to see it. And him too. "Show anyone you like," they've said to me. Certainly.' Bianca was not telling the truth, but time hung heavily on her hands in the empty penthouse and she knew she would enjoy showing Miss Winton all the flowers that Mrs Runca had so tastefully arranged, and all the curtains that had been imported specially from Thailand, and the rugs and the chairs and the pictures on the walls.

'Well,' began Miss Winton.

'Yes,' said Bianca and pressed Miss Winton and her dog into the lift.

But when the lift halted at the top and Bianca opened the gates Miss Winton experienced a small shock. 'Mr Morgan is here too,' said Bianca. 'Mending the water.'

Miss Winton felt that she could not now refuse to enter the Runcas' flat, since to do so would be to offend the friendly little Italian girl, yet she really did not wish to find herself face to face with Mr Morgan in somebody else's flat. 'Look here,' she said, but Bianca and the dog were already ahead of her. 'Come on, Miss Winton,' said Bianca.

Miss Winton found herself in the Runcas' small and fastidious hall, and then in the large room that had one side made of glass. She looked around her and noted all the low furniture and the pale Afghanistan carpet and the objects scattered economically about, and the flowers that Mrs Runca had arranged. 'Have coffee,' said Bianca, going quickly off to make some, and the little dog, noting her swift movement and registering it as a form of play, gave a single bark and darted about himself, in a small circle. 'Shh,' whispered Miss Winton. 'Really,' she protested, following Bianca to the kitchen, 'don't bother about coffee.' 'No, no,' said Bianca, pretending not to understand, thinking that there was plenty of time for herself and Miss Winton to have coffee together, sitting in the kitchen, where Mrs Runca had commanded coffee was to be drunk. Miss Winton could hear a light hammering and guessed it was Mr Morgan at work on the water-pipes. She could imagine him coming out of the Runcas' bathroom and stopping quite still as soon as he saw her. He would stand there in his brown overall, large and bulky, peering at her through his spectacles, chewing, probably, a piece of his moustache. His job was to attend to the needs of the tenants when the needs were not complicated, but whenever Miss Winton telephoned down to his basement and asked for his assistance he would sigh loudly into the telephone and say that he mightn't manage to attend to the matter for a day or two. He would come, eventually, late at night but still in his brown overall, his eyes watering, his breath rich with alcohol. He would look at whatever the trouble was and make a swift diagnosis, advising that experts should be summoned the following morning. He didn't much like her, Miss Winton thought; no doubt he considered her a poor creature, unmarried at sixty-four, thin and weak-looking, with little sign that her physical appearance had been attractive in girlhood.

'It's a lovely place,' said Miss Winton to Bianca. 'But I think perhaps we should go now. Please don't bother with coffee; and thank you most awfully.'

'No, no,' said Bianca, and while she was saying it Mr Morgan entered the kitchen in his brown overall.

One day in 1952 Miss Winton had mislaid her bicycle. It had disappeared without trace from the passage in the basement where Mr Morgan had said she might keep it. 'I have not seen it,' he had said slowly and deliberately at that time. 'I know of no cycle.' Miss Winton had reminded him that the bicycle had always had a place in the passage, since he had said she might keep it there. But Mr Morgan, thirteen years younger then, had replied that he could recall none of that. 'Stolen,' he had said. 'I dare say stolen. I should say the coke men carted it away. I cannot always be watching the place, y'know. I have me work, madam.' She had asked him to enquire of the coke men if they had in error removed her bicycle; she had spoken politely and with a smile, but Mr Morgan had repeatedly shaken his head, pointing out that he could not go suggesting that the coke men had made off with a bicycle, saying that the coke men would have the law on him. 'The wife has a cycle,' Mr Morgan had said. 'A Rudge. I could obtain it for you, madam. Fifty shillings?' Miss Winton had smiled again and had walked away, having refused this offer and given thanks for it.

'Was you wanting something, madam?' asked Mr Morgan now, his lower lip pulling a strand of his moustache into his mouth. 'This is the Runcas' flat up here.'

Miss Winton tried to smile at him. She thought that whatever she said he would be sarcastic in a disguised way. He would hide his sarcasm beneath the words he chose, implying it only with the inflection of his voice. Miss Winton said:

'Bianca kindly invited me to see the penthouse.'

'It is a different type of place from yours and mine,' replied Mr Morgan, looking about him. 'I was attending to a tap in the bathroom. Working, Miss Winton.'

'It is all to be photographed today,' said Bianca. 'Mr and Mrs Runca will return early from their businesses.'

'Was you up here doing the flowers, madam?'

He had called her madam during all the years they had known one another, pointing up the fact that she had no right to the title.

'A cup of coffee, Mr Morgan?' said Bianca, and Miss Winton hoped he would refuse.

'With two spoons of sugar in it,' said Mr Morgan, nodding his head and adding: 'D'you know what the Irish take in their coffee?' He began to laugh rumbustiously, ignoring Miss Winton and appearing to share a joke with Bianca. 'A tot of the hard stuff,' said Mr Morgan. 'Whisky.'

Bianca laughed too. She left the kitchen, and Miss Winton's dog ran after her. Mr Morgan blew at the surface of his coffee while Miss Winton, wondering what to say to him, stirred hers.

'It's certainly a beautiful flat,' said Miss Winton.

'It would be too large for you, madam. I mean to say, just you and the dog in a place like this. You'd lose one another.'

'Oh, yes, of course. No, I meant—'

'I'll speak to the authorities if you like. I'll speak on your behalf, as a tenant often asks me to do. Put a word in, y'know. I could put a word in if you like, madam.'

Miss Winton frowned, wondering what Mr Morgan was talking about. She smiled uncertainly at him. He said:

'I have a bit of influence, knowing the tenants and that. I got the left-hand ground flat for Mr McCarthy by moving the Aitchesons up to the third. I got Mrs Bloom out of the back one on the first—'

'Mr Morgan, you've misunderstood me. I wouldn't at all like to move up here.'

Mr Morgan looked at Miss Winton, sucking coffee off his moustache. His eyes were focused on hers. He said:

'You don't have to say nothing outright, madam. I understand a hint.'

Bianca returned with a bottle of whisky. She handed it to Mr Morgan, saying that he had better add it to the coffee since she didn't know how much to put in.

'Oh, a good drop,' said Mr Morgan, splashing the liquor on to his warm coffee. He approached Miss Winton with the neck of the bottle poised towards her cup. He'll be offended, she thought; and because of that she did not, as she wished to, refuse his offering. 'The Irish are heavy

53

drinkers,' said Mr Morgan. 'Cheers.' He drank the mixture and proclaimed it good. 'D'you like that, Miss Winton?' he asked, and Miss Winton tasted it and discovered to her surprise that the beverage was pleasant. 'Yes,' she said. 'I do.'

Mr Morgan held out his cup for more coffee. 'Just a small drop,' he said, and he filled the cup up with whisky. Again he inclined the neck of the bottle towards Miss Winton, who smiled and said she hadn't finished. He held the bottle in the same position, watching her drinking her coffee. She protested when Bianca poured her more, but she could sense that Bianca was enjoying this giving of hospitality, and for that reason she accepted, knowing that Mr Morgan would pour in more whisky. She felt comfortably warm from the whisky that was already in her body, and she experienced the desire to be agreeable—although she was aware, too, that she would not care for it if the Runcas unexpectedly returned.

'Fair enough,' said Mr Morgan, topping up Bianca's cup and adding a further quantity to his own. He said:

'Miss Winton is thinking of shifting up here, her being the oldest tenant in the building. She's been stuck downstairs for fifteen years.'

Bianca shook her head, saying to Miss Winton: 'What means that?'

'I'm quite happy,' said Miss Winton, 'where I am.' She spoke softly, with a smile on her face, intent upon being agreeable. Mr Morgan was sitting on the edge of the kitchen table. Bianca had turned on the wireless. Mr Morgan said:

'I came to the flats on March the twenty-first, nineteen fifty-one. Miss Winton here was already in residence. Riding about on a cycle.'

'I was six years old,' said Bianca.

'D'you remember that day, Miss Winton? March the twenty-first?'

Miss Winton shook her head. She sat down on a chair made of an ersatz material. She said:

'It's a long time ago.'

'I remember the time you lost your cycle, Miss Winton.

She come down to me in the basement,' said Mr Morgan to Bianca, 'and told me to tick off the coke deliverers for thieving her bicycle. I never seen no cycle, as I said to Miss Winton. D'you understand, missy?' Bianca smiled, nodding swiftly. She hummed the tune that was coming from the wireless. 'Do you like that Irish drink?' said Mr Morgan. 'Shall we have some more?'

'I must be going,' said Miss Winton. 'It's been terribly kind of you.'

'Are you going, madam?' said Mr Morgan, and there was in his tone a hint of the belligerency that Miss Winton knew his nature was imbued with. In her mind he spoke more harshly to her, saying she was a woman who had never lived. He was saying that she might have been a nun the way she existed, not knowing anything about the world around her; she had never known a man's love, Mr Morgan was saying; she had never borne a child.

'Oh, don't go,' said Bianca. 'Please, I'll make you a cold cocktail, like Mr Runca showed me how. Cinzano with gin in it, and lemon and ice.'

'Oh, no,' said Miss Winton.

Mr Morgan sighed, implying with the intake of his breath that her protest was not unexpected. There were other women in the block of flats, Miss Winton imagined, who would have a chat with Mr Morgan now and again, who would pass the time of day with him, asking him for racing tips and suggesting that he should let them know when he heard that a flat they coveted was going to be empty. Mr Morgan was probably a man whom people tipped quite lavishly for the performance of services or favours. Miss Winton could imagine people, people like the Runcas maybe, saying to their friends : 'We greased the caretaker's palm. We gave him five pounds.' She thought she'd never be able to do that.

Bianca went away to fetch the ingredients for the drink, and again the dog went with her.

Miss Winton stood still, determined that Mr Morgan should not consider that she did not possess the nerve to receive from the Runcas' Italian maid a midday cocktail. Mr Morgan said:

'You and me have known one another a number of years.'

'Yes, we have.'

'We know what we think of a flat like this, and the type of person. Don't we, Miss Winton?'

'To tell the truth, I don't know the Runcas at all.'

'I'll admit it to you: the whisky has loosened my tongue, Miss Winton. You understand what I mean?'

Miss Winton smiled at Mr Morgan. There was sweat, she noticed, on the sides of his face. He said with vehemence: 'Ridiculous, the place being photographed. What do they want to do that for, tell me?'

'Magazines take an interest. It's a contemporary thing. Mrs Neck was saying that this flat is well-known.'

'You can't trust Mrs Neck. I think it's a terrible place. I wouldn't be comfortable in a place like this.'

'Well—'

'You could report me for saying a thing like that. You could do that, Miss Winton. You could tell them I was intoxicated at twelve o'clock in the day, drinking a tenant's liquor and abusing the tenant behind his back. D'you see what I mean, madam?'

'I wouldn't report you, Mr Morgan. It's no business of mine.'

'I'd like to see you up here, madam, getting rid of all this trash and putting in a decent bit of furniture. How's about that?'

'Please, Mr Morgan, I'm perfectly happy—'

'I'll see what I can do,' said Mr Morgan.

Bianca returned with glasses and bottles. Mr Morgan said:

'I was telling Miss Winton here that she could report me to the authorities for misconduct, but she said she never would. We've known one another a longish time. We was never drinking together though.'

Bianca handed Miss Winton a glass that felt cold in Miss Winton's hand. She feared now what Mr Morgan was going to say. He said:

'I intoxicate easily.' Mr Morgan laughed, displaying darkened teeth. He swayed back and forth, looking at Miss Winton. 'I'll put in a word for you,' he said, 'no bother at all.'

She was thinking that she would finish the drink she'd been given and then go away and prepare lunch. She would buy some little present to give Bianca, and she would come up to the Runcas' flat one morning and hand it to her, thanking her for her hospitality and her thoughtfulness.

While Miss Winton was thinking that, Mr Morgan was thinking that he intended to drink at least two more of the drinks that the girl was offering, and Bianca was thinking that it was the first friendly morning she had spent in this flat since her arrival three weeks before. 'I must go to the W.C.,' said Mr Morgan, and he left the kitchen, saying he would be back. 'It's most kind of you,' said Miss Winton when he had gone. 'I do hope it's all right.' It had occurred to her that Bianca's giving people the Runcas' whisky and gin was rather different from her giving people a cup of coffee, but when she looked at Bianca she saw that she was innocently smiling. She felt light-headed, and smiled herself. She rose from her chair and thanked Bianca again and said that she must be going now. Her dog came to her, wishing to go also. 'Don't you like the drink?' said Bianca, and Miss Winton finished it. She placed the glass on the metal draining-board and as she did so a crash occurred in the Runcas' large sitting-room. 'Heavens!' said Miss Winton, and Bianca raised a hand to her mouth and kept it there. When they entered the room they saw Mr Morgan standing in the centre of it, looking at the floor.

'Heavens!' said Miss Winton, and Bianca widened her eyes and still did not take her hand away from her mouth. On the floor lay the flowers that Mrs Runca had earlier arranged. The huge vase was smashed into many pieces. Water was soaking into the Afghanistan carpet.

'I was looking at it,' explained Mr Morgan. 'I was touching a flower with my fingers. The whole thing gave way.'

'Mrs Runca's flowers,' said Bianca. 'Oh, Mother of God!'

'Mr Morgan,' said Miss Winton.

'Don't look at me, ma'am. Don't blame me for an instant. Them flowers was inadequately balanced. Ridiculous.'

Bianca, on her hands and knees, was picking up the broken stalks. She might have been more upset, Miss Winton thought, and she was glad that she was not. Bianca explained that Mrs Runca had stayed away from her boutique specially to arrange the flowers. 'They'll give me the sack,' she said, and instead of weeping she gave a small giggle.

The gravity of the situation struck Miss Winton forcibly. Hearing Bianca's giggle, Mr Morgan laughed also, and went to the kitchen, where Miss Winton heard him pouring himself some more of the Runcas' gin. Miss Winton realised then that neither Bianca nor Mr Morgan had any sense of responsibility at all. Bianca was young and did not know any better; Mr Morgan was partly drunk. The Runcas would return with people from a magazine and they would find that their property had been damaged, that a vase had been broken and that a large damp patch in the centre of their Afghanistan carpet would not look good in the photographs. 'Let's have another cocktail,' said Bianca, throwing down the flowers she had collected and giggling again. 'Oh, no,' cried Miss Winton. 'Please, Bianca. We must think what's best to do.' But Bianca was already in the kitchen, and Miss Winton could hear Mr Morgan's rumbustious laugh.

'I tell you what,' said Mr Morgan, coming towards her with a glass in his hand. 'We'll say the dog done it. We'll say the dog jumped at the flowers trying to grip hold of them.'

Miss Winton regarded him with surprise. 'My dog?' she said. 'My dog was nowhere near the flowers.' Her voice was sharp, the first time it had been so that morning.

Mr Morgan sat down in an armchair, and Miss Winton, about to protest about that also, realised in time that she had, of course, no right to protest at all.

'We could say,' said Mr Morgan, 'that the dog went into a hysterical fit and attacked the flowers. How's about that?'

'But that's not true. It's not the truth.'

'I was thinking of me job, madam. And of the young missy's. It's all right for others.'

'It was an accident,' said Miss Winton, 'as you have said, Mr Morgan.'

'They'll say what was I doing touching the flowers? They'll say to the young missy what was happening at all, was you giving a party? I'll have to explain the whole thing to my wife.'

'Your wife?'

'What was I doing in the Runcas' flat with the young one? The wife will see through anything.'

'You were here to mend a water-pipe, Mr Morgan.'

'What's the matter with the water-pipes?'

'Oh really, Mr Morgan. You were repairing a pipe when I came into the flat.'

'There was nothing the matter with the pipes, ma'am. Nor never has been, which is just the point. The young missy telephones down saying the pipes is making a noise. She's anxious for company. She likes to engage in a chat.'

'I shall arrange what flowers we can salvage,' said Miss Winton, 'just as neatly as they were arranged before. And we can explain to the Runcas that you came to the flat to mend a pipe and that in passing you brushed against Mrs Runca's flowers. The only difficulty is the carpet. The best way to get that damp stain out would be to lift up the carpet and put an electric fire in front of it.'

'Take it easy,' said Mr Morgan. 'Have a drink, Miss Winton.'

'We must repair the damage—'

'Listen, madam,' said Mr Morgan, leaning forward, 'you and I know what we think of a joint like this. Tricked out like they've got it—'

'It's a question of personal taste—'

'Tell them the dog done the damage, Miss Winton, and I'll see you right. A word in the ear of the authorities and them Runcas will be out on the street in a jiffy. Upsetting the neighbours with noise, bringing the flats into disrepute.

I'd say it in court, Miss Winton: I seen naked women going in and out of the penthouse. D'you see?'

Bianca returned, and Miss Winton repeated to her what she had said already to Mr Morgan about the drying of the carpet. Between them, they moved chairs and tables and lifted the carpet from the floor, draping it across two chairs and placing an electric fire in front of it. Mr Morgan moved to a distant sofa and watched them.

'I used not to be bad with flowers,' said Miss Winton to Bianca. 'Are there other vases?' They went together to the kitchen to see what there was. 'Would you like another cocktail?' said Bianca, but Miss Winton said she thought they all had had enough to drink. 'I like these drinks,' said Bianca, sipping one. 'So cool.'

'You must explain,' said Miss Winton, 'that Mr Morgan had to come in order to repair the gurgling pipe and that he brushed against the flowers on the way across the room. You must tell the truth: that you had invited me to have a look at the beautiful flat. I'm sure they won't be angry when they know it was all an accident.'

'What means gurgling?' said Bianca.

'Hey,' shouted Mr Morgan from the other room.

'I think Mr Morgan should go now,' said Miss Winton. 'I wonder if you'd say so, Bianca? He's a very touchy man.' She imagined Mr Runca looking sternly into her face and saying he could not believe his eyes: that she, an elderly spinster, still within her wits, had played a part in the disastrous proceedings in his flat. She had allowed the caretaker to become drunk, she had egged on a young foreign girl. 'Have you no responsibility?' shouted Mr Runca at Miss Winton in her imagination. 'What's the matter with you?'

'Hey,' shouted Mr Morgan. 'That carpet's burning.'

Miss Winton and Bianca sniffed the air and smelt at once the tang of singed wool. They returned at speed to the other room and saw that the carpet was smoking and that Mr Morgan was still on the sofa, watching it. 'How's about that?' said Mr Morgan.

'The fire was too close,' said Bianca, looking at Miss Winton, who frowned and felt afraid. She didn't remember putting the fire so close to the carpet, and then she thought that she was probably as intoxicated as Mr Morgan and didn't really know what she was doing.

'Scrape off the burnt bit,' advised Mr Morgan, 'and tell them the dog ate it.'

They unplugged the fire and laid the carpet flat on the floor again. Much of the damp had disappeared, but the burnt patch, though small, was eye-catching. Miss Winton felt a weakness in her stomach, as though a quantity of jelly were turning rhythmically over and over. The situation now seemed beyond explanation, and she saw herself asking the Runcas to sit down quietly, side by side with the people from the magazine, and she heard herself trying to tell the truth, going into every detail and pleading that Bianca should not be punished. 'Blame me,' she was saying, 'if someone must be blamed, for I have nothing to lose.'

'I'll tell you what,' said Mr Morgan, 'why don't we telephone for Mrs Neck? She done a carpet for her hearth, forty different wools she told me, that she shaped with a little instrument. Ring up Mrs Neck, missy, and say there's a drink for her if she'll oblige Mr Morgan with ten minutes of her time.'

'Do no such thing,' cried Miss Winton. 'There's been enough drinking, Mr Morgan, as well you know. The trouble started with drink, when you lurched against the flowers. There's no point at all in Mrs Neck adding to the confusion.'

Mr Morgan listened to Miss Winton and then rose from the sofa. He said:

'You have lived in these flats longer than I have, madam. We all know that. But I will not stand here and be insulted by you, just because I am a working man. The day you came after your cycle—'

'I must go away,' cried Bianca in distress. 'I cannot be found with a burnt carpet and the flowers like that.'

'Listen,' said Mr Morgan, coming close to Miss Winton. 'I have a respect for you. I'm surprised to hear myself insulted from your lips.'

'Mr Morgan—'

'You was insulting me, madam.'

'I was not insulting you. Don't go, Bianca. I'll stay here and explain everything to the Runcas. I think, Mr Morgan, it would be best if you went off to your lunch now.'

'How can I?' shouted Mr Morgan very loudly and rudely, sticking his chin out at Miss Winton. 'How the damn hell d'you think I can go down to the wife in the condition I'm in? She'd eat the face off me.'

'Please, Mr Morgan.'

'You and your dog: I have respect for the pair of you. You and me is on the same side of the fence. D'you understand?'

Miss Winton shook her head.

'What d'you think of the Runcas, ma'am?'

'I've said, Mr Morgan: I've never met the Runcas.'

'What d'you think of the joint they've got here?'

'I think it's most impressive.'

'It's laughable. The whole caboodle is laughable. Did you ever see the like?' Mr Morgan pointed at objects in the room. 'They're two tramps,' he shouted, his face purple with rage at the thought of the Runcas. 'They're jumped-up tramps.'

Miss Winton opened her mouth in order to speak soothingly. Mr Morgan said:

'I could put a match to the place and to the Runcas too, with their bloody attitudes. I'm only a simple caretaker, madam, but I'd see their bodies in flames.' He kicked a chair, his boot thudding loudly against pale wood. 'I hate that class of person, they're as crooked as a corkscrew.'

'You're mistaken, Mr Morgan.'

'I'm bloody not mistaken,' shouted Mr Morgan. 'They're full of hate for a man like me. They'd say I was a beast.'

Miss Winton, shocked and perturbed, was also filled with amazement. She couldn't understand why Mr Morgan had said that he and she belonged on the same side of the fence, since for the past fifteen years she had noted the scorn in his eyes.

'We have a thing in common,' said Mr Morgan. 'We have no respect whatever for the jumped-up tramps who occupy this property. I'd like to see you in here, madam, with your bits and pieces. The Runcas can go where they belong.' Mr Morgan spat into the chair which he had struck with his boot.

'Oh, no,' cried Miss Winton, and Mr Morgan laughed. He walked about the room, clearing his throat and spitting carelessly. Eventually he strolled away, into the kitchen. The dog barked, sensing Miss Winton's distress. Bianca began to sob and from the kitchen came the whistling of Mr Morgan, a noise he emitted in order to cover the sound of gin being poured into his glass. Miss Winton knew what had happened: she had read of men who could not resist alcohol and who were maddened by its presence in their bloodstream. She considered that Mr Morgan had gone mad in the Runcas' flat; he was speaking like an insane person, saying he had respect for her dog.

'I am frightened of him,' said Bianca.

'No,' said Miss Winton. 'He's a harmless man, though I wish he'd go away. We can clean up a bit. We can make an effort.'

Mr Morgan returned and took no notice of them. He sat on the sofa while they set to, clearing up all the pieces of broken vase and the flowers. They placed a chair over the burnt area of carpet so that the Runcas would not notice it as soon as they entered the room. Miss Winton arranged the flowers in a vase and placed it where the other one had been placed by Mrs Runca. She surveyed the room and noticed that, apart from the presence of Mr Morgan, it wasn't so bad. Perhaps, she thought, the explanation could be unfolded gradually. She saw no reason why the room shouldn't be photographed as it was now, with the nicely-arranged flowers and the chair over the burnt patch of carpeting. The damp area, greater in size, was still a little noticeable, but she imagined that in a photograph it mightn't show up too badly.

'You have let me get into this condition,' said Mr Morgan in an aggressive way. 'It was your place to say that the Runcas' whisky shouldn't be touched, nor their gin neither. You're a fellow-tenant, Miss Winton. The girl and I are servants, madam. We was doing what came naturally.'

'I'll take the responsibility,' said Miss Winton.

'Say the dog done it,' urged Mr Morgan again. 'The other will go against the girl and myself.'

'I'll tell the truth,' said Miss Winton. 'The Runcas will understand. They're not monsters that they won't forgive an accident. Mrs Runca—'

'That thin bitch,' shouted Mr Morgan, and added more quietly: 'Runca's illegitimate.'

'Mr Morgan—'

'Tell them the bloody dog done it. Tell them the dog ran about like a mad thing. How d'you know they're not monsters? How d'you know they'll understand, may I ask? "We was all three boozing in the kitchen," are you going to say? "and Mr Morgan took more than his share of the intox- icant. All hell broke loose." Are you going to say that, Miss Winton?'

'The truth is better than lies.'

'What's the matter with saying the dog done it?'

'You would be far better off out of this flat, Mr Morgan. No good will come of you raving on like that.'

'You have always respected me, madam. You have never been familiar.'

'Well—'

'I might strike them dead. They might enter that door and I might hit them with a hammer.'

Miss Winton began to protest, but Mr Morgan waved a hand at her. He sniffed and said: 'A caretaker sees a lot, I'll tell you that. Fellows bringing women in, hypocrisy all over the place. There's those that slips me a coin, madam, and those that doesn't bother, and I'm not to know which is the worse. Some of them's miserable and some's boozing all night, having sex and laughing their heads off. The Runcas isn't human in any way whatsoever. The Runcas is saying I was a beast that might offend their eyes.' Mr Morgan ceased to speak, and glared angrily at Miss Winton.

'Come now,' she said.

'A dirty caretaker, they've said, who's not fit to be alive—'

'They've never said any such thing, Mr Morgan. I'm sure of it.'

'They should have moved away from the flats if they hated the caretaker. They're a psychological case.'

There was a silence in the room, while Miss Winton trembled and tried not to show it, aware that Mr Morgan had reached a condition in which he was capable of all he mentioned.

'What I need,' he said after a time, speaking more calmly from the sofa on which he was relaxing, 'is a cold bath.'

'Mr Morgan,' said Miss Winton. She thought that he was at last about to go away, down to his basement and his angry wife, in order to immerse his large body in cold water. 'Mr Morgan, I'm sorry that you should think badly of me—'

'I'll have a quick one,' said Mr Morgan, walking towards the Runcas' bathroom. 'Who'll know the difference?'

'No,' cried Miss Winton. 'No, please, Mr Morgan.'

But with his glass in his hand Mr Morgan entered the bathroom and locked the door.

When the photographers arrived at half-past two to prepare their apparatus Mr Morgan was still in the bathroom. Miss Winton waited with Bianca, reassuring her from time to time, repeating that she would not leave until she herself had explained to the Runcas what had happened. The photographers worked silently, moving none of the furniture because they had been told that the furniture was on no account to be displaced.

For an hour and twenty minutes Mr Morgan had been in the bathroom. It was clear to Miss Winton that he had thrown the vase of flowers to the ground deliberately and in anger, and that he had placed the fire closer to the carpet. In his crazy and spiteful condition Miss Winton imagined that he was capable of anything: of drowning himself in the bath maybe, so that the Runcas' penthouse might sordidly feature in the newspapers. Bianca had been concerned about his continued presence in the bathroom, but Miss Winton had explained that Mr Morgan was simply being unpleasant since he was made like that. 'It is quite disgraceful,' she said, well aware that Mr Morgan realised that she was the kind of woman who would not report him to the authorities, and was taking advantage of her nature while involving her in his own. She felt that the Runcas were the victims of circumstance, and thought that she might use that very expression when she made her explanation to them. She would speak slowly and quietly, breaking it to them in the end that Mr Morgan was still in the bathroom and had probably fallen asleep. 'It is not his fault,' she heard herself saying. 'We must try to understand.' And she felt that the Runcas would nod their heads in agreement and would know what to do next.

'Will they sack me?' said Bianca, and Miss Winton shook her head, repeating again that nothing that had happened had been Bianca's fault.

At three o'clock the Runcas arrived. They came together, having met in the hallway downstairs. 'The flowers came, did they?' Mr Runca had enquired of his wife in the lift, and she had replied that the flowers had safely been delivered and that she had arranged them to her satisfaction. 'Good,' said Mr Runca, and reported to his wife some facts about the morning he had spent.

When they entered their penthouse apartment the Runcas noted the presence of the photographers and the photographers' apparatus. They saw as well that an elderly woman with a dog was there, standing beside Bianca, that a chair had been moved, that the Afghanistan carpet was stained, and that some flowers had been loosely thrust into a vase. Mr Runca wondered about the latter because his wife had just informed him that she herself had arranged the flowers; Mrs Runca thought that something peculiar was going on. The elderly woman stepped forward to greet them, announcing that her name was Miss Winton, and at that moment a man in a brown overall whom the Runcas recognised as a Mr Morgan, caretaker and odd-job man, entered the room from the direction of the bathroom. He strode towards them and coughed.

'You had trouble with the pipes,' said Mr Morgan. He spoke urgently and it seemed to Mr and Mrs Runca that the elderly woman with the dog was affected by his speaking. Her mouth was actually open, as though she had been about to speak herself. Hearing Mr Morgan's voice, she closed it.

'What has happened here?' said Mrs Runca, moving forward from her husband's side. 'Has there been an accident?'

'I was called up to the flat,' said Mr Morgan, 'on account of noise in the pipes. Clogged pipes was on the point of bursting, a trouble I've been dealing with since eleven-thirty. You'll discover the bath is full of water. Release it, sir, at five o'clock tonight, and then I think you'll find everything O.K. Your drain-away was out of order.'

Mrs Runca removed her gaze from Mr Morgan's face and passed it on to the face of Miss Winton and then on to the bowed head of Bianca. Her husband examined the silent photographers, sensing something in the atmosphere. He said to himself that he did not yet know the full story: what, for instance, was this woman with a dog doing there? A bell rang, and Bianca moved automatically from Miss Winton's side to answer the door. She admitted the woman from the magazine, the woman who was in charge of everything and was to write the article.

'Miss Winton,' said Mr Morgan, indicating Miss Winton, 'occupies a flat lower down in the building.' Mr Morgan blew his nose. 'Miss Winton wished,' he said, 'to see the penthouse, and knowing that I was coming here she came up too and got into conversation with the maid on the doorstep. The dog dashed in, in a hysterical fit, knocking down a bowl of flowers and upsetting an electric fire on the carpet.

Did you notice this?' said Mr Morgan, striding forward to display the burnt patch. 'The girl had the fire on,' added Mr Morgan, 'because she felt the cold, coming from a warmer clime.'

Miss Winton heard the words of Mr Morgan and said nothing at all. He had stood in the bathroom, she reckoned, for an hour and twenty minutes, planning to say that the girl had put on the fire because, being Italian, she had suddenly felt the cold.

'Well?' said Mr Runca, looking at Miss Winton.

She saw his eyes, dark and intent, anxious to draw a response from her, wishing to watch the opening and closing of her lips while his ears listened to the words that relayed the explanation.

'I regret the inconvenience,' she said. 'I'll pay the damage.'

'Damage?' cried Mrs Runca, moving forward and pushing the chair further away from the burnt area of carpet. 'Damage?' she said again, looking at the flowers in the vase.

'So a dog had a fit in here,' said Mr Runca.

The woman from the magazine looked from Mr Morgan to Bianca and then to Miss Winton. She surveyed the faces of Mr and Mrs Runca and glanced last of all at the passive countenances of her photographers. It seemed, she reflected, that an incident had occurred; it seemed that a dog had gone berserk. 'Well now,' she said briskly. 'Surely it's not as bad as all that? If we put that chair back who'll notice the carpet? And the flowers look most becoming.'

'The flowers are a total mess,' said Mrs Runca. 'An animal might have arranged them.'

Mr Morgan was discreetly silent, and Miss Winton's face turned scarlet.

'We had better put the whole thing off,' said Mr Runca meditatively. 'It'll take a day or two to put everything back to rights. We are sorry,' he said, addressing himself to the woman from the magazine. 'But no doubt you see that no pictures can be taken?'

The woman, swearing most violently within her mind,

smiled at Mr Runca and said it was obvious, of course. Mr Morgan said:

'I'm sorry, sir, about this.' He stood there, serious and unemotional, as though he had never suggested that Mrs Neck might be invited up to the Runcas' penthouse apartment, as though hatred and drink had not rendered him insane. 'I'm sorry, sir,' said Mr Morgan. 'I should not have permitted a dog to enter your quarters, sir. I was unaware of the dog until it was too late.'

Listening to Mr Morgan laboriously telling his lies, Miss Winton was visited by the thought that there was something else she could do. For fifteen years she had lived lonesomely in the building, her shyness causing her to keep herself to herself. She possessed enough money to exist quite comfortably; she didn't do much as the days went by.

'Excuse me,' said Miss Winton, not at all knowing how she was going to proceed. She felt her face becoming red again, and she felt the eyes of all the people on her. She wanted to explain at length, to go on talking in a manner that was quite unusual for her, weaving together the threads of an argument. It seemed to Miss Winton that she would have to remind the Runcas of the life of Mr Morgan, how he daily climbed from his deep basement, attired invariably in his long brown overall. 'He has a right to his resentment,' was what she might say; 'he has a right to demand more of the tenants of these flats. His palm is greased, he is handed a cup of tea in exchange for a racing tip; the tenants keep him sweet.' He had come to consider that some of the tenants were absurd, or stupid, and that others were hypocritical. For Miss Winton he had reserved his scorn, for the Runcas a share of his hatred. Miss Winton had accepted the scorn, and understood why it was there; they must seek to understand the other. 'The ball is in your court,' said Miss Winton in her imagination, addressing the Runcas and pleased that she had thought of a breezy expression that they would at once appreciate.

'What about Wednesday next?' said Mr Runca to the

woman from the magazine. 'All this should be sorted out by then, I imagine.'

'Wednesday would be lovely,' said the woman.

Miss Winton wanted to let Mr Morgan see that he was wrong about these people. She wanted to have it proved here and now that the Runcas were human and would understand an accident, that they, like anyone else, were capable of respecting a touchy caretaker. She wished to speak the truth, to lead the truth into the open and let it act for itself between Mr Morgan and the Runcas.

'We'll make a note of everything,' Mrs Runca said to her, 'and let you have the list of the damage and the cost of it.'

'I'd like to talk to you,' said Miss Winton. 'I'd like to explain if I may.'

'Explain?' said Mrs Runca. 'Explain?'

'Could we all sit down? I'd like you to understand. I've been in these flats for fifteen years. Mr Morgan came a year later. Perhaps I can help. It's difficult for me to explain to you.' Miss Winton paused, in some confusion.

'Is she ill?' enquired the steely voice of Mrs Runca, and Miss Winton was aware of the woman's metallic hair, and finger-nails that matched it, and the four shrewd eyes of a man and a woman who were successful in all their transactions. 'I might hit them with a hammer,' said the voice of Mr Morgan in Miss Winton's memory. 'I might strike them dead.'

'We must try to understand,' cried Miss Winton, her face burning with embarrassment. 'A man like Mr Morgan and people like you and an old spinster like myself. We are all standing in this room and we must relax and attempt to understand.' Miss Winton wondered if the words that she forced from her were making sense; she was aware that she was not being eloquent. 'Don't you see?' cried Miss Winton with the businesslike stare of the Runcas fixed harshly upon her.

'What's this?' demanded Mrs Runca. 'What's all this about understanding? Understanding what?'

'Yes,' said her husband.

'Mr Morgan comes up from his basement every day of his life. The tenants grease his palm. He sees the tenants in his own way. He has a right to do that; he has a right to his touchiness—'

Mr Morgan coughed explosively, interrupting the flow of words. 'What are you talking about?' cried Mrs Runca. 'It's enough that damage has been done without all this.'

'I'm trying to begin at the beginning.' Ahead of her Miss Winton sensed a great mound of words and complication before she could lay bare the final truth: that Mr Morgan regarded the Runcas as people who had been in some way devoured. She knew that she would have to progress slowly, until they began to guess what she was trying to put to them. Accepting that they had failed the caretaker, as she had failed him too, they would understand the reason for his small revenge. They would nod their heads guiltily while she related how Mr Morgan, unhinged by alcohol, had spat at their furniture and had afterwards pretended to be drowned.

'We belong to different worlds,' said Miss Winton, wishing the ground would open beneath her, 'you and I and Mr Morgan. Mr Morgan sees your penthouse flat in a different way. What I am trying to say is that you are not just people to whom only lies can be told.'

'We have a lot to do,' said Mrs Runca, lighting a cigarette. She was smiling slightly, seeming amused.

'The bill for damage must be paid,' added Mr Runca firmly. 'You understand, Miss Winter? There can be no shelving of that responsibility.'

'I don't do much,' cried Miss Winton, moving beyond embarrassment now. 'I sit with my dog. I go to the shops. I watch the television. I don't do much, but I am trying to do something now. I am trying to promote understanding.'

The photographers began to dismantle their apparatus. Mr Runca spoke in a whisper to the woman from the magazine, making some final arrangement for the following Wednesday. He turned to Miss Winton and said more loudly: 'Perhaps you had better return to your apartment,

71

Miss Winter. Who knows, that little dog may have another fit.'

'He didn't have a fit,' cried Miss Winton. 'He never had a fit in the whole of his life.'

There was a silence in the room then, before Mr Runca said:

'You've forgotten, Miss Winter, that your little dog had a bout of hysteria and caused a lot of trouble. Come now, Miss Winter.'

'My name is not Miss Winter. Why do you call me a name that isn't correct?'

Mr Runca threw his eyes upwards, implying that Miss Winton was getting completely out of hand and would next be denying her very existence. 'She's the Queen Mother,' whispered Mrs Runca to one of the photographers, and the photographer sniggered lightly. Miss Winton said:

'My dog did not have a fit. I am trying to tell you, but no one bothers to listen. I am trying to go back to the beginning, to the day that Mr Morgan first became caretaker of these flats—'

'Now, madam,' said Mr Morgan, stepping forward.

'I am going to tell the truth,' cried Miss Winton shrilly. Her dog began to bark, and she felt, closer to her now, the presence of Mr Morgan. 'Shall we be going, madam?' said Mr Morgan, and she was aware that she was being moved towards the door. 'No,' she cried while the movement continued. 'No,' whispered Miss Winton again, but already she was on the landing and Mr Morgan was saying that there was no point whatsoever in attempting to tell people like the Runcas the truth. 'That type of person,' said Mr Morgan, descending the stairs with Miss Winton, his hand beneath her left elbow as though she required aid, 'that type of person wouldn't know the meaning of the word.'

I have failed, said Miss Winton to herself; I have failed to do something that might have been good in its small way. She found herself at the door of her flat, feeling tired, and heard Mr Morgan saying: 'Will you be all right, madam?' She reflected that he was speaking to her as though she were the one who had been mad, soothing her in his scorn. Mr Morgan began to laugh. 'Runca slipped me a quid,' he said. 'Our own Runca.' He laughed again, and Miss Winton felt wearier. She would write a cheque for the amount of the damage, and that would be that. She would often in the future pass Mr Morgan on the stairs and there would be a confused memory between them. The Runcas would tell their friends, saying there was a peculiar woman in one of the flats. 'Did you see their faces,' said Mr Morgan, 'when I mentioned about the dog in a fit?' He threw his head back, displaying all his teeth. 'It was that amusing,' said Mr Morgan. 'I nearly smiled.' He went away, and Miss Winton stood by the door of her flat, listening to his footsteps on the stairs. She heard him on the next floor, summoning the lift that would carry him smoothly to the basement, where he would tell his wife about how Miss Winton's dog had had a fit in the Runcas' penthouse, and how Miss Winton had made a ridiculous fuss that no one had bothered to listen to.

IV

In at the Birth

ONCE UPON A TIME there lived in a remote London suburb an elderly lady called Miss Efoss. Miss Efoss was a spry person, and for as long as she could control the issue she was determined to remain so. She attended the cinema and the theatre with regularity; she read at length; and she preferred the company of men and women forty years her junior. Once a year Miss Efoss still visited Athens and always on such visits she wondered why she had never settled in Greece: now, she felt, it was rather too late to make a change; in any case, she enjoyed London.

In her lifetime, nothing had passed Miss Efoss by. She had loved and been loved. She had once, even, given birth to a child. For a year or two she had known the ups and downs of early family life, although the actual legality of marriage had somehow been overlooked. Miss Efoss's baby died during a sharp attack of pneumonia; and shortly afterwards the child's father packed a suitcase one night. He said goodbye quite kindly to Miss Efoss, but she never saw him again.

In retrospect, Miss Efoss considered that she had run the gamut of human emotions. She settled down to the lively superficiality of the everyday existence she had mapped for herself. She was quite content with it. And she hardly noticed it when the Dutts entered her life.

It was Mr Dutt who telephoned. He said: 'Ah, Miss Efoss, I wonder if you can help us. We have heard that occasionally you baby-sit. We have scoured the neighbourhood for a reliable baby-sitter. Would you be interested, Miss Efoss, in giving us a try?'

'But who are you?' said Miss Efoss. 'I don't even know you. What is your name to begin with?'

74

'Dutt,' said Mr Dutt. 'We live only a couple of hundred yards from you. I think you would find it convenient.'

'Well—'

'Miss Efoss, come and see us. Come and have a drink. If you like the look of us perhaps we can arrange something. If not, we shan't be in the least offended.'

'That is very kind of you, Mr Dutt. If you give me your address and a time I'll certainly call. In fact, I shall be delighted to do so.'

'Good, good.' And Mr Dutt gave Miss Efoss the details, which she noted in her diary.

Mr and Mrs Dutt looked alike. They were small and thin with faces like greyhounds. 'We have had such difficulty in finding someone suitable to sit for us,' Mrs Dutt said. 'All these young girls, Miss Efoss, scarcely inspire confidence.'

'We are a nervous pair, Miss Efoss,' Mr Dutt said, laughing gently as he handed her a glass of sherry. 'We are a nervous pair and that's the truth of it.'

'There is only Mickey, you see,' explained his wife. 'I suppose we worry a bit. Though we try not to spoil him.'

Miss Efoss nodded. 'An only child is sometimes a problem.'

The Dutts agreed, staring intently at Miss Efoss, as though recognising in her some profound quality.

'We have, as you see, the television,' Mr Dutt remarked. 'You would not be lonely here of an evening. The radio as well. Both are simple to operate and are excellent performers.'

'And Mickey has never woken up,' said Mrs Dutt. 'Our system is to leave our telephone behind. Thus you may easily contact us.'

'Ha, ha, ha.' Mr Dutt was laughing. His tiny face was screwed into an unusual shape, the skin drawn tightly over his gleaming cheek-bones.

'What an amusing thing to say, Beryl! My wife is fond of a joke, Miss Efoss.'

Unaware that a joke had been made, Miss Efoss smiled. 'It would be odd if we did *not* leave our telephone

75

behind,' Mr Dutt went on. 'We leave the telephone *number* behind, Beryl. The telephone number of the house where we are dining. You would be surprised, Miss Efoss, to receive guests who carried with them their telephone receiver. Eh?'

'It would certainly be unusual.'

' "We have brought our own telephone, since we do not care to use another." Or: "We have brought our telephone in case anyone telephones us while we are here". Miss Efoss, will you tell me something?'

'If I can, Mr Dutt.'

'Miss Efoss, have you ever looked up the word *joke* in the *Encyclopaedia Britannica*?'

'I don't think I have.'

'You would find it rewarding. We have the full *Encyclopaedia* here, you know. It is always at your service.'

'How kind of you.'

'I will not tell you now what the *Encyclopaedia* says on the subject. I will leave you to while away a minute or two with it. I do not think you'll find it a wasted effort.'

'I'm sure I won't.'

'My husband is a great devotee of the *Encyclopaedia*,' Mrs Dutt said. 'He spends much of his time with it.'

'It is not always pleasure,' Mr Dutt said. 'The accumulation of information on many subjects is part of my work.'

'Your work, Mr Dutt?'

'Like many, nowadays, Miss Efoss, my husband works for his living.'

'You have some interesting job, Mr Dutt?'

'Interesting, eh? Yes, I suppose it is interesting. More than that I cannot reveal. That is so, eh, Beryl?'

'My husband is on the secret list. He is forbidden to speak casually about his work. Alas, even to someone to whom we trust our child. It's a paradox, isn't it?'

'I quite understand. Naturally, Mr Dutt's work is no affair of mine.'

'To speak lightly about it would mean marching orders for me,' Mr Dutt said. 'No offence, I hope?'

'Of course not.'

'Sometimes people take offence. We have had some un-happy occasions, eh, Beryl?'

'People do not always understand what it means to be on the secret list, Miss Efoss. So little is taken seriously now-adays.'

Mr Dutt hovered over Miss Efoss with his sherry decan-ter. He filled her glass and his wife's. He said:

'Well, Miss Efoss, what do you think of us? Can you accept the occasional evening in this room, watching our television and listening for the cry of our child?'

'Naturally, Miss Efoss, there would always be supper,' Mrs Dutt said.

'With sherry before and brandy to finish with,' Mr Dutt added.

'You are very generous. I can quite easily have something before I arrive.'

'No, no, no. It is out of the question. My wife is a good cook. And I can be relied upon to keep the decanters brim-ming.'

'You have made it all so pleasant I am left with no option. I should be delighted to help you out when I can manage it.'

Miss Efoss finished her sherry and rose. The Dutts rose also, smiling benignly at their satisfactory visitor.

'Well then,' Mr Dutt said in the hall, 'would Tuesday evening be a time you could arrange, Miss Efoss? We are bidden to dine with friends near by.'

'Tuesday? Yes, I think Tuesday is all right. About seven?'

Mrs Dutt held out her hand. 'Seven would be admirable. Till then, Miss Efoss.'

On Tuesday Mr Dutt opened the door to Miss Efoss and led her to the sitting-room. His wife, he explained, was still dressing. Making conversation as he poured Miss Efoss a drink, he said:

'I married my wife when she was on the point of entering a convent, Miss Efoss. What d'you think of that?'

'Well,' Miss Efoss said, settling herself comfortably

before the cosy-stove, 'it is hard to know what to say, Mr Dutt. I am surprised, I suppose.'

'Most people are surprised. I often wonder if I did the right thing. Beryl would have made a fine nun. What d'you think?'

'I'm sure you both knew what you were doing at the time. It is equally certain that Mrs Dutt would have been a fine nun.'

'She had chosen a particularly severe order. That's just like Beryl, isn't it?'

'I hardly know Mrs Dutt. But if it is like her to have made that choice, I can well believe it.'

'You see my wife as a serious person, Miss Efoss? Is that what you mean?'

'In the short time I have known her, yes I think I do. Yet you also say she relishes a joke.'

'A joke, Miss Efoss?'

'So you remarked the other evening. In relation to a slip in her speech.'

'Ah yes. How right you are. You must forgive me if my memory is often faulty. My work is wearing.'

Mrs Dutt, gaily attired, entered the room. 'Here, Miss Efoss,' she said, proffering a piece of paper, 'is the telephone number of the house we are going to. If Mickey makes a sound please ring us up. I will immediately return.'

'Oh but I'm sure that's not necessary. It would be a pity to spoil your evening so. I could at least attempt to comfort him.'

'I would prefer the other arrangement. Mickey does not take easily to strangers. His room is at the top of the house, but please do not enter it. Were he to wake suddenly and catch sight of you he might be extremely frightened. He is quite a nervous child. At the slightest untoward sound do not hesitate to telephone.'

'As you wish it, Mrs Dutt. I only suggested—'

'Experience has taught me, Miss Efoss, what is best. I have laid you a tray in the kitchen. Everything is cold, but quite nice, I think.'

'Thank you.'

'Then we will be away. We should be back by eleven-fifteen.'

'Do have a good evening.'

The Dutts said they intended to have a good evening, whispered for a moment together in the hall and were on their way. Miss Efoss looked critically about her.

The room was of an ordinary kind. Utrillo prints on plain grey walls. Yellowish curtains, yellowish chair-covers, a few pieces of simple furniture on a thick grey carpet. It was warm, the sherry was good and Miss Efoss was comfortable. It was pleasant, she reflected, to have a change of scene without the obligation of conversation. In a few moments, she carried her supper tray from the kitchen to the fire. As good as his word, Mr Dutt had left some brandy. Miss Efoss began to think the Dutts were quite a find.

She had dropped off to sleep when they returned. Fortunately, she heard them in the hall and had time to compose herself.

'All well?' Mrs Dutt asked.

'Not a sound.'

'Well, I'd better change him right away. Thank you so much, Miss Efoss.'

'Thank you. I have spent a very pleasant evening.'

'I'll drive you back,' Mr Dutt offered. 'The car is still warm.'

In the car Mr Dutt said: 'A child is a great comfort. Mickey is a real joy for us. And company for Beryl. The days hangs heavy when one is alone all day.'

'Yes, a child is a comfort.'

'Perhaps you think we are too careful and fussing about Mickey?'

'Oh no, it's better than erring in the other direction.'

'It is only because we are so grateful.'

'Of course.'

'We have much to be thankful for.'

'I'm sure you deserve it all.'

Mr Dutt had become quite maudlin by the time he

delivered Miss Efoss at her flat. She wondered if he was drunk. He pressed her hand warmly and announced that he looked forward to their next meeting. 'Any time,' Miss Efoss said as she stepped from the car. 'Just ring me up. I am often free.'

After that, Miss Efoss baby-sat for the Dutts many times. They became more and more friendly towards her. They left her little bowls of chocolates and drew her attention to articles in magazines that they believed might be of interest to her. Mr Dutt suggested further words she might care to look up in the *Encyclopaedia* and Mrs Dutt wrote out several of her recipes.

One night, just as she was leaving, Miss Efoss said: 'You know, I think it might be a good idea for me to meet Mickey some time. Perhaps I could come in the daytime once. Then I would no longer be a stranger and could comfort him if he woke.'

'But he *doesn't* wake, Miss Efoss. He has never woken, has he? You have never had to telephone us.'

'No. That is true. But now that I have got to know you, I would like to know him as well.'

The Dutts took the compliment, smiling at one another and at Miss Efoss. Mr Dutt said: 'It is kind of you to speak like this, Miss Efoss. But Mickey is rather scared of strangers. Just at present at any rate, if you do not mind.'

'Of course not, Mr Dutt.'

'I fear he is a nervous child,' Mrs Dutt said. 'Our present arrangement is carefully devised.'

'I'm sorry,' Miss Efoss said.

'No need. No need. Let us all have a final brandy,' Mr Dutt said cheerfully.

But Miss Efoss was sorry, for she feared she had said something out of place. And then for a week or so she was worried whenever she thought of the Dutts. She felt they were mistaken in their attitude about their child; and she felt equally unable to advise them. It was not her place to speak any further on the subject, yet she was sure that to keep the child away from people just because he was nervous of them was wrong. It sounded as though there was a root to the trouble somewhere, and it sounded as though the Dutts had not attempted to discover it. She continued to baby-sit for them about once every ten days and she held her peace. Then, quite unexpectedly, something happened that puzzled Miss Efoss very much indeed.

It happened at a party given by some friends of hers. She was talking about nothing in particular to an elderly man called Summerfield. She had known him for some years but whenever they met, as on this occasion, they found themselves with little to say beyond the initial courteous greetings. Thinking that a more direct approach might yield something of interest, Miss Efoss, after the familiar lengthy silence, said: 'How are you coping with the advancing years, Mr Summerfield? I feel I can ask you, since it is a coping I have to take in my own stride.'

'Well, well, I think I am doing well enough. My life is simple since my wife died, but there is little I complain of.'

'Loneliness is a thing that sometimes strikes at us. I find one must regard it as the toothache or similar ailment, and seek a cure.'

'Ah yes. I'm often a trifle alone.'

'I baby-sit, you know. Have you ever thought of it? Do not shy off because you are a man. A responsible person is all that is required.'

'I haven't thought of baby-sitting. Not ever I think. Though I like babies and always have done.'

'I used to do quite a lot. Now I have only the Dutts, but I go there very often. I enjoy my evenings. I like to see the TV now and again and other people's houses are interesting.'

'I know the Dutts,' said Mr Summerfield. 'You mean the Dutts in Raeburn Road? A small weedy couple?'

'They live in Raeburn Road, certainly. They are small too, but you are unkind to call them weedy.'

'I don't particularly mean it unkindly. I have known Dutt a long time. One takes liberties, I suppose, in describing people.'

'Mr Dutt is an interesting person. He holds some responsible position of intriguing secrecy.'

'Dutt? 25 Raeburn Road? The man is a chartered accountant.'

'I feel sure you are mistaken—'

'I cannot be mistaken. The man was once my colleague. In a very junior capacity.'

'Oh, well . . . then I must be mistaken.'

'What surprises me is that you say you baby-sit for the Dutts. I think you must be mistaken about that too.'

'Oh no, I am completely certain about that. It is for that reason that I know them at all.'

'I cannot help being surprised. Because, Miss Efoss—and of this I am certain—the Dutts have no children.'

Miss Efoss had heard of the fantasy world with which people, as they grow old, surround themselves. Yet she could not have entirely invented the Dutts in this way because Mr Summerfield had readily agreed about their existence. Was it then for some other reason that she visited them? Did she, as soon as she entered their house, become so confused in her mind that she afterwards forgot the real purpose of her presence? Had they hired her in some other capacity altogether? A capacity she was so ashamed of that she had invented, even for herself, the euphemism of baby-sitting? Had she, she wondered, become some kind of servant to these people—imagining the warm comfortable room, the sherry, the chocolates, the brandy?

'We should be back by eleven, Miss Efoss. Here is the telephone number.' Mrs Dutt smiled at her and a moment later the front door banged gently behind her.

It is all quite real, Miss Efoss thought. There is the sherry. There is the television set. In the kitchen on a tray I shall find my supper. It is all quite real: it is old Mr Summerfield who is wandering in his mind. It was only when she had finished her supper that she had the idea of establishing her role beyond question. All she had to do was to go upstairs and peep at the child. She knew how to be quiet: there was no danger of waking him.

The first room she entered was full of suitcases and card-board boxes. In the second she heard breathing and knew she was right. She snapped on the light and looked around her. It was brightly painted, with a wallpaper with elves on it. There was a rocking horse and a great pile of coloured bricks. In one of the far corners there was a large cot. It was very large and very high and it contained the sleeping figure of a very old man.

When the Dutts returned Miss Efoss said nothing. She was frightened and she didn't quite know why she was frightened. She was glad when she was back in her flat. The next day she telephoned her niece in Devon and asked if she might come down and stay for a bit.

Miss Efoss spoke to nobody about the Dutts. She gathered her strength in the country and returned to London at the end of a fortnight feeling refreshed and rational. She wrote a note to the Dutts saying she had decided to baby-sit no more. She gave no reason, but she said she hoped they would understand. Then, as best she could, she tried to forget all about them.

A year passed and then, one grey cold Sunday afternoon, Miss Efoss saw the Dutts in one of the local parks. They were sitting on a bench, huddled close together and seeming miserable. For a reason that she was afterwards unable to fathom Miss Efoss approached them.

'Good afternoon.'

The Dutts looked up at her, their thin, pale faces unsmiling and unhappy.

'Hello, Miss Efoss,' Mr Dutt said. 'We haven't seen you for a long time, have we? How are you this nasty weather?'

'Quite well, thank you. And you? And Mrs Dutt?'

Mr Dutt rose and drew Miss Efoss a few yards away from his wife. 'Beryl has taken it badly,' he said. 'Mickey died. Beryl has not been herself since. You understand how it is?'

'Oh, I am sorry.'

'I try to cheer her up, but I'm afraid my efforts are all in vain. I have taken it hard myself too. Which doesn't make anything any easier.'

'I don't know what to say, Mr Dutt. It's a great sadness for both of you.'

Mr Dutt took Miss Efoss's arm and led her back to the seat. 'I have told Miss Efoss,' he said to his wife. Mrs Dutt nodded.

'I'm very sorry,' Miss Efoss said again.

The Dutts looked at her, their sad, intent eyes filled with a pathetic desire for comfort. There was something almost hypnotic about them.

'I must go,' Miss Efoss said. 'Goodbye.'

'They have all died, Miss Efoss,' Mr Dutt said.' One by one they have all died.'

Miss Efoss paused in her retreat. She could think of nothing to say except that she was sorry.

'We are childless again,' Mr Dutt went on. 'It is almost unbearable to be childless again. We are so fond of them and here we are, not knowing what to do on a Sunday afternoon because we are a childless couple. The human frame, Miss Efoss, is not built to carry such misfortunes.'

'It is callous of me to say so, Mr Dutt, but the human frame is pretty resilient. It does not seem so at times like this I know, but you will find it is so in retrospect.'

'You are a wise woman, Miss Efoss, but, as you say, it is hard to accept wisdom at a moment like this. We have lost so many over the years. They are given to us and then abruptly they are taken away. It is difficult to understand God's infinite cruelty.'

'Goodbye, Mr Dutt. Goodbye, Mrs Dutt.'

They did not reply, and Miss Efoss walked quickly away.

Miss Efoss began to feel older. She walked with a stick; she found the cinema tired her eyes; she read less and discovered that she was bored by the effort of sustaining long conversations. She accepted each change quite philosophically, pleased that she could do so. She found too that there were compensations; she enjoyed, more and more, thinking about the past. Quite vividly, she re-lived the parts she wished to re-live. Unlike life itself, it was pleasant to be able to pick and choose.

Again by accident, she met Mr Dutt. She was having tea one afternoon in a quiet, old-fashioned teashop, not at all the kind of place she would have associated with Mr Dutt. Yet there he was, standing in front of her. 'Hello, Miss Efoss,' he said.

'Why, Mr Dutt. How are you? How is your wife? It is some time since we met.'

Mr Dutt sat down. He ordered some tea and then he leaned forward and stared at Miss Efoss. She wondered what he was thinking about: he had the air of someone who, through politeness, makes the most of a moment but whose mind is busily occupied elsewhere. As he looked at her, his face suddenly cleared. He smiled, and when he spoke he seemed to be entirely present.

'I have great news, Miss Efoss. We are both so happy about it. Miss Efoss, Beryl is expecting a child.'

Miss Efoss blinked a little. She spread some jam on her toast and said:

'Oh, I'm so glad. How delightful for you both! Mrs Dutt will be pleased. When is it—when is it due?'

'Quite soon. Quite soon.' Mr Dutt beamed. 'Naturally Beryl is beside herself with joy. She is busy preparing all day.'

'There is a lot to see to on these occasions.'

'Indeed there is. Beryl is knitting like a mad thing. It seems as though she can't do enough.'

'It is the biggest event in a woman's life, Mr Dutt.'

'And often in a man's, Miss Efoss.'

'Yes, indeed.'

'We have quite recovered our good spirits.'

'I'm glad of that. You were so sadly low when last I saw you.'

'You gave us some wise words. You were more comfort than you think, you know.'

'Oh, I was inadequate. I always am with sorrow.'

'No, no. Beryl said so afterwards. It was a happy chance to have met you so.'

'Thank you, Mr Dutt.'

'It's not easy always to accept adversity. You helped us on our way. We shall always be grateful.'

'It is kind of you to say so.'

'The longing for a child is a strange force. To attend to its needs, to give it comfort and love—I suppose there is that in all of us. There is a streak of simple generosity that we do not easily understand.'

'The older I become, Mr Dutt, the more I realise that one understands very little. I believe one is meant not to understand. The best things are complex and mysterious. And must remain so.'

'How right you are! It is often what I say to Beryl. I shall be glad to report that you confirm my thinking.'

'On my part it is instinct rather than thinking.'

'The line between the two is less acute than many would have us believe.'

'Yes, I suppose it is.'

'Miss Efoss, may I do one thing for you?'

'What is that?'

'It is a small thing but would give me pleasure. May I pay for your tea? Beryl will be pleased if you allow me to.'

Miss Efoss laughed. 'Yes, Mr Dutt, you may pay for my tea.' And it was as she spoke this simple sentence that it dawned upon Miss Efoss just what it was she had to do.

Miss Efoss began to sell her belongings. She sold them in many directions, keeping back only a few which she wished to give away. It took her a long time, for there was much to see to. She wrote down long lists of details, finding this method the best for arranging things in her mind. She was sorry to see the familiar objects go, yet she knew that to be sentimental about them was absurd. It was for other people now to develop a sentiment for them; and she knew that the fresh associations they would in time take on would be, in the long run, as false as hers.

Her flat became bare and cheerless. In the end there was nothing left except the property of the landlord. She wrote to him, terminating her tenancy.

The Dutts were watching the television when Miss Efoss

arrived. Mr Dutt turned down the sound and went to open the door. He smiled without speaking and brought her into the sitting-room.

'Welcome, Miss Efoss,' Mrs Dutt said. 'We've been expecting you.'

Miss Efoss carried a small suitcase. She said: 'Your baby, Mrs Dutt. When is your baby due? I do hope I am in time.'

'Perfect, Miss Efoss, perfect,' said Mr Dutt. 'Beryl's child is due this very night.'

The pictures flashed silently, eerily, on the television screen. A man dressed as a pirate was stroking the head of a parrot.

Miss Efoss did not sit down. 'I am rather tired,' she said. 'Do you mind if I go straight upstairs?'

'Dear Miss Efoss, please do.' Mrs Dutt smiled at her. 'You know your way, don't you?'

'Yes,' Miss Efoss said. 'I know my way.'

V

The Original Sins of Edward Tripp

EDWARD TRIPP HAD often noticed Mrs Mayben at her sitting-room window, putting bread on the window-sills for the birds. Her hair was white and she was dressed always in the same way, in several shades of grey. She had, he considered, the kindest face in all Dunfarnham Avenue, and when she saw him she would nod at him in a dignified manner, befitting a woman of her years. He had never rung the bell of Mrs Mayben's house as he had rung the bells of the other houses; he had never held her in conversation on her doorstep, but he knew that the day would come when his sister would ask him to cross the road and speak to the old woman. Edward was notorious in Dunfarmham Avenue, yet he felt whenever he considered the fact that Mrs Mayben, who kept herself to herself and did not gossip with the other people, was perhaps—just possibly—unaware of his notoriety. He thought, too, that when the time came, when eventually he found himself face to face with Mrs Mayben, he would tell her the truth: he would speak to her bluntly, and Edward guessed that an old woman with Mrs Mayben's dignity, who was a Christian and who never forgot the birds, would listen to him and would say a word or two of comfort. He imagined how things would be after that visit, he himself passing by Mrs Mayben's house and the truth hanging between them, she nodding with a smile from her window and he giving thanks to God for her understanding heart.

On Sunday August 26th Edward Tripp's sister, Emily, spoke of Mrs Mayben and Edward knew that on this morning he would hear himself protesting in a familiar way and that in the end he would cross the road to Mrs Mayben's house.

'We have watched the neighbourhood go down,' said Emily. 'Mrs Mayben was the last who was a decent sort of person. And now she's gone too. In cold blood.'

Edward, slicing some ham that he had purchased the day before in Lipton's, had been thinking to himself that the piece of gammon was not as satisfactory as usual: there was, for instance, a certain stringiness and a confusion about the direction of the grain. Before his sister had mentioned Mrs Mayben he had been allowing his thoughts to consider the meat as once it had been, an area of living flesh on the thigh of a pig. He imagined that something might have troubled that pig, some physical disorder that caused it to wriggle and dash about its sty, banging itself against the concrete sides and causing thus the stringiness to develop in its flesh.

'In cold blood,' said Emily again.

Edward looked up and regarded her back. He stared at the blackness of the material of which her long, old-fashioned dress was composed and at the roll of her hair, neat and formal on her neck.

'No, no,' said Edward. 'Not dead, dear. Not dead.'

But his sister nodded, denying his denial, and Edward shook his head with firmness.

'I remember when she came,' said Emily. 'Fourteen years ago. Her husband with her.'

Edward agreed with that. 'Her husband,' he said, 'died in 1955.'

'Death again,' murmured Emily, and Edward sighed. His sister was standing by their dining-room window, observing through it the house of Mrs Mayben opposite. Her left hand gripped the grey curtain that had flanked the window for almost thirty years, her right hung limply by her side. Edward guessed what was in her mind and did not care to consider it, since soon, he knew, he would be obliged to consider it whether he wished to or not. Attempting to keep the workings of his sister's brain at bay, he cut deeply into the ham. The image of the living animal appeared again before him. He said:

'After lunch why don't we try to repair the sitting-room

carpet? It gets worse, you know. Quite a hole has worn through. It seems a pity.'

'The carpet?' said Emily, and Edward added:

'Father used to talk about that carpet, d'you remember? About its quality. The years have proved him right.'

Emily, continuing to stare through the window, made no comment.

'It's lasted a couple of lifetimes,' Edward said quickly. 'It's a shame to let it go.' His eyes again travelled over his sister's back, moving upwards, to the roll of her hair. Emily said:

'There was a man here yesterday. Looking at Mrs Mayben's windows.'

'A robber,' suggested Edward, again slicing the ham, and in an automatic way beginning to feel sick in his stomach. He said, in a slow, low voice, that Mrs Mayben was probably now in church, or else within her house, cooking a simple lunch for herself.

'She hasn't been about,' said Emily. 'I haven't seen Mrs Mayben for four days.'

'I thought I saw her yesterday. I'm sure, you know.'

'He came,' said Emily, 'in a light-blue motor-car. The kind that's called a tourer, is it? Out of that he stepped at a quarter to four and stood on the pavement gazing up at her house—returning to his scene, God knows. He was indecently dressed, Edward: canvas shoes and light-weight trousers that matched the blue paintwork of his motor-car, and nothing at all where a shirt should have been. He was like a lunatic, I'll tell you that, walking on the edge of the pavement in the August sunshine, his eyes uplifted to the house. And I said to myself: "There's evil there".'

'Mrs Mayben's in church,' repeated Edward, 'or maybe home already, doing her Sunday chores.'

His sister shook her head. 'It's past her time for returning from church. She hasn't returned today, for I have watched at the window, being worried about her. Mrs Mayben, as well you know, Edward, is by now in two places at once.'

Edward imagined old Mrs Mayben delayed in a traffic jam in the hired car that called for her every Sunday at half-past eleven to take her to church. He imagined the chauffeur, the sallow-faced man who always came, with a green peaked cap, apologising to her about the delay, apologising about all the traffic, since she was the kind of woman who inspired apology, he imagined. Emily said:

'You know what I mean, don't you, when I say she's in two places at once? In heaven and in some cupboard, Edward; strung to a hook.'

There was a look, Edward knew, that must be there by now in his sister's eyes as she stared through the glass, ready to inflict her punishment. He thought, as he had thought before on similar occasions, that she was like a woman entering a fit.

'Now, now,' said Edward softly.

'Read the papers,' cried his sister, turning about to face him and speaking with emotion. 'A man has killed eight nurses in Chicago.'

'Oh no,' began Edward.

'Prize fighters turn on their children. Mothers go out with the tide.'

Edward placed the ham knife on the polished mahogany of the dining-room table. Slowly, he raised his eyes to meet his sister's.

'An old woman living alone,' said Emily.

Edward watched her tongue moving over her lips, beginning at one corner and returning to it. The tip of her tongue protruded at that corner for a moment and was then withdrawn. Again he raised his eyes to hers and they looked at one another in silence for a while, a brother and a sister who had lived all their lives in this house in Dunfarnham Avenue, Number Seventeen. Edward remembered the past and he knew that his sister was remembering it too. In the past were the children they had been, two other people, a different relationship: a girl thin and tall, four years older than the brother, he a boy who had laughed and had had his way, who had grown to be a man of slight build, permitting a small moustache to accumulate on his upper lip. The house that had been the house of their parents had changed only a little over the years. Wallpaper, the colour of good oatmeal, had hung all over it for three decades, placed there one spring when Emily was fourteen. Large engravings that featured the bridges of London decorated the hall and the stairs, and in dark book-cases, dustless behind glass, were volumes by Sapper, and *The Life of a Bengal Lancer,* and poems by Austin Dobson, and the collected works of Kipling and Scott. Edward often felt strange in the house now, feeling the present dominated by the past, remembering everything. From her own private flower-bed he had pulled her pansies, roots and all, when he was five years old; and with a pair of scissors he had cut through the centre of the buds of her roses. 'I have played a trick on you,' he used to say, sidling close to her. He had given two of her books away to an old woman who came seeking alms at the door. He had lit a fire in a fireplace of her doll's house, and had been punished because it was, so they said, a dangerous thing to do. He had taken one of her guinea-pigs and put it in her bed, where by mischance it had died. 'I have played a trick on you': he had said it repeatedly, bringing out her temper and her tears and running away himself. In middle age Emily was still taller than her brother, and had a hint of beauty about her features that was not reflected in his. Edward had developed a stoop in early manhood, and the child who had been bright with darting mischief became, in his own opinion, a shrimpish creature, fond of the corners of rooms.

On that Sunday morning, August 26th, Emily continued to speak about the man who had loitered in Dunfarnham Avenue in the sunshine. She spoke of the baldness of his head and the evil that she had recognised in the pupils of his eyes. He had worn no shirt, she repeated, emphasising the fact, and she said again that his shoes, placed over bare feet, had been of light-blue canvas, the same colour as his trousers and his car.

Listening to his sister's voice, Edward prayed in his mind. He prayed that she might turn from the window and walk away from the room, saying that she was going to the kitchen to make mustard, since mustard would be necessary with the ham. But his sister only stood before him, strange and thin as she had been as a child.

'I wish you could have seen him,' said Emily. 'I think I dreamed of him last night. The man is on my mind.'

'Why not sit down, my dear? Why not rest and try to forget?' As he spoke, Edward prayed for a day that was to come, a day that God, he felt, had promised him. His sister said:

'Perhaps on Wednesday night it was, or early on Thursday morning, that he slipped into the old woman's house to do what he had to do. And in his madness, Edward, he could not resist returning later to the scene of all the violence. I have read of this kind of thing. It has happened with other men.'

'Come along now—'

'Not at all unusual,' said Emily. 'Criminal history is not being made in Dunfarnham Avenue, if that's what you're thinking. He came and acted and returned, as others have in a similar way. D'you understand? D'you follow me?'

What was there to follow? Edward thought. What was there to understand except the facts from the past?—the quiet child of four and the son who was suddenly born in the house and allowed to go his way. The son growing up and his sport becoming the game he played with her, until her days were filled to the brim with his cunning smile and the baby tricks that everyone excused. Wasn't the simple truth that those cruelties in their thousands had fallen like a blight upon her nature in the end, wrenching some bit of it out of shape, embittering the whole?

When Edward was seventeen their parents had died, one after another within a month. He remembered still standing at his mother's funeral, the second funeral of the pair, and seeing on his sister's face the look that by now he had become familiar with, a look of reproach and sorrow. They had returned together to the dark house with the oatmeal wallpaper and Emily had said: 'There was a woman in a red coat, Edward. Did you see her? I thought it odd, you know, a woman dressed up all in red at the grave of another woman.' Edward had seen no woman in red and had said so at once, but Emily, making tea, had continued about this figure, and then had ceased to make tea and had stood quite still, gazing at him and talking at length, on and on, about the woman. 'What should we do?' she said. 'Shouldn't we try to find out a thing or two?' And then, in a moment, she had seemed to forget about the woman and had poured boiling water into a china tea-pot that both of them had known as a family possession all their lives. Afterwards, in the back garden, Edward all by himself had examined in detail his early sins against his sister, and he had closed his eyes and prayed to God. He prayed for forgiveness and he prayed that she in turn might forgive him and he prayed that the damage might not mark her for ever. From the garden, that day, he returned to the house, having found his duty, to live there with her, in that cool and silent place, to keep an eye on her for ever, and to atone as best he might. God had spoken harshly to Edward in the garden, and God had spoken harshly since. Every morning and evening Edward Tripp prayed at length, kneeling by his bed, and during the day he prayed as well, seeing her before him, she who never now walked out into Dunfarnham Avenue, who dressed herself in black and forgot her beauty. No longer children, they were reticent now in what they said one to another; they were polite in their relationship as their thoughts filled the rooms of the house and were not spoken. She played her game in a vengeful way, acting a madness and saying to him in silence that this was the state she should be in, warning him that her bitter nature needed his tenderness now. And Edward prayed and often wept, accepting the punishment as his due.

'There's nothing at all to worry about,' said Edward now. 'Mrs Mayben is quite all right.'

'You have a callous mind,' murmured Edward's sister, looking at him. 'You can know of a thing like this and stand there cutting ham and saying it doesn't matter that a lunatic has walked in Dunfarnham Avenue and brought an old woman to a grim full-stop. It doesn't matter what's in that house this morning, is that it? Edward, she has not come back from church because today she's never been there; because she's been dead and rotting for eighty-four hours. We have buried our parents: we know about the deceased. They're everywhere, Edward. Everywhere.'

'Please,' muttered Edward. 'Please now, my dear.'

'Death has danced through Dunfarnham Avenue and I have seen it, a man without socks or shirt, a man who shall fry in the deep fat of Hell. For you, Edward, must put a finger on him.'

'There's nothing I can do,' said Edward, feeling his size, five foot four, as his sister towered in the room with him.

'Cross the road,' said Emily, 'and go to the back of Mrs Mayben's house. Climb through some small window and walk through the rooms until you come to the woman.'

Edward sighed. He would cross the road, he knew, as he had known when first she mentioned Mrs Mayben, and he would tell Mrs Mayben the truth because she had a face that was kind. He would not stand on her doorstep and make some lame excuse, as he had with all the others. He would not today prevaricate and pretend; he would not dishonour the woman by meting out dishonest treatment to her. 'I will ease your mind,' he said to his sister. 'I'll go and see that Mrs Mayben's quite all right.'

'Carry that ham knife with you, that you may cut her down. It's wrong, I think, don't you, that we should leave her as she is?'

'Stand by the window,' said Edward, already moving to the door, 'and watch me as I cross the road to ring her bell. You'll see her appear, my dear, and if you strain your ears you may even hear her voice.'

Emily nodded. She said:

'Telephone the police when you have cut the cord. Dial 999 and ask to speak to a sergeant. Tell him the honest truth.'

Edward walked from the room and descended the stairs of the house. He opened the front door and crossed

95

Dunfarnham Avenue, to the house of Mrs Mayben. He rang the bell, standing to one side so that his sister, from the dining-room window, would be able to see the old woman when she opened the door.

'I was trying to repair this thing,' said Mrs Mayben, holding out an electric fuse, 'with a piece of silver paper. You've been sent to me, Mr Tripp. Come in.'

Edward entered the house of Mrs Mayben, carrying the ham knife. 'I'm sorry,' he said, 'to bother you.' But Mrs Mayben seemed not to question his presence on her property. 'My husband could mend a fuse,' she said, 'with silver paper; yet I can make no hand of this.' Edward placed the ham knife on a table in the hall and took the ineffective fuse from her hand. He said there was stuff called fuse wire, and Mrs Mayben led him to a cupboard where the electric meters were and in which he discovered the wire he sought. 'I was cooking a chop,' said Mrs Mayben, a woman of eighty-two, 'when all the heat went off.'

'I was cutting ham,' said Edward, 'and I was interrupted too.' He repaired the fuse and replaced it in its socket. 'Let's go and see,' said Mrs Mayben, and led the way to her kitchen. They watched the chop for a moment, still and uninviting in the centre of a frying pan on the electric stove. In a moment a noise came from it, a spurt of sizzling that indicated to them that Edward had been successful with the fuse. 'You must take a glass of sherry,' said Mrs Mayben. 'I have one always myself, on Sundays.'

Edward followed the old woman to her sitting-room and sat down, since she wished that he should, in a comfortable arm-chair. She poured two glasses of Dry Fly sherry and then, holding hers formally in the air, she reminded Edward that she had lived in Dunfarnham Avenue for fourteen years and had never actually spoken to him before.

'I see you feeding the birds,' said Edward, 'from your sitting-room window.'

'Yes, I feed the local sparrows,' said Mrs Mayben. 'I do my bit.'

A silence fell between them, and then Mrs Mayben said:

'It is odd to have lived opposite you for all these years and yet not to have spoken. I have seen you at the windows, as you have seen me. I have seen the lady too.'

Edward felt the blood moving into his face. He felt again a sickness in his stomach and thought his hands were shivering.

'You have heard of me,' he casually said. 'I dare say you have. I am notorious in Dunfarnham Avenue.'

'I know your name is Tripp,' said Mrs Mayben. 'I know no more.'

'She is my sister, the woman you see in that house. She and I were born there, and now she never leaves it. I go out to do the shopping—well, you've seen me.'

'I have seen you, certainly,' said Mrs Mayben, 'returning from the shops with a string bag full of this and that, potatoes and tins, lettuces in season. I do not pry, Mr Tripp, but I have seen you. Have more sherry?'

Edward accepted another glass. 'I am known to every house in the road,' he said. 'Parents warn their children to cross to the other side when they see me coming. Men have approached me to issue rough warnings, using language I don't much care to hear. Women move faster when Edward Tripp's around.'

Mrs Mayben said that she was not deaf but wondered if she quite understood what Edward was talking about. 'I don't think I follow,' she said. 'I know nothing of all this. Like your sister, I don't go out much. I've heard nothing from the people of Dunfarnham Avenue about you, Mr Tripp, or how it is you have become notorious.'

Edward said he had guessed that might be so, and added that one person at least in Dunfarnham Avenue should know the truth, on this Sabbath day.

'It's very kind of you to have repaired my fuse,' said Mrs Mayben a little loudly. 'I'm most obliged to you for that.' She rose to her feet, but did not succeed in drawing her visitor to his. Edward sat on in the comfortable arm-chair, holding his sherry glass. He said:

'It is a hell for me, Dunfarnham Avenue, walking down it

and feeling all eyes upon me. I have rung the bells of all the houses. I have trumped up some story on the doorsteps, even on the doorsteps that she cannot see from the dining-room window. She always knows if I have talked to someone and have been embarrassed: I come back in a peculiar state. I suffer from nerves, Mrs Mayben.'

'Thank you,' said Mrs Mayben more loudly still. 'And how nice to meet you after all these years.'

'I am going to tell you the truth,' explained Edward, 'as I have never told a soul in all my life. It is an ugly business, Mrs Mayben. Perhaps you should sit down.'

'But, Mr Tripp,' protested the old woman, greatly puzzled, 'what on earth is all this?'

'Let me tell you,' said Edward, and he told her of his sister standing at the top of the stairs while their mother broke to her the news that her two coloured story-books had been handed out to a beggar at the front door. 'He's only little,' their mother had explained to Edward's sister. 'Forgive an imp, my dear.' But Emily had not found it in her heart to forgive him and he had sniggered at the time.

'I see,' said Mrs Mayben.

'I knew you would,' cried Edward, smiling at her and nodding his head several times. 'Of course you see. You have a kindly face; you feed the birds.'

'Yes, but—' said Mrs Mayben.

'No,' said Edward. 'Listen.'

He told her about the woman in red at the funeral of their mother, the woman his sister had seen, and how he afterwards prayed in the back garden and had been sternly answered by Almighty God. He explained how he had come upon his duty then and had accepted all that was required of him.

'It has nothing to do with the present,' said Edward. 'Do not see my sister and myself as we stand today, but as two children playing in that house across the road. I sinned against my sister, Mrs Mayben, every hour of my early life. She was stamped into the ground; she was destroyed and devoured. There's nothing left of my sister except a kind of shadow.'

'I'm sorry,' said Mrs Mayben. 'I'm sorry there have been these troubles in your life. It's difficult to accept adversity and unhappiness, I know that.'

'I was cutting ham,' repeated Edward, 'when my sister turned to me and said you had been murdered by a man in canvas shoes.'

'Murdered?' repeated Mrs Mayben, opening the door of her sitting-room and appearing to be nervous.

'She's just a shadow,' said Edward. 'You understand it?'

Mrs Mayben did not reply. Instead she said:

'Mr Tripp, you have been most gallant. I wish you would now return to your home. I have my lunch to prepare and eat.'

' "I saw a dog today," my sister said, "a vicious dog abroad in Dunfarnham Avenue. Go to the houses, Edward, and tell the mothers to look to their children until the dog is captured and set to rest." She talked for seven hours, Mrs Mayben, about that dog, one day in 1951, and in the end she watched me move from house to house ringing the bells and warning the people about a vicious animal.'

'This is no concern of mine. If your sister is unwell—'

'My sister is not unwell. My sister pretends, exacting her revenge. God has told me, Mrs Mayben, to play my part in her pretended fantasies. I owe her the right to punish me, I quite understand that.'

Mrs Mayben shook her head. She said in a quiet voice that she was an old woman and did not understand much of what went on in the world. She did not mind, she said, Edward ringing her doorbell, but she wished now that he would leave her house since she had much to do.

'I have never told anyone else,' said Edward. 'Years ago I said to myself that when I had to come to your house I would tell you the truth about everything. How I have grown up to be an understanding man, with the help of God. How the punishment must be shared between us—well, she has had hers. D'you see?'

99

Mrs Mayben shook her head and was about to speak again. Edward said:

' "There's a smell of burning," my sister said to me in 1955. "It comes from the house with the three Indian women in it." She had woken me up to tell me that, for it was half-past two in the morning. "They are women from the East," she said. "They do not understand about precautions against fire as we do." In my dressing-gown, Mrs Mayben, I walked the length of Dunfarnham Avenue and rang the bell of that house. "May I use your telephone?" I said to the Indian woman who opened the door, for I could think of nothing else to say to her. But she said no, I could not; and rightly pointed out that she could not be expected to admit into her house a man in pyjamas at half-past two in the morning. I have never told anyone because it seemed to be a family thing. I have never told the truth. It is all pretence and silence between my sister and myself. We play a game.'

'I must ask you to go now. I really must. An old woman like me can't be expected to take a sudden interest. You must do the best you can.'

'But I am telling you terrible things,' cried Edward. 'I killed my sister's guinea-pig, I pulled her pansies by the roots. Not an hour passed in my early childhood, Mrs Mayben, but I did not seek to torment her into madness. I don't know why I was given that role, but now I have the other since I've been guided towards it. She is quite sane, you know. She plays a part. I am rotten with guilt.'

Mrs Mayben clapped her hands sharply together. 'I cannot have you coming here,' she said, 'telling me you are rotten with guilt, Mr Tripp. You are a man I have seen about the place with a string bag. I do not know you. I do not know your sister. It's no concern of mine. Not at all.'

'You have a kind face to live up to,' said Edward, bowing and smiling in a sad way. 'I have seen you feeding the sparrows, and I've often thought you have a kind face.'

'Leave me alone, sir. Go from this house at once. You speak of madness and death, Mr Tripp; you tell me I've been murdered: I am unable to think about such things. My days are simple here.'

'Since I was seventeen, Mrs Mayben, since the day of my mother's funeral, I have lived alone with all this horror. Dunfarnham Avenue is the theatre of my embarrassment. You feed the sparrows, Mrs Mayben, yet for me it seems you have no crumb of comfort.'

'I cannot be expected—' began Mrs Mayben.

'I am forty-one this month. She is four years older. See us as children, Mrs Mayben, for it's absurd that I am here before you as a small man in a week-end suit. We are still children in that house, in our way: we have not grown up much. Surely you take an interest?'

'You come here saying you are notorious, Mr Tripp—'

'I am notorious, indeed I am, for God is a hard master. The house is dark and unchanged. Only the toys have gone. We eat the same kind of food.'

'Go away,' cried Mrs Mayben, her voice rising. 'For the sake of God, go away from me, Mr Tripp. You come here talking madly and carrying a ham knife. Leave my house.'

Edward rose to his feet and with his head bowed to his chest he walked past Mrs Mayben into her hall. He picked up the ham knife from the table and moved towards the front door.

'I'm sorry I can't interest myself in you and your sister,' said Mrs Mayben. 'I am too old, you see, to take on new subjects.'

Edward did not say anything more. He did not look at Mrs Mayben, but into his mind came the picture of her leaning from her sitting-room window putting crumbs of bread on the window-sills for the birds. He walked from her house with that picture in his mind and he heard behind him the closing of her hall-door.

Edward crossed Dunfarnham Avenue and entered the house he had always known, carrying the ham knife in his left hand. He moved slowly to the dining-room and saw that the table was neatly laid for lunch. The sliced ham had been placed by his sister on two blue and white plates. Salt and pepper were on the table, and a jar of pickles that he himself had bought, since they both relished them. She had washed a lettuce and cut up a few tomatoes and put chives and cucumber with the salad. 'I've made some mustard,' said Emily, smiling at him as he sat down, and he saw, as he expected, that the look had gone from her face. 'We might repair the sitting-room carpet this afternoon,' said Emily, 'before that hole becomes too large. We could do it together.'

He nodded and murmured, and then, although he was awake and eating his lunch, Edward dreamed. It seemed to him that he was still in Mrs Mayben's sitting-room and that she, changed in her attitude, was murmuring that of course she understood, and all the better because she was old. She placed a hand on Edward's shoulder and said most softly that he had made her feel a mother again. He told her then, once more, of the pansies plucked from the flower-bed, and Mrs Mayben nodded and said he must not mind. He must suffer a bit, she said in a gentle way, since that was his due; he must feel his guilt around him and know that it was rightly there. In Edward's dream Mrs Mayben's voice was soothing, like a cool balm in the sunshine that came prettily through her sitting-room window. 'My dear, do not weep,' said the voice. 'Do not cry, for soon there is the Kingdom of Heaven.' The birds sang while the sun illuminated the room in which Mrs Mayben stood. 'I will go now,' said Edward in his dream, 'since I have mended your fuse and had my sherry. We've had a lovely chat.' He spoke in a peculiar voice and when he rose and walked away his feet made little sound as they struck the floor. 'Come when you wish,' invited Mrs Mayben with tears in her eyes. 'Cross the road for comfort. It's all you have to do.'

Edward chewed lettuce and ham and a piece of tomato, staring over his sister's shoulder at the grey curtains that hung by the window. His eyes moved to his sister's face and then moved downwards to the table, towards the knife that lay now on the polished wood. He thought about this knife that he had carried into a neighbour's house, remembering its keen blade slicing through the flesh of a pig. He saw himself standing with the knife in his hand, and he heard a noise that might have been a cry from his sister's throat. 'I have played a trick on you,' his own voice said, tumbling back to him over the years.

'A pity if that carpet went,' said Emily.

Edward looked at her, attempting to smile. He heard her add:

'It's always been there. All our lives, Edward.' And then, without meaning to say it, Edward said:

'She was harsh in how she looked. Too old to take on new subjects: she was making excuses.'

'What?' murmured Emily, and Edward sighed a little, eating more of the food she had prepared. Vaguely, he told her not to worry, and as he spoke he imagined them that afternoon, sitting on the floor of the other room stitching the carpet they had always known, not saying much except to comment perhaps upon the labour and upon the carpet. And as they worked together, he knew that he would go on praying, praying in his mind for the day to come: a day when old Mrs Mayben and all the people of Dunfarnham Avenue would see his sister walking lightly in the Kingdom of Heaven. In their presence she would smile as once she had smiled as a child, offering him her forgiveness while saying she was sorry too, and releasing in sumptuous glory all the years of imprisoned truth.

VI

A Meeting in Middle Age

'I AM MRS DA TANKA,' said Mrs da Tanka. 'Are you Mr
Mileson?' The man nodded, and they walked together the
length of the platform, seeking a compartment that might
offer them a welcome, or failing that, and they knew the
more likely, simple privacy. They carried each a small suitcase, Mrs da Tanka's of white leather or some material
manufactured to resemble it, Mr Mileson's battered and
black. They did not speak as they marched purposefully:
they were strangers one to another, and in the noise and the
bustle, examining the lighted windows of the carriages, there
was little that might constructively be said.

'A ninety-nine years' lease,' Mr Mileson's father had said,
'taken out in 1862 by my grandfather, whom of course you
never knew. Expiring in your lifetime, I fear. Yet you will
by then be in a sound position to accept the misfortune. To
renew what has come to an end; to keep the property in the
family.' The property was an expression that glorified. The
house was small and useful, one of a row, one of a kind easily
found; but the lease when the time came was not renewable
—which released Mr Mileson of a problem. Bachelor, childless, the end of the line, what use was a house to him for a
further ninety-nine years?

Mrs da Tanka, sitting opposite him, drew a magazine
from an assortment she carried. Then, checking herself,
said: 'We could talk. Or do you prefer to conduct the business in silence?' She was a woman who filled, but did not
overflow from, a fair-sized, elegant, quite expensive tweed
suit. Her hair, which was grey, did not appear so; it was
tightly held to her head, a reddish gold colour. Born into
another class she would have been a chirpy woman; she

guarded against her chirpiness, she disliked the quality in her. There was often laughter in her eyes, and as often as she felt it there she killed it by the severity of her manner.

'You must not feel embarrassment,' Mrs da Tanka said. 'We are beyond the age of giving in to awkwardness in a situation. You surely agree?'

Mr Mileson did not know. He did not know how or what he should feel. Analysing his feelings he could come to no conclusion. He supposed he was excited but it was more difficult than it seemed to track down the emotions. He was unable, therefore, to answer Mrs da Tanka. So he just smiled.

Mrs da Tanka, who had once been Mrs Horace Spire and was not likely to forget it, considered those days. It was a logical thing for her to do, for they were days that had come to an end as these present days were coming to an end. Termination was on her mind: to escape from Mrs da Tanka into Mrs Spire was a way of softening the worry that was with her now, and a way of seeing it in proportion to a lifetime.

'If that is what you want,' Horace had said, 'then by all means have it. Who shall do the dirty work—you or I?' This was his reply to her request for a divorce. In fact, at the time of speaking, the dirty work as he called it was already done: by both of them.

'It is a shock for me,' Horace had continued. 'I thought we could jangle along for many a day. Are you seriously involved elsewhere?'

In fact she was not, but finding herself involved at all reflected the inadequacy of her married life and revealed a vacuum that once had been love.

'We are better apart,' she had said. 'It is bad to get used to the habit of being together. We must take our chances while we may, while there is still time.'

In the railway carriage she recalled the conversation with vividness, especially that last sentence, most especially the last five words of it. The chance she had taken was da Tanka, eight years ago. 'My God,' she said aloud, 'what a pompous bastard he turned out to be.'

Mr Mileson had a couple of those weekly publications for which there is no accurate term in the language: a touch of a single colour on the front—floppy, half-intellectual things, somewhere between a journal and a magazine. While she had her honest mags. *Harper's. Vogue.* Shiny and smart and rather silly. Or so thought Mr Mileson. He had opened them at dentists' and doctors', leafed his way through the ridiculous advertisements and aptly titled model girls, unreal girls in unreal poses, devoid it seemed of sex, and half the time of life. So that was the kind of woman she was.

'Who?' said Mr Mileson.

'Oh, who else, good heavens! Da Tanka I mean.'

Eight years of da Tanka's broad back, so fat it might have been padded beneath the skin. He had often presented it to her; he was that kind of man. Busy, he claimed; preoccupied.

'I shall be telling you about da Tanka,' she said. 'There are interesting facets to the man; though God knows, he is scarcely interesting in himself.'

It was a worry, in any case, owning a house. Seeing to the roof; noticing the paint cracking on the outside, and thinking about damp in mysterious places. Better off he was, in the room in Swiss Cottage; cosier in winter. They'd pulled down the old house by now, with all the others in the road. Flats were there instead: bulking up to the sky, with a million or so windows. All the gardens were gone, all the gnomes and the Snow White dwarfs, all the winter bulbs and the little paths of crazy paving; the bird-baths and bird-boxes and bird-tables; the miniature sandpits, and the metal edging, ornate, for flower-beds.

'We must move with the times,' said Mrs da Tanka, and he realized that he had been speaking to her; or speaking aloud and projecting the remarks in her direction since she was there.

His mother had made the rockery. Aubretia and sarsaparilla and pinks and Christmas roses. Her brother, his uncle

Edward, bearded and queer, brought seaside stones in his motor-car. His father had shrugged his distaste for the project, as indeed for all projects of this nature, seeing the removal of stones from the seashore as being in some way disgraceful, even dishonest. Behind the rockery there were loganberries: thick, coarse, inedible fruit, never fully ripe. But nobody, certainly not Mr Mileson, had had the heart to pull away the bushes.

'Weeks would pass,' said Mrs da Tanka, 'without the exchange of a single significant sentence. We lived in the same house, ate the same meals, drove out in the same car, and all he would ever say was: "It is time the central heating was on." Or: "These windscreen-wipers aren't working".'

Mr Mileson didn't know whether she was talking about Mr da Tanka or Mr Spire. They seemed like the same man to him: shadowy, silent fellows who over the years had shared this woman with the well-tended hands.

'He will be wearing city clothes,' her friend had said, 'grey or nondescript. He is like anyone else except for his hat, which is big and black and eccentric.' An odd thing about him, the hat: like a wild oat almost.

There he had been, by the tobacco kiosk, punctual and expectant; gaunt of face, thin, fiftyish; with the old-fashioned hat and the weekly papers that somehow matched it, but did not match him.

'Now would you blame me, Mr Mileson? Would you blame me for seeking freedom from such a man?'

The hat lay now on the luggage-rack with his carefully folded overcoat. A lot of his head was bald, whitish and tender like good dripping. His eyes were sad, like those of a retriever puppy she had known in her childhood. Men are often like dogs, she thought; women more akin to cats. The train moved smoothly, with rhythm, through the night. She thought of da Tanka and Horace Spire, wondering where Spire was now. Opposite her, he thought about the ninety-nine-year lease and the two plates, one from last night's supper, the other from breakfast, that he had left unwashed in the room at Swiss Cottage.

'This seems your kind of place,' Mr Mileson said, surveying the hotel from its ornate hall.

'Gin and lemon, gin and lemon,' said Mrs da Tanka, matching the words with action: striding to the bar.

Mr Mileson had rum, feeling it a more suitable drink though he could not think why. 'My father drank rum with milk in it. An odd concoction.'

'Frightful, it sounds. Da Tanka is a whisky man. My previous liked stout. Well, well, so here we are.'

Mr Mileson looked at her. 'Dinner is next on the agenda.'

But Mrs da Tanka was not to be moved. They sat while she drank many measures of the drink; and when they rose to demand dinner they discovered that the restaurant was closed and were ushered to a grill-room.

'You organized that badly, Mr Mileson.'

'I organized nothing. I know the rules of these places. I repeated them to you. You gave me no chance to organize.'

'A chop and an egg or something. Da Tanka at least could have got us soup.'

In 1931 Mr Mileson had committed fornication with the maid in his parents' house. It was the only occasion, and he was glad that adultery was not expected of him with Mrs da Tanka. In it she would be more experienced than he, and he did not relish the implication. The grill-room was lush and vulgar. 'This seems your kind of place,' Mr Mileson repeated rudely.

'At least it is warm. And the lights don't glare. Why not order some wine?'

Her husband must remain innocent. He was a person of importance, in the public eye. Mr Mileson's friend had repeated it, the friend who knew Mrs da Tanka's solicitor. All expenses paid, the friend had said, and a little fee as well. Nowadays Mr Mileson could do with little fees. And though at the time he had rejected the suggestion downright, he had later seen that friend—acquaintance really—in the pub he went to at half past twelve on Sundays, and had agreed to take part in the drama. It wasn't just the little fee; there was something rather like prestige in the thing;

his name as co-respondent—now *there* was something you'd never have guessed! The hotel bill to find its way to Mrs da Tanka's husband who would pass it to his solicitor. Breakfast in bed, and remember the face of the maid who brought it. Pass the time of day with her, and make sure she remembered yours. Oh very nice, the man in the pub said, very nice Mrs da Tanka was—or so he was led to believe. He batted his eyes at Mr Mileson; but Mr Mileson said it didn't matter, surely, about Mrs da Tanka's niceness. He knew his duties: there was nothing personal about them. He'd do it himself, the man in the pub explained, only he'd never be able to keep his hands off an attractive middle-aged woman. That was the trouble about finding someone for the job.

'I've had a hard life,' Mrs da Tanka confided. 'Tonight I need your sympathy, Mr Mileson. Tell me I have your sympathy.' Her face and neck had reddened: chirpiness was breaking through.

In the house, in a cupboard beneath the stairs, he had kept his gardening boots. Big, heavy army boots, once his father's. He had worn them at week-ends, poking about in the garden.

'The lease came to an end two years ago,' he told Mrs da Tanka. 'There I was with all that stuff, all my gardening tools, and the furniture and bric-à-brac of three generations to dispose of. I can tell you it wasn't easy to know what to throw away.'

'Mr Mileson, I don't like that waiter.'

Mr Mileson cut his steak with care: a three-cornered piece, neat and succulent. He loaded mushroom and mustard on it, added a sliver of potato and carried the lot to his mouth. He masticated and drank some wine.

'Do you know the waiter?'

Mrs da Tanka laughed unpleasantly; like ice cracking. 'Why should I know the waiter? I do not generally know waiters. Do you know the waiter?'

'I ask because you claim to dislike him.'

'May I not dislike him without an intimate knowledge of the man?'

'You may do as you please. It struck me as a premature decision, that is all.'

'What decision? What is premature? What are you talking about? Are you drunk?'

'The decision to dislike the waiter I thought to be premature. I do not know about being drunk. Probably I am a little. One has to keep one's spirits up.'

'Have you ever thought of wearing an eye-patch, Mr Mileson? I think it would suit you. You need distinction. Have you led an empty life? You give the impression of an empty life.'

'My life has been as many other lives. Empty of some things, full of others. I am in possession of all my sight, though. My eyes are real. Neither is a pretence. I see no call for an eye patch.'

'It strikes me you see no call for anything. You have never lived, Mr Mileson.'

'I do not understand that.'

'Order us more wine.'

Mr Mileson indicated with his hand and the waiter approached. 'Some other waiter, please,' Mrs da Tanka cried. 'May we be served by another waiter?'

'Madam?' said the waiter.

'We do not take to you. Will you send another man to our table?'

'I am the only waiter on duty, madam.'

'It's quite all right,' said Mr Mileson.

'It's not quite all right. I will not have this man at our table, opening and dispensing wine.'

'Then we must go without.'

'I am the only waiter on duty, madam.'

'There are other employees of the hotel. Send us a porter or the girl at the reception.'

'It is not their duty, madam—'

'Oh nonsense, nonsense. Bring us the wine, man, and have no more to-do.'

Unruffled, the waiter moved away. Mrs da Tanka hummed a popular tune.

'Are you married, Mr Mileson? Have you in the past been married?'

'No, never married.'

'I have been married twice. I am married now. I am throwing the dice for the last time. God knows how I shall find myself. You are helping to shape my destiny. What a fuss that waiter made about the wine!'

'That is a little unfair. It was you, you know—'

'Behave like a gentleman, can't you? Be on my side since you are with me. Why must you turn on me? Have I harmed you?'

'No, no. I was merely establishing the truth.'

'Here is the man again with the wine. He is like a bird. Do you think he has wings strapped down beneath his waiter's clothes? You are like a bird,' she repeated, examining the waiter's face. 'Has some fowl played a part in your ancestry?'

'I think not, madam.'

'Though you cannot be sure. How can you be sure? How can you say you think not when you know nothing about it?'

The waiter poured the wine in silence. He was not embarrassed, Mr Mileson noted; not even angry.

'Bring coffee,' Mrs da Tanka said.

'Madam.'

'How servile waiters are! How I hate servility, Mr Mileson! I could not marry a servile man. I could not marry that waiter, not for all the tea in China.'

'I did not imagine you could. The waiter does not seem your sort.'

'He is your sort. You like him, I think. Shall I leave you to converse with him?'

'Really! What would I say to him? I know nothing about the waiter except what he is in a professional sense. I do not wish to know. It is not my habit to go about consorting with waiters after they have waited on me.'

'I am not to know that. I am not to know what your sort is, or what your personal and private habits are. How could I know? We have only just met.'

'You are clouding the issue.'

'You are as pompous as da Tanka. Da Tanka would say issue and clouding.'

'What your husband would say is no concern of mine.'

'You are meant to be my lover, Mr Mileson. Can't you act it a bit? My husband must concern you dearly. You must wish to tear him limb from limb. Do you wish it?'

'I have never met the man. I know nothing of him.'

'Well then, pretend. Pretend for the waiter's sake. Say something violent in the waiter's hearing. Break an oath. Blaspheme. Bang your fist on the table.'

'I was not told I should have to behave like that. It is against my nature.'

'What is your nature?'

'I'm shy and self-effacing.'

'You are an enemy to me. I don't understand your sort. You have not got on in the world. You take on commissions like this. Where is your self-respect?'

'Elsewhere in my character.'

'You have no personality.'

'That is a cliché. It means nothing.'

'Sweet nothings for lovers, Mr Mileson! Remember that.'

They left the grill-room and mounted the stairs in silence. In their bedroom Mrs da Tanka unpacked a dressing-gown. 'I shall undress in the bathroom. I shall be absent a matter of ten minutes.'

Mr Mileson slipped from his clothes into pyjamas. He brushed his teeth at the wash-basin, cleaned his nails and splashed a little water on his face. When Mrs da Tanka returned he was in bed.

To Mr Mileson she seemed a trifle bigger without her daytime clothes. He remembered corsets and other containing garments. He did not remark upon it.

Mrs da Tanka turned out the light and they lay without touching between the cold sheets of the double bed.

He would leave little behind, he thought. He would die and there would be the things in the room, rather a number of useless things with sentimental value only. Ornaments and ferns. Reproductions of paintings. A set of eggs, birds' eggs he had collected as a boy. They would pile all the junk together and probably try to burn it. Then perhaps they would light a couple of those fumigating candles in the room, because people are insulting when other people die.

'Why did you not get married?' Mrs da Tanka said.

'Because I do not greatly care for women.' He said it, throwing caution to the winds, waiting for her attack.

'Are you a homosexual?'

The word shocked him. 'Of course I'm not.'

'I only asked. They go in for this kind of thing.'

'That does not make me one.'

'I often thought Horace Spire was more that way than any other. For all the attention he paid to me.'

As a child she had lived in Shropshire. In those days she loved the country, though without knowing, or wishing to know, the names of flower or plants or trees. People said she looked like Alice in Wonderland.

'Have you ever been to Shropshire, Mr Mileson?'

'No. I am very much a Londoner. I lived in the same house all my life. Now the house is no longer there. Flats replace it. I live in Swiss Cottage.'

'I thought you might. I thought you might live in Swiss Cottage.'

'Now and again I miss the garden. As a child I collected birds' eggs on the common. I have kept them all these years.'

She had kept nothing. She cut the past off every so often, remembering it when she cared to, without the aid of physical evidence.

'The hard facts of life have taken their toll of me,' said Mrs da Tanka. 'I met them first at twenty. They have been my companions since.'

'It was a hard fact the lease coming to an end. It was hard to take at the time. I did not accept it until it was well upon me. Only the spring before I had planted new delphiniums.'

'My father told me to marry a good man. To be happy

and have children. Then he died. I did none of those things. I do not know why except that I did not care to. Then old Horry Spire put his arm around me and there we were. Life is as you make it, I suppose. I was thinking of homosexual in relation to that waiter you were interested in downstairs.'

'I was not interested in the waiter. He was hard done by, by you, I thought. There was no more to it than that.'

Mrs da Tanka smoked and Mr Mileson was nervous; about the situation in general, about the glow of the cigarette in the darkness. What if the woman dropped off to sleep? He had heard of fires started by careless smoking. What if in her confusion she crushed the cigarette against some part of his body? Sleep was impossible: one cannot sleep with the thought of waking up in a furnace, with the bells of fire brigades clanging a death knell.

'I will not sleep tonight,' said Mrs da Tanka, a statement which frightened Mr Mileson further. For all the dark hours the awful woman would be there, twitching and puffing beside him. *I am mad. I am out of my mind to have brought this upon myself.* He heard the words. He saw them on paper, written in his handwriting. He saw them typed, and repeated again as on a telegram. The letters jolted and lost their order. The words were confused, skulking behind a fog. 'I am mad,' Mr Mileson said, to establish the thought completely, to bring it into the open. It was a habit of his; for a moment he had forgotten the reason for the thought, thinking himself alone.

'Are you telling me now you are mad?' asked Mrs da Tanka, alarmed. 'Gracious, are you worse than a homo? Are you some sexual pervert? Is that what you are doing here? Certainly that was not my plan, I do assure you. You have nothing to gain from me, Mr Mileson. If there is trouble I shall ring the bell.'

'I am mad to be here. I am mad to have agreed to all this. What came over me I do not know. I have only just realised the folly of the thing.'

'Arise then, dear Mileson, and break your agreement,

your promise and your undertaking. You are an adult man,
you may dress and walk from the room.'

They were all the same, she concluded: except that while
others had some passing superficial recommendation, this
one it seemed had none. There was something that made
her sick about the thought of the stringy limbs that were
stretched out beside her. What lengths a woman will go to
to rid herself of a horror like da Tanka!

He had imagined it would be a simple thing. It had
sounded like a simple thing: a good thing rather than a bad
one. A good turn for a lady in need. That was as he had
seen it. With the little fee already in his possession.

Mrs da Tanka lit another cigarette and threw the match
on the floor.

'What kind of a life have you had? You had not the nerve
for marriage. Nor the brains for success. The truth is you
might not have lived.' She laughed in the darkness, determined to hurt him as he had hurt her in his implication
that being with her was an act of madness.

Mr Mileson had not before done a thing like this. Never
before had he not weighed the pros and cons and seen that
danger was absent from an undertaking. The thought of it
all made him sweat. He saw the future further deeds: worse
deeds, crimes and irresponsibilities.

Mrs da Tanka laughed again. But she was thinking of
something else.

'You have never slept with a woman, is that it? Ah, you
poor thing! What a lot you have not had the courage for!'
The bed heaved with the raucous noise that was her
laughter, and the bright spark of her cigarette bobbed
about in the air.

She laughed, quietly now and silently, hating him as she
hated da Tanka and had hated Horace Spire. Why could
he not be some young man, beautiful and nicely-mannered
and gay? Surely a young man would have come with her?
Surely there was one amongst all the millions who would
have done the chore with relish, or at least with charm?

'You are as God made you,' said Mr Mileson. 'You can-

THE DAY WE GOT DRUNK ON CAKE

not help your shortcomings, though one would think you might by now have recognised them. To others you may be all sorts of things. To me you are a frightful woman.'

'Would you not stretch out a hand to the frightful woman? Is there no temptation for the woman's flesh? Are you a eunuch, Mr Mileson?'

'I have had the women I wanted. I am doing you a favour. Hearing of your predicament and pressed to help you, I agreed in a moment of generosity. Stranger though you were I did not say no.'

'That does not make you a gentleman.'

'And I do not claim it does. I am gentleman enough without it.'

'You are nothing without it. This is your sole experience. In all your clerkly subservience you have not paused to live. You know I am right, and as for being a gentleman—well, you are of the lower middle classes. There has never been an English gentleman born of the lower middle classes.'

She was trying to remember what she looked like; what her face was like, how the wrinkles were spread, how old she looked and what she might pass for in a crowd. Would men not be cagey now and think that she must be difficult in her ways to have parted twice from husbands? Was there a third time coming up? Third time lucky, she thought. Who would have her, though, except some loveless Mileson?

'You have had no better life than I,' said Mr Mileson. 'You are no more happy now. You have failed, and it is cruel to laugh at you.'

They talked and the hatred grew between them.

'In my childhood young men flocked about me, at dances in Shropshire that my father gave to celebrate my beauty. Had the fashion been duels, duels there would have been. Men killed and maimed for life, carrying a lock of my hair on their breast.'

'You are a creature now, with your face and your finger-nails. Mutton dressed as lamb, Mrs da Tanka!'

Beyond the curtained windows the light of dawn broke

into the night. A glimpse of it crept into the room, noticed and welcomed by its occupants.

'You should write your memoirs, Mr Mileson. To have seen the changes in your time and never to know a thing about them! You are like an occasional table. Or a coat-rack in the hall of a boarding-house. Who shall mourn at your grave, Mr Mileson?'

He felt her eyes upon him; and the mockery of the words sank into his heart with intended precision. He turned to her and touched her, his hands groping about her shoulders. He had meant to grasp her neck, to feel the muscles struggle beneath his fingers, to terrify the life out of her. But she, thinking the gesture was the beginning of an embrace, pushed him away, swearing at him and laughing. Surprised by the misunderstanding, he left her alone.

The train was slow. The stations crawled by, similar and ugly. She fixed her glance on him, her eyes sharpened; cold and powerful.

She had won the battle, though technically the victory was his. Long before the time arranged for their breakfast Mr Mileson had leaped from bed. He dressed and breakfasted alone in the dining-room. Shortly afterwards, after sending to the bedroom for his suitcase, he left the hotel, informing the receptionist that the lady would pay the bill. Which in time she had done, and afterwards pursued him to the train, where now, to disconcert him, she sat in the facing seat of an empty compartment.

'Well,' said Mrs da Tanka, 'you have shot your bolt. You have taken the only miserable action you could. You have put the frightful woman in her place. Have we a right,' she added, 'to expect anything better of the English lower classes?'

Mr Mileson had foolishly left his weekly magazines and the daily paper at the hotel. He was obliged to sit bare-faced before her, pretending to observe the drifting land-scape. In spite of everything, guilt gnawed him a bit. When

117

he was back in his room he would borrow the vacuum cleaner and give it a good going over: the exercise would calm him. A glass of beer in the pub before lunch; lunch in the ABC; perhaps an afternoon cinema. It was Saturday today: this, more or less, was how he usually spent Saturday. Probably from lack of sleep he would doze off in the cinema. People would nudge him to draw attention to his snoring; that had happened before, and was not pleasant.

'To give you birth,' she said, 'your mother had long hours of pain. Have you thought of that, Mr Mileson? Have you thoughts of that poor woman crying out, clenching her hands and twisting the sheets? Was it worth it, Mr Mileson? You tell me now, was it worth it?'

He could leave the compartment and sit with other people. But that would be too great a satisfaction for Mrs da Tanka. She would laugh loudly at his going, might even pursue him to mock in public.

'What you say about me, Mrs da Tanka, can equally be said of you.'

'Are we two peas in a pod? It's an explosive pod in that case.'

'I did not imply that. I would not wish to find myself sharing a pod with you.'

'Yet you shared a bed. And were not man enough to stick to your word. You are a worthless coward, Mr Mileson. I expect you know it.'

'I know myself, which is more than can be said in your case. Do you not think occasionally to see yourself as others see you? An ageing woman, faded and ugly, dubious in morals and personal habits. What misery you must have caused those husbands!'

'They married me, and got good value. You know that, yet dare not admit it.'

'I will scarcely lose sleep worrying the matter out.'

It was a cold morning, sunny with a clear sky. Passengers stepping from the train at the intermediate stations muffled up against the temperature, finding it too much after the warm fug within. Women with baskets. Youths. Men with children, with dogs collected from the guard's van.

Da Tanka, she had heard, was living with another woman. Yet he refused to admit being the guilty party. It would not do for someone like da Tanka to be a public adulterer. So he had said. Pompously. Crossly. Horace Spire, to give him his due, hadn't given a damn one way or the other.

'When you die, Mr Mileson, have you a preference for the flowers on your coffin? It is a question I ask because I might send you off a wreath. That lonely wreath. From ugly, frightful Mrs da Tanka.'

'What?' said Mr Mileson, and she repeated the question.

'Oh well—cowparsley, I suppose.' He said it, taken off his guard by the image she created; because it was an image he often saw and thought about. Hearse and coffin and he within. It would not be like that probably. Anticipation was not in Mr Mileson's life. Remembering, looking back, considering events and emotions that had been at the time mundane perhaps—this kind of thing was more to his liking. For by hindsight there was pleasure in the stream of time. He could not establish his funeral in his mind; he tried often but ended up always with a funeral he had known: a repetition of his parents' passing and the accompanying convention.

'Cowparsley?' said Mrs da Tanka. Why did the man say cowparsley? Why not roses or lilies or something in a pot? There had been cowparsley in Shropshire; cowparsley on the verges of dusty lanes; cowparsley in hot fields buzzing with bees; great white swards rolling down to the river. She had sat among it on a picnic with dolls. She had lain on it, laughing at the beautiful anaemic blue of the sky. She had walked through it by night, loving it.

'Why did you say cowparsley?'

He did not know, except that once on a rare family outing to the country he had seen it and remembered it. Yet in his garden he had grown delphiniums and wallflowers and asters and sweet-pea.

She could smell it again: a smell that was almost noth-

119

ing: fields and the heat of the sun on her face, laziness and summer. There was a red door somewhere, faded and blistered, and she sat against it, crouched on a warm step, a child dressed in the fashion of the time.

'Why did you say cowparsley?'

He remembered, that day, asking the name of the white powdery growth. He had picked some and carried it home; and had often since thought of it, though he had not come across a field of cowparsley for years.

She tried to speak again, but after the night there were no words she could find that would fit. The silence stuck between them, and Mr Mileson knew by instinct all that it contained. She saw an image of herself and him, strolling together from the hotel, in this same sunshine, at this very moment, lingering on the pavement to decide their direction and agreeing to walk to the promenade. She mouthed and grimaced and the sweat broke on her body, and she looked at him once and saw words die on his lips, lost in his suspicion of her.

The train stopped for the last time. Doors banged; the throng of people passed them by on the platform outside. They collected their belongings and left the train together. A porter, interested in her legs, watched them walk down the platform. They passed through the barrier and parted, moving in their particular directions. She to her new flat where milk and mail, she hoped, awaited her. He to his room; to the two unwashed plates on the draining board and the forks with egg on the prongs; and the little fee propped up on the mantelpiece, a pink cheque for five pounds, peeping out from behind a china cat.

VII

The Introspections of J. P. Powers

J. P. POWERS, BIG, FORTY-THREE, his face a mass of moustache, said: 'You must depress the clutch, Miss Hobish.
It is impossible to change from one gear to another without
you depress the clutch.'

J. P. Powers was aware of his grammatical lapse. *It is impossible to change from one gear to another unless you
depress the clutch. It is impossible to change from one gear
to another without depressing the clutch.* Either variant
would have done: both were within his idiom. *Without you
depress* was foreign to him, the way the Irish talk. Despite
the Celtic ring of his name, Justin Parke Powers was not
Irish.

Miss Hobish drove the Austin in a jagged manner down
Cave Crescent and into Mortimer Road. Ahead lay Putney
Hill and an awkward right turn, across both streams of
traffic. Powers prepared himself for the moment, feet ready
for the dual controls, fingers poised to jab the starter when
the engine stalled.

'Slowing down signal,' said J. P. Powers. Then: 'Change
to second, hand signal, indicator. Always the old hand
signal: never rely on the indicator, Miss Hobish.'

Miss Hobish edged the car forwards, aiming at a bus.

'Wait for a gap, Miss Hobish. All that traffic has the right
of way.'

He had said *without you depress* just for the novelty
sound of it, because he had become so used to the usual
patter of words, because his tongue grew tired of forming
them.

'Now, Miss Hobish.' He seized the steering wheel and
swung it, giving the engine a spurt of petrol.

The Austin bore to the left at the traffic lights, along Upper Richmond Road, and later turned right, into the quiet roads of Barnes Common. Powers relaxed then, telling her to take it calmly. Miss Hobish was always happy on Barnes Common.

He lit a cigarette and lowered the window so that the smoke would be carried away. He sat in silence, watching the road. Occasionally he glanced at Miss Hobish and occasionally at parts of himself. He saw his fingernails splayed on his two thick knees. He was not a particularly clean man, and this was a fact he now thought about. He visualised his grey-brown underclothes and the tacky yellow on the underarms of his shirts. Once his wife had commented on this yellow, saying he was a dirty man, running baths for him and pushing deodorants at him. She did all this no longer, only sighing when by chance she came upon his socks, stiff like little planks, in the big cardboard carton she used as a laundry basket. A complaint had come in one summer from a fastidious man called Hopker. Roche had had him in and told him about it, with the typing girl still in the room. 'Wash out your armpits, old son. Get Lifebuoy and Odo-ro-no or Mum.' Roche was a little fellow; it was easy for Roche, there wasn't an ounce of sweat in him. Powers was fifteen stone : rolls of fat and muscle, grinding out the perspiration, secreting it in fleshy caches. To keep himself sweet he'd have to take a shower every two hours.

During his daily periods of boredom J. P. Powers was given to thought. It was thought of a depressing quality, being concerned with his uselessness. Fifty years ago there were no driving instructors in the world : what would he have done fifty years ago, how would he have made a living? The truth was he brought no skill to the job, he had no interest in it. How could one be interested in so unnecessary an occupation as teaching people to drive motor-cars? People could walk, they had legs. People could avail themselves of public transport. He gave no real service; better to be a booking clerk for British Railways. Not that people weren't grateful to him. They waved to him afterwards, implying that he had helped them on their way. But J. P. Powers was thinking of himself; there was nothing expert in what he did, anyone could teach the gears and the knack.

'Well, that was nice,' said Miss Hobish. 'I do enjoy it, Mr Powers. Now, will you take a cup of tea with me?'

Miss Hobish had been learning to drive for five years. It was an outing for her: Miss Hobish was seventy-three.

There was a job that was waiting for J. P. Powers, preserved for him by Ransome, with whom he had served in the Royal Air Force. 'Any time you're ready, J. P.,' was how Ransome put it. Ransome with an amber pint in his paw, down at the Saracen's Head on a Sunday morning. Ransome was sorry for him, remembering how he had driven a Spitfire during the war, thinking of him being driven by inept drivers now. Ransome felt he owed him something, some vague debt incurred in 1945. 'Your day's your own,' said Ransome. 'We supply the car.' The task was to sell baby requisites from door to door: gripe water and talcum powder, disinfectant and baby oil. Ransome was expanding: he'd just bought up a concern that manufactured nappies; he was taking a look at the plastic toy business. 'Let me ask you a question,' said Ransome. 'Doesn't it send you up the wall hawking these learner drivers about?' Ransome had a nice little patch keeping warm for Powers out Kingston way. 'Look at the commission,' said Ransome. 'You won't find commissions like that in your front garden.'

Justin Parke Powers, a man unclean and not entirely satisfied with himself, said yes to Miss Hobish; said yes, he would take the cup of tea, and held the car door open for her and followed her into her small house. Miss Hobish paid for her lessons in advance, by the quarter, but each lesson lasted only twenty minutes instead of the full hour: Miss Hobish at seventy-three could rarely sustain more.

Darker than the strands that crossed his scalp, softer than the bristle of moustache, was the mat of hair beneath the arms of J. P. Powers. 'A growth that traps, a growth that sours,' said Roche, referring to the twin clumps and Powers' perspiration. The hair overflowed from the armpits like stuffing from a mattress—yet his chest was naked as a girl's. Smooth and white; a suggestion of breasts; pitted, if you cared to look, with blackheads. Earlier in his life J. P. Powers had been concerned about it: a big man like him with so unmanly an expanse. He had turned his back on the company in changing rooms, whistling to cover the gesture.

In the bath on Sunday mornings he washed this body with passing diligence, watching the milky scum form on the water, lathering himself with Lifebuoy as Roche had counselled. As he bathed he could hear the cry of the radio in the kitchen and the quarrelling sounds of his two small daughters. It was a Sunday ritual, accepted by his wife who took no part in it; ritual that the geyser should snarl and the water flow, that scum should form, radio play, daughters quarrel; ritual that at midday precisely J. P. Powers should emerge from the bathroom temporarily cleansed, should leave his rented house by the back door and board a bus to the Saracen's Arms. It was ritual too that he should later return with four pints of beer in his barrel stomach and eat a lunch that had been kept for him in a low oven.

When he got going he couldn't stop himself. The images of himself, of his daily work and of his body, rose often and unbidden before him. They bloomed in Mortimer Road and Cave Crescent, among the similar houses, detached or partly so. They hovered then over conversation and instruction; they were there in the Austin, like fog. He saw houses and roads being built and wished he had the courage to join a labour gang. He saw his big hands on the steering wheel and considered afresh their function.

On Tuesday September the twenty-first, Justin Parke Powers gave Miss Hobish her two hundred and forty-first driving lesson. He sat beside her, feet and hands alerted.

'We've had no summer, Mr Powers.' She sighed, settling herself. 'One, two, three, four, up and back for reverse. Are we ready, Mr Powers?'

She drove raggedly from Cave Crescent to Amervale Avenue.

'Hand signals,' said Powers, and Miss Hobish extended a scrawny arm and waved it arbitrarily about.

He fancied the typing girl in Roche's office. When the weather was cold she wore knitted jumpers that shaped her breasts. They quivered as she typed, but there was nothing he could do about them now. Probably she'd giggled with Roche afterwards, about what fastidious Hopker had said, about Roche so bold as to recommend Odo-ro-no or Mum.

'You're forgetting those hand signals,' said Powers.

'So difficult,' murmured Miss Hobish.

'Come and have a drink,' a woman had said to him once, at the end of a lesson; and his heart had fluttered in his naked chest, for he had heard from the other men of such approaches made. Nothing had come of it though, because with the drink in his hand he had laughed and been himself, had told her a few jokes and moved around the room so that he was positioned to give her an exploratory slap on the bottom. All this the woman had not welcomed, and had requested a different tutor for future lessons.

'Slow down for the crossing,' Powers said.

'I beg your pardon?' said Miss Hobish, turning to look at him, jerking the Austin onwards, missing a woman with a pram.

'Turn right. We'll go up Mortimer Road. Hand signal, indicator. Draw out to the centre of the road.'

Excited, Miss Hobish allowed the car to stall.

'More gas, more gas,' cried J. P. Powers, apologising to the traffic.

'Tell me about the R.A.F.,' said Miss Hobish in Mortimer Road. 'I love to hear your tales.'

'We must concentrate on our driving, Miss Hobish.'

'Shall we have a cup of coffee afterwards and shall you tell me then?'

'Yes, Miss Hobish; a coffee would be nice.'

He closed his eyes and within seconds Miss Hobish had driven the Austin into the back of a stationary van.

'Oh dear, oh dear,' said Miss Hobish.

Powers got out and examined the damage. Both wings and

the radiator grill had suffered considerably. The bumper had folded like a length of cardboard.

'I'd better drive,' said Powers. 'The steering may be wonky.'

He drove in silence, reflecting upon what the incident would cost in terms of himself. Then he wondered idly, as he often did, what it would be like to be a solicitor or a bank manager. He couldn't fit himself into either role; he couldn't hear himself advising on the purchase of a house, or lending money, or retailing the details of the divorce laws. It seemed a truth that his tasks were destined to be expendable; only in war had he established himself.

'Coffee now?' Miss Hobish asked with meekness.

He looked at the front of the car again. Both headlights were smashed.

'I'm going to give you a cheque,' said Miss Hobish. She handed him coffee, and biscuits with icing on them. 'For that damage to your motor. I suppose it would be two hundred pounds?'

'Two hundred,' said Powers, falling in with the plan. 'J. P. the initials are.'

'Now we'll forget about it?' She was anxious, and he nodded, tucking the cheque away and thinking about it.

Ransome would be at the Saracen's Head at lunch-time. He'd park the Austin round at the back where Ransome wouldn't see it and wouldn't guess anything. Two hundred: he could make it last a long time, nice to have it by him, nice to be able to draw on it now and again.

'Lovely biscuits, Miss Hobish.'

'So forgiving, Mr Powers! I thought you mightn't speak to me, your beautiful motor all broken up.'

'Not at all—'

'Have some more of these biscuits, I know you like them. I get them at Sainsbury's.'

He dunked the biscuit in his coffee and sucked off the coloured icing. It was a comfortable room. The arm-chair he sat in was large and soft. Once he had fallen asleep in it.

Once Miss Hobish, recognising his fatigue, had invited him to take off his shoes.

'Goodbye, Miss Hobish.'

'More coffee? Biscuits?'

'I fear I must make my way, Miss Hobish.'

'Goodbye then, Mr Powers.' They shook hands as they always did.

It was the boredom, he thought; it was that that prevented him from being the easy extrovert he was born to be. The boredom of repeating, the boredom of talking in simple terms. Hand signals and gear changes: the boredom gave him time to think, it made him think. Powers did not employ these words in his survey of his trouble, but that was the meaning he arrived at. Thoughts ran around in his brain like hares. He didn't know how to catch them.

'I couldn't be happier,' said Ransome.

Powers examined the beer in his tankard. He nodded, smiling to display enthusiasm.

'Do you know,' queried Ransome, 'what I'm going to do next?'

In three months' time Powers knew he'd be beginning to think Ransome a swine. Ransome had the makings of another Roche; probably he was worse.

'I'm going to fire Jack Clay,' said Ransome.

It was one thing knowing the man in the Saracen's Head, talking over a beer about days in the R.A.F.; it was rather different having him in charge of one's daily life. *I'm going to fire J. P. Powers*. He could hear the man saying it, in this very bar, to some youthful figure who might make a better hand of distributing the requisites.

'I'm going to fire Jack Clay and put J. P. Powers in his car. What d'you think of that, a big Consul?'

'Fine,' said J. P. Powers. 'Fine, fine, a Consul's lovely.'

'I've got a concern making rubber sheets and hot-water bottles shaped like a bunny rabbit. I'd like to have the lot, you know; carry-cots, everything, a full service. I've got a fellow in Hoxton working on a wee-control.'

The old, tired thoughts began all over again. He couldn't

see himself clearly; he couldn't see how his pattern was cut or what he was meant to do, or had ever been meant to do. He began to worry and he hated himself for it; because he didn't want to worry, because the thoughts were forced upon him.

'A pregnant woman,' Ransome was going on, 'will buy anything. Apples off a tree, old boy. Two days out and by God, you'll *know* you never had it so good.'

Powers nodded.

'Two pints,' Ransome said to the barmaid.

If he worked on the public transport he'd be a cog in a big machine, getting people to work in the morning, taking them home at night. Otherwise they'd have to walk. He'd seen them during a transport strike, walking from Regent Street to Wimbledon. You couldn't do that more than once a week.

'Will I be all right?'

'Old boy?'

'Will I fit the bill?'

'Haven't I said so? Haven't I been plaguing you to come in for years? I mean what I say, old boy.'

It occurred to him that Ransome, far from being kind, was deliberately being cruel. Ransome was pointing the moral. They had walked out of the R.A.F. together on the same day. They had gone their separate ways, he to teach learner drivers, Ransome to set up in business. And now Ransome was going to employ him. For years, all those Sunday mornings in the pub, Ransome's persuasive talk had been designed to needle him. He had been Ransome's superior in the R.A.F.

'Drink to it.'

He raised his tankard to meet Ransome's.

'Get a nice new suit,' suggested Ransome, smiling. 'Spick and span, with a polish on the shoes. They'll love you, old boy.'

He sat in the Austin, thinking about the last three hours. The pints of beer had darkened the hue of his face. He could feel them in his stomach, thick and comforting—a moat against Roche who was talking in his mind. He saw his flat mouth open and close, and the words lay between them, above Roche's tidy desk, eavesdroppings for the typing girl. So that was that: Powers must nod and understand, and go away and never return, must be forgotten by Roche, and by the typist whose breasts he had so much desired. Already he was a man of another trade, a good-hearted man who talked to the pregnant woman about what was to come, taking an interest and selling a requisite.

The sun was hot on his face as he sat in the Austin. His skin relaxed, that part of him happy in the heat. He closed his eyes and gave himself up to the tiny moment. The sun touched his hands on the steering wheel and warmed them too. Beer in his stomach, sun on his skin: he had felt such cosseting before. He had lain in bed, stretched and at peace, warmly covered. The warmth of his wife had welcomed him and given him another version of simple sensuality. Blearily, an awareness stirred in J. P. Powers. He did not think in so many words that the excuse for his life lay in moments like these: only in what he received, since he contributed nothing. He did not think it because it was absurd when it was put like that, clarified and clinical. The feeling hammered at his brain but no tendril stretched out to fashion it into thought. A cloud obscured the shaft of sunlight and the feeling evaporated, giving way to an afternoon depression. He switched on the ignition and drove the Austin for the last time, past Cave Crescent and Mortimer Road, out on to Putney Hill and into the stream of traffic.

VIII

A School Story

EVERY NIGHT AFTER lights-out in the dormitory there was
a ceremonial story-telling. One by one we contributed our
pieces, holding the stage from the gloom for five or six
minutes apiece. Many offerings were of a trite enough
order: the Englishman, the Irishman and the Scotsman on
a series of desert islands, and what the drunk said to the
Pope. But often the stories were real: reminiscences from
a short past, snippets of overheard conversation, descriptions
of the naked female body in unguarded moments. Only
Markham deliberately repeated himself, telling us again and
again, and by unanimous demand, about the death of his
mother. On a night when no one had much to say, Markham would invariably be called upon; and none of us ever
expected to hear anything new. We were satisfied that it
was so; because Markham told his story well and it was, to
us, a fascinating one.

'It was like this, you see. One Sunday morning my father
and I were walking up Tavistock Hill and I asked him to tell
me about my mother. It was a good sunny morning in early
May and my father looked up at the sky and started on
about how beautiful she'd been. So then, when I could get
a word in, I asked him about how she'd died and that. Well,
he took an extra breath or two and said to prepare myself. I
assured him I was well prepared, and then he told me about
how they had been staying with these friends in Florence
and how they had set out to the hills to do some shooting.
They rode out in a great Italian shooting-brake and soon
they were slaying the birds like nobody's business. But in
the middle of everything there was this accident and my
mother was lying in a pool of blood and all the Italians were

throwing up their hands and saying "Blessed Mother of Jesus, what a terrible thing!" I said: "Did her gun go off by accident? Was she not carrying it correctly or what?" And my father said it wasn't like that at all, it was his gun that went off by accident and what a shocking thing it was to be the instrument of one's wife's slaughter. Well, sharp as a knife I could see the lie in his face and I said to myself: "Accident, forsooth! Murder more like." Or, anyway, words to that effect. You'll understand with a discovery like that fresh on the mind one is in an emotional tizzy and apt to forget the exact order of thinking. Why was I certain? I'll tell you, boys, why I was certain: because within a six-month the father had married the dead mother's sister. My stepmother to this day. And I'll tell you another thing: I have plans laid to wipe out those two with a couple of swoops of a butcher's knife. Am I not, when all's said and done, a veritable pocket Hamlet? And isn't it right that I should dream at night of the sharpening of the knife?'

Markham had a long, rather serious face; deeply set, very blue eyes; and smooth fair hair the colour of yellow terra-cotta. People liked him, but nobody knew him very well. His stories about his family and the threats they exposed were taken only half seriously; and when he talked in this way he seemed to be speaking outside his role. Markham was too quiet, too pleasant, too attractive to be mixed up in this way. There was something wrong, not so much with what he said—which we quite understood, whether we thought of it as fact or not—as with Markham's saying it. That at least is how it appears in retrospect, to me and to the others with whom I have since discussed it. Then, we scarcely analysed our feelings; after all, we were only fifteen at the time of the Markham affair.

'I've got some bread from Dining Hall,' Williams said. 'Let's toast it in the boilerhouse.' He drew from beneath his jacket four rounds of hard-looking bread and a couple of pieces of straightened wire. His small red-rimmed eyes darted about my face as though seeking some minute, mislaid article. He held out a piece of wire and I took it from him, already recognising its utter uselessness for the task in hand. One had to open the top of the boiler and toast from above, guiding the bread far into the bowels of the ironwork until it was poised neatly above the glowing coke. It was a business of expertise, and a single length of wire in place of an expanding toasting fork indicated rudimentary disaster.

It was mid-afternoon and, recovering from a cold, I was 'off games'. Williams, who suffered from asthma, was rarely seen on the games field. He disliked any form of physical exercise and he used his disability as an excuse to spend solitary afternoons hanging around the classrooms or enjoying a read and a smoke in the lavatories. He was despised for his laziness, his unprepossessing appearance, and his passion for deception. I said I would join him on his expedition to the boiler-house.

'I've snitched some jam,' he said, 'and a pat or two of butter.'

We walked in silence, Williams occasionally glancing over his shoulder in his customary furtive manner. In the boiler-house he laid the bread on the seat of the boilerman's chair and extracted the jam and butter from the depths of his clothes. They were separately wrapped in two sheets of paper torn from an exercise book. The jam was raspberry and contact with the paper had caused the ruled lines to run. Fearing the effects of this, I said at once that as far as I was concerned the addition of butter was quite sufficient.

The toast was badly burnt and tasted of smoke. Williams ate his ravenously, wiping his fingers on his trouser pockets. I nibbled at mine and eventually threw it into the corner. At this Williams expostulated, picked up the discarded piece, wiped it and smeared on the remains of the jam. He made a crunching noise as he ate, and explained that his inordinate appetite was due to the presence of worms in his body.

There was a footfall on the steps outside and a moment later a figure appeared, sharply silhouetted in the doorway. We could not at first establish its identity, and Williams, speaking loudly, said to me: 'It has been well worth while. The knowledge we have gained of our school's heating system will stand us in good stead. It is well to put a use to one's time in this way.' The figure advanced, and Williams, seeing that it was not the headmaster, sniggered. 'It's only bloody Markham,' he said. 'I thought it was Bodger at least.'

'I have come to smoke,' Markham announced, offering each of us a small, thin cigar.

'When I am fully grown and equipped for life,' Williams said, 'I intend to pursue a legal career. As well, I shall smoke only the most expensive cigars. One can well afford such a policy if one makes a success of the law.'

Markham and I, concerned with the lighting of our tobacco, heard this pronouncement in silence.

'It may be,' Williams went on, 'that I shall learn in time to roll the leaves together myself. The female thigh, I understand, is just the instrument for such a chore.'

'Williams will make an excellent lawyer,' Markham remarked.

'Certainly he will be splendid beneath his wig,' I said.

'And what,' Williams asked, 'do you intend to do with your years, Markham?'

'Oh, they are well numbered. I shall hang quite soon for the slaughter of my father.'

'Would you not wait a while that I might defend you?'

'It is not an action you could readily defend surely? I am guilty already. I would prefer not to die, but I would not wish to dissociate myself from my crime.'

Williams, puffing hard and with the cigar clamped in the centre of his teeth, said:

'Markham's a bloody madman, eh?'

'Damn it, isn't it correct that I should be hatching schemes of vengeance? Wasn't it my own mother? Would you do less, Mr Williams? Answer me now, would you do less?'

'Ah Markham, I wouldn't go about with the noose around my neck before it was time for it. I'd hold my peace on that account.'

'Puny, Williams, puny.'

'But wise, none the less.' He kicked a piece of coke across

the floor, following it with his glance. He said: 'Anyway, Markham will never do it. Markham is all talk.'

'This is a good cigar,' Markham said. 'May we enjoy many another.'

'Yes,' said Williams agreeably enough. 'A fine drag.'

We smoked in silence. Looking back on it, it seems certain that it all began that afternoon in the boiler-house. Had I not met Williams on the way to his toasting session, had Markham not later shared his cigars with us, how different the course of events might have been. My friendship with Markham might never have come about; Williams might never have been transformed from a cunning nonentity into a figure of mystery and power; and Markham, somehow, might have dodged the snare he had already set for himself.

Becoming friends with Markham was an odd thing. Markham was so silent, so unforthcoming on any subject except the death of his mother. Yet he was sunny rather than sullen; thoughtful rather than brooding. We walked together on the hills behind the school, often without exchanging more than a dozen words. In spite of this our friendship grew. I discovered that Markham's father and stepmother were now in Kenya. Markham saw them only once a year, during the summer holidays; he spent Easter and Christmas with a grandmother on the south coast.

The other odd aspect of this new relationship between Markham and me was the attitude of Williams. He hung around us. Often, uninvited, he accompanied us on our walks. He took to sidling up to us and whispering: 'Markham will never do it. Markham's just a madman, eh?' Markham rarely replied. He stared at Williams with a puzzled expression and smiled.

When he came on walks with us Williams would ask Markham to tell us about the shooting accident in Florence, and this of course Markham never tired of doing. He didn't seem to resent Williams. I think he was more generous than the rest of us about people like Williams. Certainly he was more generous than I was. Frankly, Williams used to set my teeth on edge. I found him alone one day and asked him bluntly what he was up to. He sniffed at me and asked me what I meant.

'Why do you follow Markham and me around?' I said. 'Why don't you leave Markham alone?'

Williams laughed. 'Markham's an interesting bird.'

'What are you up to, Williams?'

But he wouldn't tell me. He said: 'I'm an unhealthy personage.' He laughed again and walked away.

This exchange had no effect on Williams. He still haunted our movements, chattering of his future in the legal world or retailing the fruits of an hour's eavesdropping. When we were alone together Markham no longer repeated his famous story or made any allusion to this particular aspect of life. I came to realize that although he truly hated his father it had become a joke with him to talk about it. I was the first close friend Markham had known, and he was quite unused to the communication that such a relationship involved. It was only very gradually that new topics of conversation developed between us.

But there was always Williams, devotedly determined, it seemed, to wrap Markham and his story closer and closer together. We formed, I suppose, an odd kind of triangle.

At the beginning of the autumn term the headmaster, Bodger, addressed us at length about this and that, announcing the names of the new prefects and supplying us with fresh items of school routine. When he had finished this part of his peroration he paused for a suitable moment and then he said:

'There are times, boys, in the lives of us all when we must display the ultimate bravery. When we must face the slings and arrows with a fortitude we may perhaps have never had call to employ before. Such a fearful moment has come to one of our number. I would ask you to show him kindness and understanding. I would ask you this term to help him on his way; to make that way as easy as you may. For us it is a test as it is for him. A test of our humanity. A test of our Christian witness. It is with the greatest grief, boys, that I must report to you the sudden and violent death of Ian Markham's father and stepmother.'

Markham had not yet returned. During the fortnight of his absence speculation and rumour ran high. Neither Bodger nor his henchmen seemed to know about the threats he had been wont to issue. Only we who were in their care questioned the accuracy of the facts as they had been presented to us: that a Mau Mau marauder armed with a heavy knife had run berserk through the Markham farm in Kenya. Was not the coincidence too great? Was it not more likely that Markham had finally implemented his words with action?

'Markham's a madman, eh?' Williams said to me.

When he did return, Markham was changed. He no longer smiled. Waiting expectantly in the dormitory for a new and gory story, his companions received only silence from Markham's bed. He spoke no more of his mother; and when anyone sympathised with him on his more recent loss he seemed not to know what was being spoken of. He faded into the background and became quite unremarkable. Pointedly rejecting my companionship, he ended our brief friendship. Instead, he and Williams became inseparable.

It was, I remember, a particularly beautiful autumn. Red, dead leaves gleamed all day in the soft sunlight. On warm afternoons I walked alone through the gorse-covered hills. I did not make friends easily; and I missed the company of Markham.

As the weeks passed it became clear the murder of Markham's parents by Mau Mau was now generally accepted. It might be thought that against a background of Markham's stories and avowed intentions a certain fear would have

developed; an uneasiness about sharing one's daily existence with such a character. It was not so. Markham seemed
almost dead himself; he was certainly not a figure to inspire
terror. The more one noticed him the more unlikely it
appeared that he could possibly have had any hand in the
events in Kenya, although he had been in the house at the
time and had himself escaped undamaged.

I thought that only I must have been aware of the
ominous nature of Markham's association with Williams.
Williams, I knew, was up to no good. He whispered con-
stantly to Markham, grinning slyly, his small eyes drilling
into Markham's face. I didn't like it and I didn't know what
to do.

One afternoon I walked into the town with a boy called
Block. We went to a café with the intention of passing an
hour over tea and cakes and, if the coast seemed clear, a
surreptitious smoke.

'This is an uncivilised place,' Block remarked as we sat
down. 'I cannot imagine why we came here.'

'There is nowhere else.'

'It is at least too revolting for the Bodger or any of his
band. Look, there's our dreaded Williams. With Markham.'

They were sitting at a table in an alcove. Williams, talking
as usual, was fiddling with the spots on his face. As I watched
him, he picked a brightly coloured cake from the plate
between them. It looked an uninviting article, indeed scarcely
edible. He nibbled at one corner and replaced it on the plate.

'Whatever does Markham see in him?' Block asked.

I shook my head. Block was a simple person, but when
he next spoke he revealed a depth I had not before had
evidence of. He cocked his head to one side and said:
'Williams hates Markham. You can see it easily enough. And
I believe Markham's terrified of him. You used to know
Markham rather well. D'you know why?'

Again I shook my head. But there was no doubt about it,
Block was quite right.

The nub of the relationship was William's hatred. It was
as though hatred of some kind was essential to Markham;

as though, since he had no father to hate now, he was feeding on this unexplained hatred of himself. It all seemed a bit crazy, but I felt that something of the kind must be true.

'I feel I should do something about it all,' I said. 'Williams is a horribly untrustworthy fellow. God knows what his intentions are.'

Did Williams know something that we others were ignorant of? Something of the double death in Kenya?

'What can you do?' Block said, lighting the butt of a cigarette.

'I wonder if I should talk to Pinshow?'

Block laughed. Pinshow was a fat, middle-aged master who welcomed the personal problems of his pupils. He was also a bit of an intellectual. It was enough to tell Mr Pinshow that one had an ambition to become a writer or an actor to ensure endless mugs of black coffee in Mr Pinshow's room.

'I often wonder if we don't underestimate Pinshow,' I said. 'There's lots of goodwill in the man. And good ideas quite often originate in unexpected quarters. He just might be able to suggest something.'

'Perhaps. You know more about Markham than I do. I mean, you probably know more about what the matter is. He doesn't seem much good at anything any more, does he?'

I looked across the room at his sad, lost-looking face. 'No, I'm afraid he doesn't.'

Block suddenly began to laugh. 'Have you heard Butler's one about the sick budgerigar?'

I said I didn't think I had, and he leaned forward and told me. Listening to this obscene account of invalid bird-life, I made up my mind to see Pinshow as soon as possible.

The evening light faded and Mr Pinshow continued to talk. I tried in the gloom to take some biscuits without his observing my action. He pushed the box closer to me, oblivious, or so I hoped, of my deceit. 'Out of the slimy mud of words,' said Mr Pinshow, 'out of the sleet and hail of verbal imprecision, come approximate thoughts and feelings, words that have taken the place of thoughts and feelings, and the beauty of incantation.' Mr Pinshow often said this. I think it may have been his favourite quotation. I drained my coffee mug, filling my mouth with bitter sediment as I did so.

I said: 'There is a land of the living and a land of the dead and the bridge is love.'

'Ah, Wilder.' Mr Pinshow drew a large coloured handkerchief from his trouser pocket and blew his nose.

'The only survival,' I added, 'the only meaning.'

Mr Pinshow replaced his handkerchief. He scratched a match along the side of its box and held the flame to his pipe. 'Love,' he said, puffing, 'or love? One sort or the other sort?'

'The other sort, sir?'

'You question such a division? Good. Good.'

I said: 'I wanted to speak to you, sir.'

'Quite right. Fire away, then.'

'In confidence, sir, I think Williams is a bad influence on Markham.'

'Ah.'

'I think Markham may be very upset about his parents' death, sir. Williams is the last person . . .'

'Come now, in what way a bad influence? Speak freely, my friend. We must straightway establish the facts of the case.'

I knew then that the whole thing was going to be useless. It had been a mistake to come to Pinshow. I could not reveal to him the evidence on which my fears were based. I said nothing, hoping he would not press me.

'I see,' he said.

'Perhaps I am making a mountain out of a molehill, sir.'

Mr Pinshow, however, did not think so at all. 'This is a serious business,' he said. 'Though it is unusual in these matters, I am glad you came to me.'

Clearly, I had given the man a completely false impression. I attempted to rectify this, but Mr Pinshow waved me to silence.

'Say no more, my friend. Leave the matter with me. You can rely on me to speak with discretion in the right directions.'

'Sir, I hope I have not misled you.'

'No, no, no.'

'It is not a *serious* thing, sir. It is just that Markham was once a friend of mine and I am sure that now he . . .'

Mr Pinshow held up his hand. He smiled. 'You are a good fellow. Do not despair. All will be well.'

God knows, I thought, what damage I have done.

'Mind your own bloody business,' Williams muttered to me. 'Any more of this kind of stuff to Pinshow and I'll have you for slander. Don't you know that man's a menace?'

'Go to hell, Williams.' And Williams, seeming a fit candidate for such a destination, shuffled angrily away.

After that, I decided to forget about Markham and Williams. After all, it had nothing to do with me; and in any case I appeared to have no option. I settled down to concentrating a little harder on my work and then, when I really had forgotten all about this strange alliance, I was summoned from class one day by the headmaster.

He stood by the window of his study, a terrible, sickly figure of immense height. He remained with his back to me when I entered the room and spoke to me throughout the interview from this position. 'You will tell me what you know about Markham and the boy Williams,' he said. 'Do not lie, boy. I know a lie. I feel a lie on its utterance. Likewise, do not exaggerate. You will repeat to me simply and honestly all that is apposite. Unburden yourself, boy, that you may leave the room with your duty well done.'

I did not intend to lie. To conceal three-quarters of the story was not to lie. I said: 'The whole truth, sir, is that . . .' I paused not knowing how to go on. The headmaster said:

'Well, boy, let us have haste with the whole truth.'

'I can tell you nothing, sir.'

'Nothing?'

'Yes, sir. I know nothing of Markham and Williams.'

'They are boys in this school. You know that, I presume? You have associated with them. You have spoken to Mr Pinshow of these boys. If their relationship is an illicit one I wish to know it. You will achieve little by reticence.'

'There is nothing illicit, sir, in their friendship. I spoke to Mr Pinshow merely because I felt Williams to be the wrong sort of friend for Markham at this particular time.'

'That is a presumptuous decision for you to make, boy.'

'Yes, sir.'

'Why, then, did you so perversely make it?'

'I like Markham, sir.'

'Why, then, did you not see to it that his days were made easier by persuading him personally against an ill influence?'

'Markham no longer wished for my companionship, sir.'

'You had harmed him in some manner?'

'No, sir. At least not that I know of.'

'Yes or no, boy? Do not leave yourself a cowardly loophole.'

'No, sir. I had not harmed him.'

'Well then, why did he not wish to converse with you?'

'I'm afraid I don't know.'

'You do not know. It is unnecessary to be afraid as well.'

'Yes, sir.'

'You see, boy, that you have placed me in an intolerable position with your wild irresponsibilities? I am the fount of authority in this school. You have made me uneasy in my mind. You have forced me to pursue a course I see no good reason for pursuing. Yet because there may be one tittle of reality in your guarded suspicions I must act as I do not wish to act. Have you ever placed yourself in a headmaster's shoes?'

'No, sir.'

'No, sir. I had sensed as much. They are shoes that pinch, boy. It is well to remember that.'

'Yes, sir.'

'Walk forward to my desk, boy, and press the bell you see there. We will order this affair one way or the other.'

Markham and Williams were summoned. When they entered, the headmaster turned from the window and faced us. He said to them:

'Your friendship is in dispute. Your accuser stands beside you. Do not lie, boys. I know a lie. I can feel a lie on its utterance. Have you reason for shame?'

Williams, whose eyes were fastened on the legs of the headmaster's desk, shook his head. Markham replied that he had no cause to be ashamed.

'On what then is your relationship based? Have you like interests? Of what do you speak together?'

'Of many things, sir,' Williams said. 'Politics and affairs of state. Of our ambitions, sir. And our academic progress as the term passes.'

'We talk of one subject only, sir,' Markham said. 'The death of my father and stepmother.'

'Yet you, boy,' the headmaster said to Williams, 'would claim a wider conversational field. The air is blackened with the lie. Which boy are we to believe?'

'Markham is ill, sir. He is not at all himself. I give him what help I can. He does not recall the full extent of our conversation.'

'We speak of one subject,' Markham repeated.

'Why, boy, do you speak of this subject to the exclusion of all others?'

'Because I killed my father, sir. And my stepmother too.'

'Markham is ill, sir. He ...'

'Leave the room, you boys. Markham, you shall remain.'

Neither Williams nor I spoke as we walked away from the headmaster's door. Then, as our ways were about to divide, I said:

'You know he didn't. You know it is not true.'

Williams did not look at me. He said: 'That's right. Why didn't you tell Bodger that?'

'You've made him believe he did it, Williams.'

'Markham's all talk. Markham's a madman, eh?'

'You're an evil bastard, Williams.'

'That's right. I'm an unhealthy personage.'

He went on his way and I stood where he had left me, looking back at the closed door of the headmaster's study. The little red light which indicated that for no reason whatsoever should the headmaster be disturbed gleamed above it. Within, I guessed that the curtains were by now closely drawn, since to do so was the headmaster's practice on all grave occasions.

Suddenly I had the absurd notion of returning to this darkened room and demanding to be heard, since now I was free to speak. I felt for the moment that I could put his case more clearly, more satisfactorily than Markham himself. I felt that I knew everything: the horror of the thought that had leapt in Markham's mind when first his father told him of the accident in Florence; the game he had made of it, and the later fears that Williams had insidiously played upon. But as I paused in doubt I heard the urgent chiming of a bell, and, like the object of some remote control, I answered the familiar summons.

That same evening Markham was driven away. He was seen briefly in the headmaster's hall, standing about in his overcoat, seeming much as usual.

'They've sent him up to Derbyshire,' said Mr Pinshow when later I attempted to elicit information. 'Poor lad; so healthy in the body, too.' He would say no more, but I knew what he was thinking; and often since I have thought of Markham, still healthy in his body, growing up and getting older in the place they had found for him in Derbyshire. I have thought of Williams too, similarly growing older though in other circumstances, marrying perhaps and begetting children, and becoming in the end the man he had said he would one day be.

IX

The Day We Got Drunk on Cake

GARBED IN A CRUSHED tweed suit, fingering the ragged end of a tie that might well have already done a year's service about his waist, Swann de Courcey uttered a convivial obscenity in the four hundred cubic feet of air they euphemistically called my office. I had not seen him for some years: he is the kind of person who is often, for no reason one can deduce, out of the country. In passing, one may assume that his lengthy absences are due in some way to the element of disaster that features so commandingly in his make-up.

I should have known when I saw him standing there that I must instantly be on my guard. In my prevailing condition of emotional delicacy I could not hope to cope with whatever entertainment Swann had in mind for me. For, to give him his due, Swann never came empty-handed. Swann was a great one for getting the best out of life; and he offered one, invariably, a generous part of his well-laid plans. This time, he explained, he was offering me an attractive afternoon. In turn, I explained that I did not feel like an attractive afternoon, that I was too busy to gild the hours in the manner he was suggesting. But Swann was sitting down, well entrenched; and in the end he talked me into it.

I wrote a note and put it on my typewriter: *Tuesday p.m. Am under surgeon's knife.* Then I made a telephone call.

'Lucy?'

'Hullo, Mike.'

'How are you?'

'Very well, Mike. How are you?'

'Very well, too. Just thought I'd ring—'

'Thank you, Mike.'

'We must meet again soon.'

'Yes, we must.'

'I'd invite you to lunch only an old and valued friend has just transpired.'

'That's nice for you.'

'Well, yes.'

'Thanks for ringing, Mike.'

'Goodbye, Lucy.'

'Goodbye, Mike.'

Swann was drawing designs on the varnish of my desk with a straightened-out paper-clip.

'That wasn't your wife,' he said.

'Wife? Far from it.'

'You haven't married or anything?'

'No.'

'Good. I've got a couple in a hostelry. They tell me they know you.' We sauntered out into the September sun to meet them.

I thought I might cheat a little here. I have always wanted to invent pert shorthand typists with good figures and pretty lips whose heads may easily be turned by the crisp jingle of money, puritan maids who have done the stint at Pitman's and do not believe in anticipating marriage. It might quite easily have been such girls with whom we found ourselves wasting away that afternoon. As it happened, it was Margo and Jo, a smart pair who drew pictures for the glossy magazines.

'When I was eleven,' Jo told me, 'I wrote this children's book and drew all the pictures. Somebody published it, and that of course made me terribly unpopular with everyone.'

'You must have been hugely clever.'

'No, honestly. It was terribly bad, as you can imagine. Just chance that it got published.'

'Words,' said Margo, 'mean a lot to Jo. She has a real sense.'

'She's bonkers,' said Swann.

'For God's sake, Swann,' said Margo.

Jo and Swann moved together. Swann was bored and he began to tell Jo a joke. Margo said, specifically to me: 'Jo is the most talented person I've ever met.' I nodded, not caring one way or the other. The bar was full of uniformed men: dark grey suits, waistcoats, white shirts, striped ties of some club or school.

'Have a drink, Margo?'

Margo said that was a good idea and I squeezed through to the wet counter and floated a ten-shilling note on a pool of beer. When I returned to her Margo said:

'Tell me straight, what do you think of Nigel?'

Nigel? Playing for time I sipped my beer, wondering why I drank the stuff since I disliked it so much. I said:

'Oh, I like Nigel.'

'Do you *really*?'

'Well, he's all right. I mean—'

'Sometimes, Mike, I think Nigel is the most God-awful bore I ever met.'

I remembered. Nigel was plump and talkative. Nigel would tell you anything you might ever wish to know. When Nigel got going there was, in truth, no stopping Nigel. Nigel was Margo's husband.

I drank some more beer. It was cold and tasteless. I said nothing.

'Nigel and I had a barney last night.'

'Oh God!'

Margo told me about the barney. I listened dejectedly. Then I bought some more drink, and this time I made mine whisky. As I've said, Nigel was Margo's husband. She and Jo had one apiece. Both marriages were, as the saying goes, on the rocks.

Suddenly Margo stopped about Nigel. She leered at me and said something I didn't catch. From the next few sentences, I realised she was telling me I'd make a good husband.

'I suppose I would,' I said.

'I'm not in love with you or anything,' Margo said, swaying.

'Of course not.'

After the pub we went off to have some lunch. All the way in the taxi I thought about Lucy.

We went to an Italian place in Soho that was too expensive and not particularly good. Swann told us the history of his life and ate only series of cassatas. I found a telephone on the stairs and rang up Lucy.

'Hullo, Lucy. What are you doing?'

'What d'you mean, what am I doing? I'm standing here talking to you on the telephone.'

'I'm getting drunk with people in Soho.'

'Well, that's nice for you.'

'Is it? Wish you were here.'

Lucy would be bored by this. 'I've been reading *Adam Bede*,' she said.

'A good story.'

'Yes.'

'Have you had lunch?'

'I couldn't find anything. I had some chocolate.'

'I telephoned to see how you were.'

'I'm fine, thanks.'

'I wanted to hear your voice.'

'Oh come off it. It's just a voice.'

'Shall I tell you about it?'

'I'd rather you didn't. I don't know why.'

'Shall we meet some time?'

'I'm sure we shall.'

'I'll ring you when I'm sober.'

'Do that. I must get back to *Adam Bede*.'

'Goodbye.'

'Goodbye.'

I replaced the receiver and stood there looking down the steep stairs. Then I descended them.

'What on earth shall we do now?' Swann said. 'It's four o'clock.'

'I want to talk to Mike,' Margo announced. 'Nobody's to listen.'

I sat beside her and she began to speak in a limping whisper. 'I want your advice about Nigel, Mike.'

'Honestly, I scarcely know him.'

'Doesn't matter. Look, I think there's something the matter with Nigel.'

I asked her to be specific. Instead she turned her assertion into a question. 'Mike, do *you* think there's something wrong with Nigel?'

'Well—'

'Be frank now.'

'I tell you, I don't know him. For all I know he may have an artificial stomach.'

'Nigel hasn't an artificial stomach, actually.'

'Good.'

'I don't know why you should think that about him. He doesn't even have trouble with his stomach.'

'Well, then, what's the matter with the man?'

'I think he's probably mental.'

'Well, for God's sake get him attended to, Margo.'

'You think I should?'

'Certainly I do. Unless you like his being mental.'

Margo giggled. 'Well, actually, you know, I rather do.'

'In that case you've got no problem, have you?'

'Old Nigel's become funny.'

'How jolly for you, Margo.'

'He's taken to doing such odd things. I mean, I don't know where this is going to stop.'

'Odd things like what?'

'Like bringing home elderly women. He comes in with these women, explaining that he has been attending some meeting with them and has brought them back for coffee. It's quite alarming—Nigel with four or five old ladies trailing behind him. They stay for ages—sometimes weeks. I've no idea where he gets them from. I think he imagines he's being kind.'

'What does Nigel say?'

'He says they haven't finished their meeting. They all sit round writing little notes. Nobody *says* anything.'

'I think it's all very interesting. I'm sure there's some quite simple explanation. I don't think you've really investigated the matter, Margo.'

'Let's leave this place,' Swann said.

We went to another place, called the Blue Goat. It was one of these clubs where you can drink in the afternoon without having to watch strip-tease. Margo tried to go on about Nigel, but I said firmly that I didn't want to hear anything more about Nigel. I talked to Jo.

'Jo,' I said, 'do you know a girl called Lucy Anstruth?'

'Small, plump, balding a little?'

'No. Lucy is a very beautiful person.'

'Not the same girl.'

'Tall, fair, very blue eyes. Moves like a cat.'

'Don't know her.'

'She says unexpected things. She's half Swedish or something.'

'Mike, would you guess I was half Welsh?'

'No. I want to ask you about Lucy—'

'But I don't know her.'

'I don't know what to do about Lucy.'

'You sound like Margo. Margo doesn't know what to do about Nigel. Nobody knows what to do about anyone else. God! May I have some more vodka?'

'Yes. As I say—'

'I want a triple vodka.'

I ordered the vodka. Beside us, Swann and Margo were sitting in preoccupied silence; they weren't even listening to what we were saying. Margo caught my eye and opened her mouth to speak. I turned my back and handed Jo her drink.

'Something's the matter with Margo's husband,' Jo said. 'Poor old Margo's terribly worried.'

'Yes, I know all about it. Margo has been telling me. In detail.'

'I like Nigel, you know.'

'Perhaps you can help him straighten himself out. We

were talking about something else. I was telling you—'

'Seems Nigel brings women home.'

'Yes I know, Jo.'

'Bit rough on Margo.'

Margo heard this. She shouted: 'What's rough on Margo?' and then the conversation became general. I went away to telephone Lucy.

'Lucy?'

'Hullo. Is that Mike?'

'Yes.'

'Hullo, Mike.'

'Hullo, Lucy.'

'How are you?'

'I'm feeling funny. But Lucy?'

'Yes?'

'I'm not trying to be funny. I'm not being amusing.'

'Where are you?'

'In the Blue Goat.'

'Wherever's that?'

'It's lined with leopard skin. Jo and Margo and Swann are here too.'

'Who are they?'

'Just other people.'

'Nice of you to ring, Mike.'

'Margo's husband Nigel brings women home. I wondered perhaps if you had a word of advice I could give her. She's worried about the women. They're elderly and they come in groups.'

'Oh, Mike, I don't know about things like that. I wouldn't know what to do. Honestly.'

'Sorry, Lucy; I just thought you might.'

'The doorbell's ringing. Goodbye, Mike. If I were you I'd go home.'

Swann said he wanted tea. We left the Blue Goat and walked in dazzling sunshine towards Floris.

Margo began again about Nigel.

Swann said he knew a man who would do Nigel a world of good. He couldn't remember the treatment this man offered, but he said it was highly thought of.

I went away to telephone Lucy.

'Lucy?'

A man's voice answered. I said: 'May I speak to Lucy? Is that the right number?'

The man didn't reply and in a moment Lucy came on. 'Is that Mike again?'

'Hullo, Lucy. How are you?'

'I'm fine, Mike.'

'Good.'

'Mike, you telephoned me at four-fifteen. Do you know what time it is now?'

'What time is it now?'

'Four-thirty-five.'

'Am I being a nuisance, is that it?'

'No, no. Just, is there anything I can do for you? I mean, do you want something and feel unable to express yourself?'

'I'm bored. I'm with these people. Lucy.'

'Yes?'

'Who's that in your flat?'

'A friend called Frank. You don't know him.'

'What's he doing there?'

'What d'you mean, what's he doing?'

'Well—'

'Look, I'll ask him. Frank, what are you doing?'

'What's he say?'

'He says he's making a cup of tea.'

'I'm having tea too. In Floris. I wish you were here.'

'Goodbye, Mike.'

'Don't go, Lucy.'

'Goodbye, Mike.'

'Goodbye, Lucy.'

When I got back to the others I found them laughing in an uproarious manner. Swann said the cake they were eating was making them drunk. 'Smell it,' he said. It smelt of rum. I tasted some: it tasted of rum too. We all ate a lot of the cake, laughing at the thought of getting drunk on cake. We ordered some more, and told the waitress it was delicious. When the enthusiasm had melted a bit Swann said:

'Mike, we want your advice about Margo's husband.'

'I've told Margo—'

'No, Mike—seriously now. You know about these things.'

'Why do you think I know about these things? Quite emphatically, I do not know about these things.'

'All right, Mike, I'll tell you. Margo's husband Nigel keeps turning up with groups of old females. Margo's worried in case the thing develops a bit—you know, tramps, grocers, one-legged soldiers. What d'you think she should do?'

'I don't know what Margo should do. Margo, I don't know what you should do. Except perhaps ask Nigel what he's up to. In the meantime, have some more cake.'

'Now there's an idea,' Swann shouted excitedly. 'Margo love, why don't you ask old Nigel what he's up to?'

Jo hacked affectionately at my face with her great spiked fingers. I guessed it was an expression of admiration rather than attack because she smiled as she did so.

'But all Nigel says,' Margo said, 'is that they haven't finished their meeting.'

'Ah yes,' said Swann, 'but you don't press him. You don't say: "What meeting?" You don't indicate that you are in the dark as to the nub of their business. Nigel may well imagine that you accept the whole state of affairs without question and expect little else of married life. When you were at the Gents,' Swann said to me, 'Margo confessed she was worried.'

'She had previously confessed as much to me. I wasn't at the Gents. I was making a telephone call.'

'Shall *I* do that?' Margo said. 'Shall I ring up Nigel and ask him to explain everything?'

We all nodded. Margo rose, hesitated, and sat down

again. She said she couldn't. She explained she was too shy
to telephone her husband in this way. She turned to me.

'Mike, would you do it?'

'Me?'

'Mike, would you telephone?'

'Are you asking me to telephone your husband and
enquire about his relationship with some elderly women
who are entirely unknown to me?'

'Mike, for my sake.'

'Think of the explanations it would involve me in. Think
of the confusion. Nigel imagining I was the husband
of one of these women. Nigel imagining I was the police.
Nigel asking me question after question. For goodness'
sake, how do you think I would get some kind of answer
out of *him*?'

Swann said: 'All you have to do is to say: "Is that Nigel?
Now look here, Nigel, what's all this I hear about these
women who come to your house at all hours of the day
and night?" Say you represent the Ministry of Pensions.'

'I can't address the man as Nigel and then say I'm from
the Ministry of Pensions.'

'Mike, Margo's husband's name *is* Nigel. He'll be expecting you to address him as Nigel. If you don't address
him as Nigel, he'll simply tell you to go to hell. He'll say
you've got a wrong number.'

'So I say: "Hullo, Nigel, this is the Ministry of Pensions."
The man'll think I'm crazy.'

Margo said: 'Mike, you just do it your own way. Take
no notice of Swann. Swann's been eating too much cake.
Come on, you know where the telephone is.' She gave me a
piece of paper with a number on it.

'Oh God,' I said; and unable to bear it any longer I
borrowed fourpence and marched off to the telephone.

'Hullo?' said the voice at the other end.

'Hullo. Can I speak to Lucy? Please.'

'Hullo,' Lucy said.

'Hullo, Lucy.'

'Well?' said Lucy.

'It's Mike.'

'I know it's Mike.'

'They wanted me to telephone this man I was telling you about, but I can't go telephoning people in this way—'

'Why don't you go home to bed?'

'Because I wouldn't sleep. Remember the man with the elderly women? Well, they wanted me to telephone him and ask him what he's up to. Lucy, I can't do that, can I?'

'No, quite honestly I don't believe you can.'

'They told me to pose as the Ministry of Pensions.'

'Goodbye, Mike.'

'Just a—Lucy?'

'Yes?'

'Isn't that man still there?'

'Which man is this?'

'The man in your flat.'

'Frank. He's still here.'

'Who is he, Lucy?'

'He's called Frank.'

'Yes, but what does he do?'

'I don't know what he does. Frank, what do you do? For a living? He says he's a—what, Frank? A freight agent, Mike.'

'A freight agent.'

'Goodbye.'

'Goodbye, Lucy.'

When I arrived back at the tea-table everyone was very gay. Nobody asked me what Nigel had said. Swann paid the bill and said he was anxious to show us a display of Eastern horrors somewhere in Euston and would afterwards take us to a party. In the taxi Margo said:

'What did Nigel say?'

'He was out.'

'Was there no reply?'

'A woman answered. She said I was interrupting the meeting. I said "What meeting?" but she wanted to know who I was before she would answer that. I said I was the Ministry of Pensions and she said "Oh my God" and rang off.'

We were hours early for the party, but nobody seemed to mind. I helped a woman in slacks to pour bottles of wine into a crock. Swann, Margo and Jo played with a tape recorder, and after a time the woman's husband arrived and we all went out to eat.

About eight, people began to arrive. The place filled with tobacco smoke, music and fumes; and the party began to swing along at a merry enough pace. A girl in ringlets talked to me earnestly about love. I think she must have been feeling much the same as I was, but I didn't fancy her as a soulmate, not even a temporary one. She said: 'It seems to me that everyone has a quality that can get the better of love. Is stronger, you see. Like pride. Or honesty. Or moral, even intellectual, even emotional integrity. Take two people in love. The only thing that can really upset things is this personal quality in one of them. Other people don't come into it at all. Except in a roundabout way—as instruments of jealousy, for instance. Don't you agree?'

I wasn't sure about anything, but I said yes.

'Another thing about love,' the girl with the ringlets said, 'is its extraordinary infection. Has it ever occurred to you that when you're in love with someone you're really wanting to be loved yourself? Because that, of course, is the law. I mean, it would be odd if every time one person loved another person the first person wasn't loved in return. There's only a very tiny percentage of that kind of thing.'

An aggressive young man, overhearing these remarks, began to laugh. He went on laughing, looking at the girl in ringlets and looking at me.

I went away and filled my glass from the crock, and asked a pretty middle-aged woman what she did. Her answer was coy; I smiled and passed on. Margo caught my arm and dragged me off to a corner. 'Mike, you'll ring Nigel again?'

'I've been thinking about that,' I said. 'Honestly, I don't think I can interfere.'

'Oh but, dear, you promised.'

'Promised? I didn't promise anything.'

'Oh Mike.'

'Really, the whole affair—oh all right.'

'Now, Mike?'

'All right. Now.'

'Lucy?'

'Is that Mike?'

'Who else?'

'Who indeed? Where are you now?'

'I'm at a party.'

'A good party?'

'Yes, I suppose so. Why don't you come along?'

'I can't, Mike. I'm doing things.'

'With the bloody freight agent, I suppose.'

'The what agent?'

'Freight. Your friend the freight agent. Frank.'

'He's not a freight agent. He's in publishing.'

'What'd he say he was a freight agent for?'

A lengthy explanation followed. Calling himself a freight agent was a sample of Frank's humour. I thought about this as I made my way back to Margo.

'What'd he say, Mike?'

'A woman said Nigel wasn't in.'

'Is that all?'

'I said the house was being watched. I said the local authorities weren't at all happy.'

'What'd she say?'

'She began to moan, so I said "I mean it," and rang off.'

'Thank you, Mike.'

'That's all right. Any time.'

Swann joined us and Margo said: 'Mike's been on to Nigel again. Mike's being wonderful.'

Swann patted me on the back and said: 'Any joy?'

Margo started to tell him. I went away.

Jo was pretending to listen to a couple of men who were between them retailing a complicated story. She said to me in a low voice: 'Don't worry about Margo. I'll see she comes through the other side.'

I stared at her, wondering why she should imagine I was worried about Margo. 'I'm sure you will, Jo,' I said.

'Trust Jo,' she whispered.

I said I considered her a trustworthy person. I began to elaborate on the thought. One of the men said: 'D'you mind, old boy?'

I shrugged and pushed a path back to the telephone. I dialled three times to be certain, but on each occasion there was no reply.

A ragged form of dancing was now taking place. Pausing by the crock, I found myself once again in the company of the girl with the ringlets. She smiled at me and in a boring way I said: 'Do you know a girl called Lucy Anstruth?'

The girl with the ringlets shook her head. 'Should I?'

'I suppose not,' I said. The girl examined me closely and passed on.

I went upstairs and discovered a quiet room with a bed in it. A lamp on a dressing-table gave out a weak light. The bed, which looked comfortable, was almost in darkness. I stretched out on it, welcoming the gloom. In a few moments I dropped off to sleep. When I awoke the luminous dial of my watch indicated that I had been asleep for two hours. Two girls were tidying their faces at the dressing-table. They drew head-scarves with horses on them from their handbags and placed them about their heads. They spoke in a whisper and left the room. I lay there considering the events of the day and wondering how I was going to feel about them at breakfast. How one feels at breakfast about the preceding day has always seemed to be important to me.

A man with a glass in his hand entered the room and placed himself before the mirror on the dressing-table. He combed his hair and tightened his tie. Then he took a handkerchief from his pocket and wrapped it around his right forefinger. He inserted this into each ear, twisting his forefinger back and forth. He remarked to himself on the outcome of this operation, examining his handkerchief. I closed my eyes; when I opened them he was gone. I lit a cigarette and set off to the telephone again.

'What is it?' a voice said. It was the publishing man. I asked to speak to Lucy.

'Hullo, Lucy.'

'Oh Mike, really—'

'Lucy, that man's there again.'

'I know, Mike.'

'It's two o'clock in the morning.'

'Two o'clock in the morning. I'm sorry, Mike.' Her voice was so gentle that I said:

'Stop trying not to hurt me.'

'I think I'd better ring off.'

'I'll ring off, damn it.'

I stood by the telephone, considering, and feeling sick. I felt something between my fingers and looked down at the piece of paper with Nigel's telephone number on it. I lifted the receiver and dialled it.

I waited almost a minute and then a woman's voice said: 'Yes? Who is that please?'

I think I said: 'I want to know what's going on.'

The woman said quickly: 'Who is that speaking? You haf the wrong number.'

'I do not,' I retaliated briskly. 'Please bring Nigel to the phone.'

'Nigel is in the Chair. You are interrupting our meeting with this demand. There is much on the agenda. I cannot attend to you, sir.'

'This is the Ministry of Pensions,' I said, and I heard the woman breathing laboriously. Then she cut me off.

I walked back through the party and looked for the front door. I was thinking that everything had been more or less resolved. Margo's grievance had had its airing; she felt the better for it, and all anyone had to do now was to ask Nigel what he was up to and press the point until a satisfactory answer was achieved. After that, it was up to the relevant experts. As for me, time would heal and time would cure. I knew it, and it was the worst thing of all. I didn't want to be cured. I wanted the madness of my love for Lucy to go on lurching at me from dreams; to mock at me from half-empty glasses; to leap at me unexpectedly. In time Lucy's face would fade to a pin-point; in time I would see her on the street and greet her with casualness, and sit with her over coffee, quietly discussing the flow beneath the bridges since last we met. Today—not even that, for already it was tomorrow—would slide away like all the other days. Not a red letter day. Not the day of my desperate bidding. Not the day on which the love of my life was snaffled away from me. I opened the front door and looked out into the night. It was cold and uncomforting. I liked it like that. I hated the moment, yet I loved it because in it I still loved Lucy. Deliberately I swung the door and shut away the darkness and drizzle. As I went back to the party the sadness of all the forgetting stung me. Even already, I thought, time is at work; time is ticking her away; time is destroying her, killing all there was between us. And with time on my side I would look back on the day without bitterness and without emotion. I would remember it only as a flash on the brittle surface of nothing, as a day that was rather funny, as the day we got drunk on cake.

X

Raymond Bamber and Mrs Fitch

FOR FIFTEEN YEARS, ever since he was twenty-seven, Raymond Bamber had attended the Tamberleys' autumn cocktail party. It was a function to which the Tamberleys inclined to invite their acquaintances rather than their friends, so that every year the faces changed a bit: no one except Raymond had been going along to the house in Eaton Square for as long as fifteen years. Raymond, the Tamberleys felt, was a special case, for they had known him since he was a boy, having been close friends of his father's.

Raymond was a tall man, six foot two inches, with spectacles and a small moustache. He was neat in all he did, and he lived what he himself referred to as tidy life.

'I come here every year,' said Raymond at the Tamberleys', to a woman he had not met before, a woman who was tall too, with a white lean face and lips that were noticeably scarlet. 'It is an occasion for me almost, like Christmas or Easter. To some extent, I guide my life by the Timberleys' autumn party, remembering on each occasion what has happened in the year gone by.'

'My name is Mrs Fitch,' said the woman, poking a hand out for a drink. 'Is that vermouth and gin?' she enquired of the Tamberleys' Maltese maid, and the maid agreed that it was. 'Good,' said Mrs Fitch.

'Raymond, Raymond,' cried the voice of Mrs Tamberley as Mrs Tamberley materialised suddenly beside them. 'How's Nanny Wilkinson?'

'She died,' murmured Raymond.

'Of course she did,' exclaimed Mrs Tamberley. 'How silly of me!'

'Oh no—'

160

'You put that sweet notice in *The Times*. His old nurse,' explained Mrs Tamberley to Mrs Fitch. 'Poor Nanny Wilkinson,' she said, and smiled and bustled off.

'What was all that?' asked Mrs Fitch.

'It's one of the things that happened to me during the year. The other was—'

'What's your name, anyway?' the woman interrupted. 'I don't think I ever caught it.'

Raymond told her his name. He saw that she was wearing a black dress with touches of white on it. Her shoulders were bare and bony; she had, Raymond said to himself, an aquiline face.

'The other thing was that an uncle died and left me a business in his will. That happened, actually, before the death of Nanny Wilkinson and to tell you the truth, Mrs Fitch, I just didn't know what to do. "What could I do with a business?" I said to myself. So I made my way to Streatham where the old lady lived. "Run a business, Raymond? You couldn't run a bath," she said.' Raymond laughed, and Mrs Fitch smiled frostily, looking about her for another drink. 'It rankled, that, as you may imagine. Why couldn't I run a business? I thought. And then, less than a week later, I heard that she had died in Streatham. I went to her funeral, and discovered that she'd left me a prayer-book in her will. All that happened in the last year. You see, Mrs Fitch?'

Mrs Fitch, her eyes on her husband, who was talking to a woman in yellow in a distant corner of the room, said vaguely:

'What about the business?'

'I sold the business. I live alone, Mrs Fitch, in a flat in Bayswater; I'm forty-two. I'm telling you that simply because I felt that I could never manage anything like taking on a business so suddenly. That's what I thought when I had considered the matter carefully. No good being emotional, I said to myself.'

'No,' said Mrs Fitch. She watched the woman move quite close to her husband and engage him in speech that had all the air of confidential talk. The woman wasn't young, Mrs

Fitch noticed, but had succeeded in giving the impression of youth. She was probably forty-four, she reckoned; she looked thirty.

So Mrs Tamberley had seen the notice in *The Times*, Raymond thought. He had worded it simply and had stated in a straightforward manner the service that Nanny Wilkinson had given over the years to his family. He had felt it her due, a notice in *The Times*, and there was of course only he who might do it. He remembered her sitting regally in his nursery teaching him his tidiness. Orderliness was the most important thing in life, she said, after a belief in the Almighty.

'Get me a drink, dear,' said Mrs Fitch suddenly, holding out an empty glass and causing Raymond to note that this woman was consuming the Tamberleys' liquor at a faster rate than he.

'Gin and vermouth,' ordered Mrs Fitch. 'Dry,' she added. 'Not that red stuff.'

Raymond smiled and took her glass while Mrs Fitch observed that her husband was listening with rapt care to what the woman in yellow was saying to him. In the taxi-cab on the way to the Tamberleys', he had remarked as usual that he was fatigued after his day's work. 'An early night,' he had suggested. And now he was listening carefully to a female: he wouldn't leave this party for another two hours at least.

'It was quite a blow to me,' said Raymond, handing Mrs Fitch a glass of gin and vermouth, 'hearing that she was dead. Having known her, you see, all my life—'

'Who's dead now?' asked Mrs Fitch, still watching her husband.

'Sorry,' said Raymond. 'How silly of me! No, I meant, you see, this old lady whom I had known as Nanny Wilkinson. I was saying it was a blow to me when she died, although of course I didn't see much of her these last few years. But the memories are there, if you see what I mean; and you cannot of course erase them.'

'No,' said Mrs Fitch.

'I was a particularly tall child, with my spectacles of course, and a longish upper lip. "When you're a big man," I remember her saying to me, "you'll have to grow a little moustache to cover up all that lip." And declare, Mrs Fitch, I did.'

'I never had a nanny,' said Mrs Fitch.

' "He'll be a tennis-player," people used to say—because of my height, you see. But in fact I turned out to be not much good on a tennis court.'

Mrs Fitch nodded. Raymond began to say something else, but Mrs Fitch, her eyes still fixed upon her husband, interrupted him. She said:

'Interesting about your uncle's business.'

'I think I was right. I've thought of it often since, of sitting down in an office and ordering people to do this and that, instead of remaining quietly in my flat in Bayswater. I do all my own cooking, actually, and cleaning and washing up. Well, you can't get people, you know. I couldn't even get a simple char, Mrs Fitch, not for love nor money. Of course it's easy having no coal fires to cope with: the flat is all-electric, which is what, really, I prefer.'

Raymond laughed nervously, having observed that Mrs Fitch was, for the first time since their conversation had commenced, observing him closely. She was looking into his face, at his nose and his moustache and his spectacles. Her eyes passed up to his forehead and down the line of his right cheek, down his neck until they arrived at Raymond's Adam's apple. He continued to speak to her, telling of the manner in which his flat in Bayswater was furnished, how he had visited the Sanderson showrooms in Berners Street to select materials for chair-covers and curtains. 'She made them for me,' said Raymond. 'She was almost ninety then.'

'What's that?' said Mrs Fitch. 'Your nurse made them?'

'I measured up for her and wrote everything down just as she had directed. Then I travelled out to Streatham with my scrap of paper.'

'On a bicycle.'

Raymond shook his head. He thought it odd of Mrs Fitch to suggest, for no logical reason, that he had cycled from Bayswater to Streatham. 'On a bus actually,' he explained. He paused, and then added: 'I could have had them made professionally, of course, but I preferred the other. I thought it would give her an interest, you see.'

'Instead of which it killed her.'

'No, no. No, you've got it confused. It was in 1964 that she made the curtains and the covers for me. As I was saying, she died only a matter of months ago.'

Raymond noticed that Mrs Fitch had ceased her perusal of his features and was again looking vacantly into the distance. He was glad that she had ceased to examine him because had she continued he would have felt obliged to move away from her, being a person who was embarrassed by such intent attention. He said, to make it quite clear about the covers and the curtains:

'She died in fact of pneumonia.'

'Stop,' said Mrs Fitch to the Tamberleys' Maltese maid who happened to be passing with a tray of drinks. She lifted a glass to her lips and consumed its contents while reaching out a hand for another. She repeated the procedure, drinking two glasses of the Tamberleys' liquor in a gulping way and retaining a third in her left hand.

'Nobody tells the truth,' said Mrs Fitch after all that. 'We come to these parties and everything's a sham.'

'What?' said Raymond.

'You know what I mean.'

Raymond laughed, thinking that Mrs Fitch was making some kind of joke. 'Of course,' he said, and laughed again, a noise that was more of a cough.

'You told me you were forty-two,' said Mrs Fitch. 'I in fact am fifty-one, and have been taken for sixty-five.'

Raymond thought he would move away from this woman in a moment. He had a feeling she might be drunk. She had listened pleasantly enough while he told her a thing or two about himself, yet here she was now speaking most peculiarly. He smiled at her and heard her say:

'Look over there, Mr Bamber. That man with the woman in yellow is my husband. We were born in the same year and in the same month, January 1915. Yet he could be in his thirties. That's what he's up to now; pretending the thirties with the female he's talking to. He's praying I'll not approach and give the game away. D'you see, Mr Bamber?'

'That's Mrs Anstey,' said Raymond. 'I've met her here before. The lady in yellow.'

'My husband has eternal youth,' said Mrs Fitch. She took a mouthful of her drink and reached out a hand to pick a fresh one from a passing tray. 'It's hard to bear.'

'You don't look fifty-one,' said Raymond. 'Not at all.'

'Are you mocking me?' cried Mrs Fitch. 'I do not look fifty-one. I've told you so: I've been taken for sixty-five.'

'I didn't mean that. I meant—'

'You were telling a lie, as well you know. My husband is telling lies too. He's all sweetness to that woman, yet it isn't his nature. My husband cares nothing for people, except when they're of use to him. Why do you think, Mr Bamber, he goes to cocktail parties?'

'Well—'

'So that he may make arrangements with other women. He desires their flesh and tells them so by looking at it.'

Raymond looked serious, frowning, thinking that that was expected of him.

'We look ridiculous together, my husband and I. Yet once we were a handsome couple. I am like an old crow while all he has is laughter lines about his eyes. It's an obsession with me.'

Raymond pursed his lips, sighing slightly.

'He's after women in this room,' said Mrs Fitch, eyeing her husband again.

'Oh, no, now—'

'Why not? How can you know better than I, Mr Bamber? I have had plenty of time to think about this matter. Why shouldn't he want to graze where the grass grows greener, or appears to grow greener? That Anstey woman is a walking confidence trick.'

'I think,' said Raymond, 'that I had best be moving on. I have friends to talk to.' He made a motion to go, but Mrs Fitch grasped part of his jacket in her right hand.

'What I say is true,' she said. 'He is practically a maniac. He has propositioned women in this very room before this. I've heard him at it.'

'I'm sure——'

'When I was a raving beauty he looked at me with his gleaming eye. Now he gleams for all the others. I'll tell you something, Mr Bamber.' Mrs Fitch paused. Raymond noticed that her eyes were staring over his shoulder, as though she had no interest in him beyond his being a person to talk at. 'I've gone down on my bended knees, Mr Bamber, in order to have this situation cleared up: I've prayed that that man might look again with tenderness on his elderly wife. But God has gone on,' said Mrs Fitch bitterly, 'in His mysterious way, not bothering Himself.'

Raymond did not reply to these observations. He said instead that he hadn't liked to mention it before but was Mrs Fitch aware that she was clutching in her right hand part of his clothes?

'He shall get to know your Anstey woman,' said Mrs Fitch. 'He shall come to know that her father was a bear-like man with a generous heart and that her mother, still alive in Guildford, is difficult to get on with. My husband shall come to know all the details about your Anstey woman: the plaster chipping in her bathroom, the way she cooks an egg. He shall know what her handbags look like, and how their clasps work—while I continue to wither away in the house we share.'

Raymond asked Mrs Fitch if she knew the Griegons, who were, he said, most pleasant people. He added that the Griegons were present tonight and that, in fact, he would like to introduce them to her.

'You are trying to avoid the truth. What have the Griegons to recommend them that we should move in their direction and end this conversation? Don't you see the situation, Mr Bamber? I am a woman who is obsessed because of the state of her marriage, how I have aged while he has not. I am obsessed by the fact that he is now incapable of love or tenderness. I have failed to keep all that alive because I lost my beauty. There are lines on my body too, Mr Bamber: I would show you if we were somewhere else.'

Raymond protested again, and felt tired of protesting. But Mrs Fitch, hearing him speak and thinking that he was not yet clear in his mind about the situation, supplied him with further details about her marriage and the manner in which, at cocktail parties, her husband made arrangements for the seduction of younger women, or women who on the face of it seemed younger. 'Obsessions are a disease,' said Mrs Fitch, drinking deeply from her glass.

Raymond explained then that he knew nothing whatsoever about marriage difficulties, to which Mrs Fitch replied that she was only telling him the truth. 'I do not for a moment imagine,' she said, 'that you are an angel come from God, Mr Bamber, in order to settle the unfortunateness. I didn't mean to imply that when I said I had prayed. Did you think I thought you were a messenger?' Mrs Fitch, still holding Raymond's jacket and glancing still at her husband and the woman in yellow, laughed shrilly. Raymond said :

'People are looking at us, the way you are pulling at my clothes. I'm a shy man—'

'Tell me about yourself. You know about me by now : how everything that once seemed rosy has worked out miserably.'

'Oh, come now,' said Raymond, causing Mrs Fitch to repeat her laughter and to call out for a further drink. The Tamberleys' maid hastened towards her. 'Now then,' said Mrs Fitch. 'Tell me.'

'What can I tell you?' asked Raymond.

'I drink a lot these days,' said Mrs Fitch, 'to help matters along. Cheers, Mr Bamber.'

'Actually I've told you quite a bit, you know. One thing and another—'

'You told me nothing except some nonsense about an

old creature in Streatham. Who wants to hear that, for Christ's sake? Or is it relevant?'

'Well, I mean, it's true, Mrs Fitch. Relevant to what?'

'I remember you, believe it or not, in this very room on this same occasion last year. "Who's that man?" I said to the Tamberley woman and she replied that you were a bore. You were invited, year by year, so the woman said, because of some friendship between the Tamberleys and your father. In the distant past.'

'Look here,' said Raymond, glancing about him and noting to his relief that no one appeared to have heard what Mrs Fitch in her cups had said.

'What's the matter?' demanded Mrs Fitch. Her eyes were again upon her husband and Mrs Anstey. She saw them laugh together and felt her unhappiness being added to as though it were a commodity within her body. 'Oh yes,' she said to Raymond, attempting to pass a bit of the unhappiness on. 'A grinding bore. Those were the words of Mrs Tamberley.'

Raymond shook his head. 'I've known Mrs Tamberley since I was a child,' he said.

'So the woman said. You were invited because of the old friendship: the Tamberleys and your father. I cannot tell a lie, Mr Bamber: she said you were a pathetic case. She said you hadn't learned how to grow up. I dare say you're a pervert.'

'My God!'

'I'm sorry I cannot tell lies,' said Mrs Fitch, and Raymond felt her grip tighten on his jacket. 'It's something that happens to you when you've been through what I've been through. That man up to his tricks with women while the beauty drains from my face. What's it like, d'you think?'

'I don't know,' said Raymond. 'How on earth could I know? Mrs Fitch, let's get one thing clear: I am not a pervert.'

'Not? Are you sure? They may think you are, you know,' said Mrs Fitch, glancing again at her husband. 'Mrs Tamberley has probably suggested that very thing to everyone in this room. Crueller, though, I would have thought, to say you were a grinding bore.'

'I am not a pervert—'

'I can see them sniggering over that all right. Unmentionable happenings between yourself and others. Elderly newspaper-vendors—'

'Stop!' cried Raymond. 'For God's sake, woman—'

'You're not a Jew, are you?'

Raymond did not reply. He stood beside Mrs Fitch, thinking that the woman appeared to be both drunk and not of her right mind. He did not wish to create a scene in the Tamberleys' drawing-room, and yet he recognised that by the look of her she intended to hold on to his jacket for the remainder of the evening. If he attempted to pull it away from her, she would not let go: she did not, somehow, seem to be the kind of woman who would. She wouldn't mind a scene at all.

'Why,' said Mrs Fitch, 'did you all of a sudden begin to tell me about that woman in Streatham, Mr Bamber, and the details about your chair-covers and curtains? Why did you tell me about your uncle dying and trying to leave you a business and your feeling that in your perverted condition you were unfit to run a business?'

Raymond's hands began to shake. He could feel an extra tug on his jacket, as though Mrs Fitch was now insisting that he stand closer to her. He pressed his teeth together, grinding his molars one upon another, and then opened his mouth and felt his teeth and his lips quivering. He knew that his voice would sound strange when he spoke. He said:

'You are being extremely offensive to me, Mrs Fitch. You are a woman who is a total stranger to me, yet you have seen fit to drive me into a corner at a cocktail party and hold me here by force. I must insist that you let go my jacket and allow me to walk away.'

'What about me, Mr Bamber? What about my husband and your Anstey woman? Already they are immoral on a narrow bed somewhere; in a fifth-class hotel near King's Cross station.'

'Your husband is still in this room, Mrs Fitch. As well you know. What your husband does is not my business.'

'Your business is your flat in Bayswater, is it? And curtains and covers from the Sanderson showrooms in Berners Street. Your world is people dying and leaving you stuff in wills—money and prayer-books and valuable jewellery that you wear when you dress yourself up in nurse's uniform.'

'I must ask you to stop, Mrs Fitch.'

'I could let you have a few pairs of old stockings if they interest you. Or garments of my husband's.'

Mrs Fitch saw Raymond close his eyes. She watched the flesh on his face redden further and watched it twitch in answer to a pulse that throbbed in his neck. There was sweat on his forehead. Her husband, a moment before, had reached out a hand and placed it briefly on the female's arm.

'So your nanny was a guide to you,' said Mrs Fitch. 'You hung on all her words, I dare say?'

Raymond did not reply. He turned his head away, trying to control the twitching in his face. The sweat poured freely now. Eventually he said, quietly and with the suspicion of a stammer:

'She was a good woman. She was kind in every way.'

'She taught you neatness.'

Raymond was aware, as Mrs Fitch spoke that sentence, that she had moved appreciably closer to him. He could feel her knee pressing against his. He felt a second knee, and felt next that his leg had been cleverly caught by her, between her own legs.

'Look here,' said Raymond.

'Yes?'

'Mrs Fitch, what are you trying to do?'

Mrs Fitch increased the pressure of her knees. Her right hand moved into Raymond's jacket pocket. 'I am a little the worse for wear,' she said, 'but I can still tell the truth.'

'You are embarrassing me.'

'What are your perversions? Tell me, Mr Bamber.'

'I have no perversions of any kind. I live a normal life.'

'Shall I come to you with a pram? I'm an unhappy woman, Mr Bamber. I'll wear black woollen stockings. I'll show you those lines on my body.'

'Please,' said Raymond, thinking he would cry in a moment.

Already people were glancing at Mrs Fitch's legs gripping his so strongly. Her white face and her scarlet lips were close to his eyes. He could see the lines on her cheeks, but he turned his glance away from them in case she mentioned again the lines on her body. She is a mad, drunken nymphomaniac, said Raymond to himself, and thought that never in all his life had anything so upsetting happened to him.

'Embrace me,' said Mrs Fitch.

'Please, I beg you,' said Raymond.

'You are a homosexual. A queer. I had forgotten that.'

'I'm not a homosexual,' shouted Raymond, aware that his voice was piercingly shrill. Heads turned and he felt the eyes of the Tamberleys' guests. He had been heard to cry that he was not a homosexual, and people had wished to see for themselves.

'Excuse me,' said a voice. 'I'm sorry about this.'

Raymond turned his head and saw Mrs Fitch's husband standing behind him. 'Come along now, Adelaide,' said Mrs Fitch's husband. 'I'm sorry,' he said again to Raymond. 'I didn't realise she'd had a tankful before she got here.'

'I've been telling him the truth,' said Mrs Fitch. 'We've exchanged life-stories.'

Raymond felt her legs slip away, and he felt her hand withdraw itself from the pocket of his jacket. He nodded in a worldly way at her husband and said in a low voice that he understood how it was.

'He's a most understanding chap,' said Mrs Fitch. 'He has a dead woman in Streatham.'

'Come along now,' ordered her husband in a rough voice, and Raymond saw that the man's hand gripped her arm in a stern manner.

'I was telling that man the truth,' said Mrs Fitch again,

seeming to be all of a sudden in an ever greater state of in-
ebriation. Very slowly she said: 'I was telling him what I am
and what you are, and what the Tamberleys think about him.
It has been home-truths corner here, for the woman with
an elderly face and for the chap who likes to dress himself
out as a children's nurse and go with women in chauffeur's
garb. Actually, my dear, he's a homosexual.'

'Come along now,' said Mrs Fitch's husband. 'I'm truly
sorry,' he added to Raymond. 'It's a problem.'

Raymond saw that it was all being conducted in a most
civilised manner. Nobody shouted in the Tamberleys' drawing-room, nobody noticed the three of them talking quite
quietly in a corner. The Maltese maid in fact, not guessing
for a moment that anything was amiss, came up with her
tray of drinks and before anyone could prevent it, Mrs Fitch
had lifted one to her lips. *In vino veritas,* she remarked.

Raymond felt his body cooling down. His shirt was damp
with sweat, and he realised that he was panting slightly and
he wondered how long that had been going on. He watched
Mrs Fitch being aided through the room by her husband.
No wonder, he thought, the man had been a little severe
with her, if she put up a performance like that very often;
no wonder he treated her like an infant. She was little more
than an infant, Raymond considered, saying the first thing
that came into her head, and going on about sex. He saw her
lean form briefly again, through an opening in the crowded
room, and he realised without knowing it that he had craned
his neck for a last glimpse. She saw him too, as she smiled
and bowed at Mrs Tamberley, appearing to be sober and
collected. She shook her head at him, deploring him or suggesting, even, that he had been the one who had misbehaved.
Her husband raised a hand in the air, thanking Raymond
for his understanding.

Raymond edged his way through all the people and went
to find a bathroom. He washed his face, taking his spectacles
off and placing them beside a piece of lime-green soap. He
was thinking that her husband was probably just like any
other man at a cocktail party. How could the husband help

it, Raymond thought, if he had not aged and if other women found him pleasant to talk to? Did she expect him to have all his hair plucked out and have an expert come to line his face?

Leaning against the wall of the bathroom, Raymond thought about Mrs Fitch. He thought at first that she was a fantastic woman given to fantastic statements, and then he embroidered on the thought and saw her as being more subtle than that. 'By heavens!' said Raymond aloud to himself. She was a woman, he saw, who was pathetic in what she did, transferring the truth about herself to other people. She it was, he guessed, who was the grinding bore, so well known for the fact that she had come to hear the opinion herself and in her unbalanced way sought to pretend that others were bores in order to push the thing away from her. She was probably even, he thought, a little perverted the way in which she had behaved with her knees, and sought to imbue others with this characteristic too, so that she, for the moment, might feel rid of it : Mrs Fitch was clearly a case for a psychiatrist. She had said that her husband was a maniac where women were concerned; she had said that he had taken Mrs Anstey to a bed in King's Cross when Mrs Anstey was standing only yards away, in front of her eyes. *In vino veritas,* she had said, for no reason at all.

One morning, Raymond imagined, poor Mr Fitch had woken up to find his wife gabbling in that utterly crazy manner about her age and her hair and the lines on her body. Probably the woman was a nuisance with people who came to the door, the deliverers of coal and groceries, the milkman and the postman. He imagined the Express Dairy on the telephone to Mrs Fitch's husband, complaining that the entire milkround was daily being disorganised because of the antics of Mrs Fitch, who was a bore with everyone.

It accounted for everything, Raymond thought, the simple fact that the woman was a psychological case. He closed his eyes and sighed with relief, and remembered then that he had read in newspapers about women like Mrs Fitch. He opened his eyes again and looked at himself in the mirror of the Tamberleys' smallest bathroom. He touched his neat moustache with his fingers and smiled at himself to ascertain that his teeth were not carrying a piece of cocktail food. 'You have a tea-leaf on your tooth,' said the voice of Nanny Wilkinson, and Raymond smiled, remembering her.

Raymond returned to the party and stood alone watching the people talking and laughing. His eyes passed from face to face, many of which were familiar to him. He looked for the Griegons with whom last year he had spent quite some time, interesting them in a small sideboard that he had just had french polished, having been left the sideboard in the will of a godmother. The man, a Mr French amusingly enough, had come to Raymond's flat to do the job there in the evenings, having explained that he had no real facilities or premises, being a postman during the day. 'Not that he wasn't an expert polisher,' Raymond had said. 'He did a most beautiful job. I heard of him through Mrs Adams who lives in the flat below. I thought it was reasonable, you know: seven guineas plus expenses. The sideboard came up wonderfully.'

'Hullo,' said Raymond to the Griegons.

'How d'you do?' said Mrs Griegon, a pleasant, smiling woman, not at all like Mrs Fitch. Her husband nodded at Raymond, and turned to a man who was talking busily.

'Our name is Griegon,' said Mrs Griegon. 'This is my husband, and this is Dr Oath.'

'I know,' said Raymond, surprised that Mrs Griegon should say who she was since they had all met so pleasantly a year ago. 'How do you do, Dr Oath?' he said, stretching out a hand.

'Yes,' said Dr Oath, shaking the hand rapidly while continuing his conversation.

Mrs Griegon said: 'You haven't told us your name.'

Raymond, puzzled and looking puzzled, said that his name was Raymond Bamber. 'But surely you remember our nice talk last year?' he said. 'I recall it all distinctly: I was telling you about Mr French who came to polish a sideboard, and how he charged only seven guineas.'

'Most reasonable,' said Mrs Griegon. '*Most* reasonable.'

'We stood over there,' explained Raymond, pointing. 'You and I and Mr Griegon. I remember I gave you my address and telephone number in case if you were ever in Bayswater you might like to pop in to see the sideboard. You said to your husband at the time, Mrs Griegon, that you had one or two pieces that could do with stripping down and polishing, and Mr French, who'll travel anywhere in the evenings and being, as you say, so reasonable—'

'Of course,' cried Mrs Griegon. 'Of course I remember you perfectly, and I'm sure Archie does too.' She looked at her husband, but her husband was listening carefully to Dr Oath.

Raymond smiled. 'It looks even better now that the initial shine has gone. I'm terribly pleased with it.' As he spoke, he saw the figure of Mrs Fitch's husband entering the room. He watched him glance about and saw him smile at someone he'd seen. Following the direction of this smile, Raymond saw Mrs Anstey smiling back at Mrs Fitch's husband, who at once made his way to her side.

'French polishing's an art,' said Mrs Griegon.

What on earth, Raymond wondered, was the man doing back at the Tamberleys' party? And where was Mrs Fitch? Nervously, Raymond glanced about the crowded room, looking for the black and white dress and the lean aquiline features of the woman who had tormented him. But although, among all the brightly-coloured garments that the women wore there were a few that were black and white, none of them contained Mrs Fitch. 'We come to these parties and everything's a sham,' her voice seemed to say, close to him. 'Nobody tells the truth.' The voice came to him in just the same way as Nanny Wilkinson's had a quarter of an hour ago, when she'd been telling him that he had a tea-leaf on his tooth.

'Such jolly parties,' said Mrs Griegon. 'The Tamberleys are wonderful.'

'Do you know a woman called Mrs Fitch?' said Raymond. 'She was here tonight.'

'Mrs Fitch!' exclaimed·Mrs Griegon with a laugh.

'D'you know her?'

'She's married to that man there,' said Mrs Griegon. She pointed at Mr Fitch and sniffed.

'Yes,' said Raymond. 'He's talking to Mrs Anstey.'

He was about to add that Mr Fitch was probably of a social inclination. He was thinking already that Mr Fitch probably had a perfectly sound reason for returning to the Tamberleys'. Probably he lived quite near and having seen his wife home had decided to return in order to say goodbye properly to his hosts. Mrs Anstey, Raymond had suddenly thought, was for all he knew Mr Fitch's sister: in her mentally depressed condition it would have been quite like Mrs Fitch to pretend that the woman in yellow was no relation whatsoever, to have invented a fantasy that was greater even than it appeared to be.

'He's always up to that kind of carry-on,' said Mrs Griegon. 'The man's famous for it.'

'Sorry?' said Raymond.

'Fitch. With women.'

'Oh but surely—'

'Really,' said Mrs Griegon.

'I was talking to Mrs Fitch earlier on and she persisted in speaking about her husband. Well, I felt she was going on rather. Exaggerating, you know. A bit of a bore.'

'He has said things to me, Mr Bamber, that would turn your stomach.'

'She has a funny way with her, Mrs Fitch has. She too said the oddest things—'

'She has a reputation,' said Mrs Griegon, 'for getting drunk and coming out with awkward truths. I've heard it said.'

'Not the truth,' Raymond corrected. 'She says things about herself, you see, and pretends she's talking about another person.'

'What?' said Mrs Griegon.

'Like maybe, you see, she was saying that she herself is a bore the way she goes on—well, Mrs Fitch wouldn't say it just like that. What Mrs Fitch would do is pretend some other person is the bore, the person she might be talking to. D'you see? She would transfer all her own qualities to the person she's talking to.'

Mrs Griegon raised her thin eyebrows and inclined her head. She said that what Raymond was saying sounded most interesting.

'An example is,' said Raymond, 'that Mrs Fitch might find herself unsteady on her feet through drink. Instead of saying that she was unsteady she'd say that you, Mrs Griegon, were the unsteady one. There's a name for it, actually. A medical name.'

'Medical?' said Mrs Griegon.

Glancing across the room, Raymond saw that Mr Fitch's right hand gripped Mrs Anstey's elbow. Mr Fitch murmured in her ear and together the two left the room. Raymond saw them wave at Mrs Tamberley, implying thanks with the gesture, implying that they had enjoyed themselves.

'I can't think what it is now,' said Raymond to Mrs Griegon, 'when people transfer the truth about themselves to others. It's some name beginning with an R, I think.'

'How nice of you,' said Mrs Tamberley, gushing up, 'to put that notice in *The Times*.' She turned to Mrs Griegon and said that, as Raymond had probably told her, a lifelong friend of his, old Nanny Wilkinson, had died a few months ago. 'Every year,' said Mrs Tamberley, 'Raymond told us all how she was bearing up. But now, alas, she's died.'

'Indeed,' said Mrs Griegon, and smiled and moved away.

Without any bidding, there arrived in Raymond's mind a picture of Mrs Fitch sitting alone in her house, refilling a glass from a bottle of Gordon's gin. '*In vino veritas*,' said Mrs Fitch, and began to weep.

'I was telling Mrs Griegon that I'd been chatting with Mrs Fitch,' said Raymond, and then he remembered that

Mrs Tamberley had very briefly joined in that chat. 'I found her strange,' he added.

'Married to that man,' cried Mrs Tamberley. 'He drove her to it.'

'Her condition?' said Raymond, nodding.

'She ladles it into herself,' said Mrs Tamberley, 'and then tells you what she thinks of you. It can be disconcerting.'

'She really says anything that comes into her head,' said Raymond, and gave a light laugh.

'Not actually,' said Mrs Tamberley. 'She tells the truth.'

'Well, no, you see—'

'You haven't a drink,' cried Mrs Tamberley in alarm, and moved at speed towards her Maltese maid to direct the girl's attention to Raymond's empty glass.

Again the image of Mrs Fitch arrived in Raymond's mind. She sat as before, alone in a room, while her husband made off with a woman in yellow. She drank some gin.

'Sherry, sir?' said the Maltese maid, and Raymond smiled and thanked her, and then, in an eccentric way and entirely on an impulse, he said in a low voice:

'Do you know a woman called Mrs Fitch?'

The girl said that Mrs Fitch had been at the party earlier in the evening, and reminded Raymond that he had in fact been talking to her.

'She has a peculiar way with her,' explained Raymond. 'I just wondered if ever you had talked to her, or had listened to what she herself had to say.' But the Maltese maid shook her head, appearing not to understand.

'Mrs Fitch's a shocker,' said a voice behind Raymond's back, and added: 'That poor man.'

There was a crackle of laughter as a response, and Raymond, sipping his sherry, turned about and moved towards the group that had caused it. The person who had spoken was a small man with shiny grey hair. 'I'm Raymond Bamber,' said Raymond, smiling at him. 'By the sound of things, you saw my predicament earlier on.' He laughed, imitating the laughter that had come from the group. Extremely awkward.'

'She gets tight,' said the small man. 'She's liable to tell a home truth or two.' He began to laugh again. *'In vino veritas,'* he said.

Raymond looked at the people and opened his mouth to say that it wasn't quite so simple, the malaise of Mrs Fitch. 'It's all within her,' he wished to say. 'Everything she says is part of Mrs Fitch, since she's unhappy in a marriage and has lost her beauty.' But Raymond checked that speech, uttering in fact not a word of it. The people looked expectantly at him, and after a long pause the small man said:

'Mrs Fitch can be most embarrassing.'

Raymond heard the people laugh again with the same sharpness and saw their teeth for a moment harshly bared and noted that their eyes were like polished ice. They would not understand, he thought, the facts about Mrs Fitch, any more than Mrs Griegon had seemed to understand, or Mrs Tamberley. It surprised Raymond, and saddened him, that neither Mrs Griegon nor Mrs Tamberley had cared to accept the truth about the woman. It was, he told himself, something of a revelation that Mrs Griegon, who had seemed so pleasant the year before, and Mrs Tamberley whom he had known almost all his life, should turn out to be no better than this group of hard-eyed people. Raymond murmured and walked away, still thinking of Mrs Griegon and Mrs Tamberley. He imagined them laughing with their husbands over Mrs Fitch, repeating that she was a bore and a drunk. Laughter was apparently the thing, a commodity that reflected the shallowness of minds too lazy to establish correctly the facts about people. And they were minds, as had been proved to Raymond, that didn't even bother to survey properly the simple explanations of eccentric conduct —as though even that constituted too much trouble.

Soon afterwards, Raymond left the party and walked through the autumn evening, considering everything. The air was cool on his face as he strode towards Bayswater, thinking that as he continued to live his quiet life Mrs Fitch would be attending parties that were similar to the Tamberleys', and she'd be telling the people she met there that they were grinding bores. The people might be offended, Raymond thought, if they didn't pause to think about it, if they didn't understand that everything was confused in poor Mrs Fitch's mind. And it would serve them right, he reflected, to be offended—a just reward for allowing their minds to become lazy and untidy in this modern manner. 'Orderliness,' said the voice of Nanny Wilkinson, and Raymond paused and smiled, and then walked on.

XI

The Hotel of the Idle Moon

THE WOMAN CALLED Mrs Dankers placed a rose-tipped
cigarette between her lips and lit it from the lighter on the
dashboard. The brief spurt of light revealed a long, handsome face with a sharpness about it that might often have
been reminiscent of the edge of a chisel. In the darkness a
double funnel of smoke streamed from her nostrils, and she
gave a tiny gasp of satisfaction. On a grass verge two hundred miles north of London the car was stationary except
for the gentle rocking imposed by the wind. Above the per-
sistent lashing of the rain the radio played a popular tune
of the Thirties, quietly and without emotion. It was two
minutes to midnight.

'Well?'

The car door banged and Dankers was again beside her.
He smelt of rain; it dripped from him on to her warm knees.

'Well?' Mrs Dankers repeated.

He started the engine. The car crept on to the narrow
highway, its wipers slashing at the rain, its powerful headlights drawing the streaming foliage startlingly near. He
cleared the windscreen with his arm. 'It'll do,' he murmured. He drove on slowly, and the sound of the engine
was lost in a medley of wind and rain and the murmur of
music and the swish of the wipers.

'It'll do?' said Mrs Dankers. 'Is it the right house?'

He twisted the car this way and that along the lane. The
lights caught an image of pillars and gates, closed in upon
them and lost them as the car swung up the avenue.

'Yes,' he murmured. 'It's the right house.'

Within that house, an old man lying stiffly in bed heard
the jangle of the bell at the hall-door and frowned over

this unaccustomed sound. At first he imagined that the noise had been caused by the wind, but then the bell rang again, sharply and in a peremptory manner. The old man, called Cronin, the only servant in the house, rose from his bed and dragged an overcoat on to his body, over his pyjamas. He descended the stairs, sighing to himself.

The pair outside saw a light go on in the hall, and then they heard the tread of Cronin's feet and the sound of a bar being pulled back on the door. Dankers threw a cigarette away and prepared an expression for his face. His wife shivered in the rain.

'It's so late,' the old man in pyjamas said when the travellers had told him their tale. 'I must wake the Marstons for guidance, sir. I can't do this on my own responsibility.'

'It's wet and cold as well,' Dankers murmured, smiling at the man through his widely-spread moustache. 'No night to be abroad, really. You must understand our predicament.'

'No night to be standing on a step,' added Mrs Dankers. 'At least may we come in?'

They entered the house and were led to a large drawing-room. 'Please wait,' the man invited. 'The fire is not entirely out. I'll question the Marstons as you warm yourselves.'

The Dankerses did not speak. They stood where the man had left them, staring about the room. Their manner one to the other had an edge of hostility to it, as though they were as suspicious in this relationship as they were of the world beyond it.

'I am Sir Giles Marston,' said another old man. 'You've sustained some travelling difficulty?'

'Our car has let us down—due, I suppose, to some penetration of the weather. We left it by your gates. Sir Giles, we're at your mercy. Dankers the name is. The lady is my good wife.' Dankers stretched his arm towards his host in a manner that might have suggested to an onlooker that he, and not Sir Giles, was the welcomer.

'Our need is simple,' said Mrs Dankers. 'A roof over our heads.'

'Some outhouse maybe,' Dankers hazarded, overplaying his part. He laughed. 'Anywhere we can curl up for an hour or two. We cannot be choosers.'

'I'd prefer a chair,' his wife interceded sharply. 'A chair and a rug would suit me nicely.'

'I'm sure we can do better than that. Prepare two beds, Cronin; and light our guests a fire in their room.'

Sir Giles Marston moved into the centre of the room and in the greater light the Dankerses saw a small, hunched man, with a face like leather that has been stretched for a lifetime and is suddenly slackened; as lined as a map.

'Oh, really,' Dankers protested in his soft voice, 'you mustn't go to such trouble. It's imposition enough to rouse you like this.'

'Are there sheets?' Cronin asked. 'Sheets and bedding: God knows where I shall find them, sir.'

'Brandy,' Sir Giles suggested. 'Am I right, Mrs Dankers, in thinking that strong refreshment would partly answer the situation?'

Cronin left the room, speaking to himself. Sir Giles poured the brandy. 'I'm ninety years of age,' he told his guests, 'But yet aware that inhospitality is a sin to be ashamed of. I bid you good-night.'

'Who are they?' Lady Marston asked in the morning, having heard the tale from her husband.

'My dear, they are simply people. They bear some unpleasant name. More than that I do not really wish to know.'

'It's a sunny day by the look of it. Your guests will have breakfasted and gone by now. I'm sorry in a way, for I would welcome fresh faces and a different point of view. We live too quiet a life, Giles. We are too much thrown in upon each other. It's hardly a healthy manner in which to prepare for our dying.'

Sir Giles, who was engaged in the drawing up of his trousers, smiled. 'Had you seen these two, my dear, you would not have said they are the kind to make our going any easier. The man has a moustache of great proportions, the woman you would describe as smart.'

'You're intolerant, love. And so high-handed that you didn't even discover the reason for this visit.'

'They came because they could move in neither direction. Trouble with their motor-car.'

'They've probably left with all our little bits and pieces. You're a sitting bird for a confidence trick. Oh, Giles, Giles!'

Sir Giles departed, and in the breakfast-room below discovered the pair called Dankers still at table.

'Your man has been most generous,' Dankers said. 'He's fed us like trenchermen: porridge, coffee, bacon and eggs. Two for me, one for my good wife. And toast and marmalade. And this delicious butter.'

'Are you trying to say that an essential commodity was lacking? If so, I fear you must be more precise. In this house we are now past subtlety.'

'You've made a fool of yourself,' Mrs Dankers said to her husband. 'Who wishes to know what two strangers have recently digested?'

'Pardon, pardon,' murmured Dankers. 'Sir Giles, forgive a rough diamond!'

'Certainly. If you have finished, please don't delay on my account. Doubtless you are anxious to be on your way.'

'My husband will attend to the car. Probably it's necessary to send for help to a garage. In the meantime I'll keep you company if I may.'

Dankers left the room, passing on the threshold an elderly lady whom he did not address, wishing to appear uncertain in his mind as to her identity.

'This is the woman who came in the night,' Sir Giles said to his wife. 'Her husband is seeing to their motor-car so that they may shortly be on their way. Mrs Dankers, my wife, Lady Marston.'

'We're more than grateful, Lady Marston. It looked as though we were in for a nasty night.'

'I hope Cronin made you comfortable. I fear I slept

through everything. "My dear, we have two guests," my husband said to me this morning. You may imagine my surprise.'

Cronin entered and placed plates of food before Sir Giles and Lady Marston.

Conversationally, Mrs Dankers said: 'You have a fine place here.'

'It's cold and big,' Sir Giles replied.

The Marstons set about their breakfast, and Mrs Dankers, unable to think of something to say, sat in silence. The smoke from her cigarette was an irritation to her hosts, but they did not remark on it, since they accepted its presence as part of the woman herself. When he returned Dankers sat beside his wife again. He poured some coffee and said: 'I am no mechanic, Sir Giles. I would like to use your 'phone to summon help.'

'We are not on the telephone.'

'Not?' murmured Dankers in simulated surprise, for he knew the fact already. 'How far in that case is the nearest village? And does it boast a garage?'

'Three miles. As to the presence of a garage, I have had no cause to establish that point. But I imagine there is a telephone.'

'Giles, introduce me please. Is this man Mrs Dankers' husband?'

'He claims it. Mr Dankers, my wife, Lady Marston.'

'How d'you do?' Dankers said, rising to shake the offered hand. 'I'm afraid we're in a pickle.'

'You should walk it in an hour,' Sir Giles reminded him.

'There's no way of forwarding a message?'

'No.'

'The postman?'

'He hardly ever comes. And then brings only a circular or two.'

'Perhaps your man?'

'Cronin's days as Hermes are over. You must see that surely for yourself?'

'In that case there's nothing for it but a tramp.'

185

This conclusion of Dankers' was received in silence.

'Walk, Mr Dankers,' Lady Marston said eventually, and added to her husband's dismay, 'and return for lunch. Afterwards you can leave us at your leisure.'

'How kind of you,' the Dankerses said together. They smiled in unison too. They rose and left the room.

Cronin watched and listened to everything. 'Prepare two beds,' his master had said, and from that same moment Cronin had been on his guard. He had given them breakfast the following morning, and had hoped that once they had consumed it they would be on their way. He took them to be commercial travellers, since they had the air of people who were used to moving about and spending nights in places. 'You have a fine place here,' Mrs Dankers had said to the Marstons, and Cronin had narrowed his eyes, wondering why she had said it, wondering why she was sitting there, smoking a cigarette while the Marstons breakfasted. He had examined their motor-car and had thought it somehow typical of the people. They were people, thought Cronin, who would know what to do with all the knobs and gadgets on the motor-car's dashboard; they would take to that dashboard like ducks to water.

For forty-eight years Cronin had lived in the house, serving the Marstons. Once, there had been other servants, and in his time he had watched over them and over the house itself. Now he contented himself with watching over the Marstons. 'Some outhouse maybe,' Dankers had said, and Cronin had thought that Dankers was not a man who knew much about outhouses. He saw Dankers and Mrs Dankers sitting together in a café connected with a cinema, a place such as he had himself visited twenty-odd years ago and had not cared for. He heard Dankers asking the woman what she would take to eat, adding that he himself would have a mixed grill with chips, and a pot of strong tea, and sliced bread and butter. Cronin observed these people closely and memorised much of what they said.

'Clearly,' Dankers remarked at lunch, 'we're not in training. Or perhaps it was the fascination of your magnificent orchard.'

'Are you saying you didn't walk to the village?' Sir Giles enquired, a trifle impatiently.

'Forgive these city folk,' cried Dankers loudly. 'Quite frankly, we got no distance at all.'

'What are you to do then? Shall you try again this afternoon? There are, of course, various houses on the route. One of them may have a telephone.'

'Your orchard has greatly excited us. I've never seen such trees.'

'They're the finest in England.'

'A pity,' said Mrs Dankers, nibbling at fish on a fork, 'to see it in such rack and ruin.'

Dankers blew upwards into his moustache and ended the activity with a smile. 'It is worth some money, that orchard,' he said.

Sir Giles eyed him coolly. 'Yes, sir; it is worth some money. But time is passing and we are wasting it in conversation. You must see to the affair of your motor-car.'

The storm had brought the apples down. They lay in their thousands in the long grass, damp and glistening, like immense unusual jewels in the afternoon sun. The Dankerses examined them closely, strolling through the orchard, noting the various trees and assessing their yield. For the purpose they had fetched Wellington boots from their car and had covered themselves in water-proof coats of an opaque plastic material. They did not speak, but occasionally, coming across a tree that pleased them, they nodded.

'A lot could be done, you know,' Dankers explained at dinner. 'It is a great orchard and in a mere matter of weeks it could be set on the road to profit and glory.'

'It has had its glory,' replied Sir Giles, 'and probably its profit too. Now it must accept its fate. I cannot keep it up.'

'Oh, it's a shame! A terrible shame to see it as it is. Why, you could make a fortune, Sir Giles.'

'You didn't get to the village?' Lady Marston asked.

'We could not pass the orchard!'

'Which means,' Sir Giles said, 'that you'll be with us for another night.'

'Could you bear it?' Mrs Dankers smiled a thin smile. 'Could you bear to have us all over again?'

'Of course, of course,' said Lady Marston. 'Perhaps tomorrow you'll feel a little stronger. I understand your lethargy. It's natural after an unpleasant experience.'

'They have been through neither flood nor fire,' her husband reminded her. 'And the village will be no nearer tomorrow.'

'Perhaps,' Dankers began gently, 'the postman will call in the morning—'

'We have no living relatives,' Sir Giles cut in, 'and most of our friends are gone. The circulars come once a month or so.'

'The groceries then?'

'I have enquired of Cronin about the groceries. They came yesterday. They will come again next week.'

'The daily milk is left at the foot of the avenue,' Lady Marston suggested. 'Cronin walks to fetch it. You could leave a message there. It is the arrangement we have for emergencies, such as summoning the doctor.'

'The doctor? But surely by the time he got here—?'

'In greater emergency one of the three of us would walk to the nearest house. We do not,' Sir Giles added, 'find it so difficult to pass one leg before the other. Senior though we may be.'

'Perhaps the milk is an idea,' Lady Marston said.

'Oh no, we could never put anyone to so much trouble. It would be too absurd. No, tomorrow we shall have found our feet.'

But tomorrow when it came was a different kind of day, because with something that disagreed with him in his stomach Sir Giles died in the night. His heart was taxed by sharp little spasms of pain and in the end they were too much for it.

'We're going to see to you for a bit,' Mrs Dankers said after the funeral. 'We'll pop you in your room, dear, and Cronin shall attend to all your needs. You can't be left to suffer your loss alone; you've been so kind to us.'

Lady Marston moved her head up and down. The funeral had been rather much for her. Mrs Dankers led her by the arm to her room.

'Well,' said Dankers, speaking to Cronin with whom he was left, 'so that's that.'

'I was his servant for forty-eight years, sir.'

'Indeed, indeed. And you have Lady Marston, to whom you may devote your whole attention. Meals in her room, Cronin, and pause now and then for the occasional chat. The old lady'll be lonely.'

'I'll be lonely myself, sir.'

'Indeed. Then all the more reason to be good company. And you, more than I, understand the business of being elderly. You know by instinct what to say, how best to seem soothing.'

'Your car is repaired, sir? At least it moved today. You'll be on your way? Shall I pack some sandwiches?'

'Come, come, Cronin, how could we leave two lonely people so easily in the lurch? Chance has sent us to your side in this hour of need : we'll stay to do what we can. Besides, there are Sir Giles's wishes.'

What's this? thought Cronin, examining the eyes of the man who had come in the night and had stayed to see his master buried. They were eyes he would not care to possess himself, for fear of what went with them. He said :

'His wishes, sir?'

'That his orchard should again be put in use. The trees repaired and pruned. The fruit sold for its true value. An old man's dying wish won't go unheeded.'

'But, sir, there's so much work in it. The trees run into many hundreds—'

'Quite right, Cronin. That's observant of you. Many men are needed to straighten the confusion and waste. There's much to do.'

'Sir Giles wished this, sir?' said Cronin, playing a part, knowing that Sir Giles could never have passed on to Dankers his dying wish. 'It's unlike him, sir, to think about his orchard. He watched it dying.'

'He wished it, Cronin. He wished it, and a great deal else. You who have seen some changes in your time are in for a couple more. And now, my lad, a glass of that good brandy would not go down amiss. At a time like this one must try to keep one's spirits up.'

Dankers sat by the fire in the drawing-room, sipping his brandy and writing industriously in a notebook. He was shortly joined by his wife, to whom he handed from time to time a leaf from this book so that she might share his plans. When midnight had passed they rose and walked through the house, measuring the rooms with a practised eye and noting their details on paper. They examined the kitchens and outhouses, and in the moonlight they walked the length of the gardens. Cronin watched them, peeping at them in all their activity.

'There's a pretty little room next to Cronin's that is so much sunnier,' Mrs Dankers said. 'Cosier and warmer, dear. We'll have your things moved there, I think. This one is dreary with memories. And you and Cronin will be company for one another.'

Lady Marston nodded, then changing her mind said: 'I like this room. It's big and beautiful and with a view. I've become used to it.'

'Now, now, my dear, we mustn't be morbid, must we? And we don't always quite know what's best. It's good to be happy, dear, and you'll be happier there.'

'I'll be happier, Mrs Dankers? Happier away from all my odds and ends, and Giles's too?'

'My dear, we'll move them with you. Come, now, look on the bright side. There's the future too, as well as the past.'

Cronin came, and the things were moved. Not quite everything though, because the bed and the wardrobe and the heavy dressing-table would not fit into the new setting.

In the orchard half a dozen men set about creating order out of chaos. The trees were trimmed and then treated, paths restored, broken walls rebuilt. The sheds were cleared and filled with fruit-boxes in readiness for next year's harvest.

'There's a wickedness here,' Cronin reported to Lady Marston. 'There's a cook in the kitchen, and a man who waits on them. My only task, they tell me, is to carry your food and keep your room in order.'

'And to see to yourself, Cronin, to take it easy and to watch your rheumatics. Fetch a pack of cards.'

Cronin recalled the house as it once had been, a place that was lively with week-end guests and was regularly wall-papered. Then there had been the years of decline and the drifting towards decay, and now there was a liveliness of a different order; while the days passed by, the liveliness established itself like a season. Mrs Dankers bustled from room to room, in tune with the altered world. Dankers said: 'It's good to see you seeming so sprightly, Cronin. The weather suits you, eh? And now that we've made these few little changes life is easier, I think.' Cronin replied that it was certainly true that he had less to do. 'So you should have less to do,' said Dankers. 'Face the facts: you cannot hope to undertake a young chap's work.' He smiled, to release the remark of its barb.

Cronin was worried about the passive attitude of Lady Marston. She had gone like a lamb to the small room, which now served as her sitting-room and bedroom combined. She had not stirred from the top of the house since the day of the move; she knew nothing save what he told her of all that was happening.

'The builders are here,' he had said; but quite often, mid-way through a game of cards, she would pause with her head a little to one side, listening to the distant sound of hammering. 'It is the noise of the builders,' he would remind her; and she would place a card on the table and say: 'I did not know that Sir Giles had ordered the builders.' In the mornings she was well aware of things, but as the day passed on she spoke more often of Sir Giles; of Sir Giles's plans for the orchard and the house. Cronin feared that, day by day, Lady Marston was sinking into her dotage; the morning hours of her clarity were shrinking even as he thought about it.

One afternoon, walking to the foot of the avenue to stretch his legs, Cronin found a small, elegantly painted board secured to one of the pillars. It faced the road, inviting those who passed to read the words it bore. He read them himself and expostulated angrily, muttering the words, repeating them as he made his way back to the house.

'M'lady, this cannot happen. They've turned your house into an hotel.'

Lady Marston looked at Cronin, whom she had known for so many years, who had seen with her and her husband a thousand details of change and reconstruction. He was upset now, she could see it. His white, sparse hair seemed uncombed, which was unusual for Cronin. There was a blush of temper on his cheeks; and in his eyes a wildness one did not associate with so well-trained a servant.

'What is it, Cronin?'

'There's a notice at the gate announcing "The Hotel of the Idle Moon".'

'Well?'

'The Dankerses—'

'Ah, the Dankerses. You talk so much about the Dankerses, Cronin. Yet as I remember them they are surely not worth it. Sir Giles said the man had repeated to him every mouthful of his breakfast. In the end he had to make short shrift of the pair.'

'No, no—'

'Yes, Cronin: they tried his patience. He gave them their marching orders, reminding them that the night was fine and the moon was full. There was a coolness between us, for I believed he had gone too far.'

'No, no. You must remember: the Dankerses are still

here. They've tidied up the orchard and now have turned your house into an hotel.'

Lady Marston made her impatient little shaking of the head. 'Of course, of course. Cronin, I apologise. You must find me very trying.'

'It has no meaning: The Hotel of the Idle Moon. Yet I fear, m'lady, it may in time mean much to us.'

Lady Marston laughed quite gaily. 'Few things have meaning, Cronin. It is rather much to expect a meaning for everything.'

They played three games of cards, and the matter was not again referred to. But in the night Lady Marston came to Cronin's bedside and shook him by the shoulder. 'I'm upset,' she said, 'by what you tell me. This isn't right at all. Cronin, listen carefully: tomorrow you must inform Sir Giles. Tell him of our fears. Beg him to reconsider. I'm far too old to act. I must leave it all to you.'

The house was busy then with visitors, and cars up and down the avenue. It thrived as the orchard thrived; it had a comfortable and sumptuous feel, and Cronin thought again of the past.

'Ah, Cronin,' Mrs Dankers said, pausing on the back stairs one day. 'Tell me, how is poor Lady Marston? She does not come down at all, and we're so on the go here that it's hard to find time to make the journey to the top of the house.'

'Lady Marston is well, madam.'

'She's welcome in the lounges. Always welcome. Would you be good enough to tell her, Cronin?'

'Yes, madam.'

'But keep an eye on her, like a good man. I would not like her upsetting the guests. You understand?'

'Yes, madam. I understand. I don't think Lady Marston is likely to make use of the lounges.'

'She would find the climb up and down too much, I dare say.'

'Yes, madam. She would find it too much.'

Cronin made many plans. He thought that one day when Dankers was away he would approach the orchard with Sir Giles's rifle and order the men to cut down the trees. That at least would bring one part of the sadness to an end. He saw the scene quite clearly: the trees toppling one against the other, their branches webbed as they hung in the air above the fresh stumps. But when he searched for the rifle he could not find it. He thought that he might wreak great damage in the house, burning carpets and opening up the upholstery. But for this he found neither opportunity nor the strength it demanded. Stropping his razor one morning, he hit upon the best plan of all: to creep into the Dankerses' bedroom and cut their throats. It had once been his master's bedroom and now it was theirs; which made revenge the sweeter. Every day for forty-eight years he had carried to the room a tray of tea-cups and a pot of Earl Grey tea. Now he would carry his sharpened razor; and for the rest of his life he would continue his shaving with it, relishing every scrape. The idea delighted him. Sir Giles would have wished to see the last of them, to see the last of all these people who strayed about the house and grounds, and to see the orchard settle down again to being the orchard he had left behind. And was not he, Cronin, the living agent of the dead Sir Giles? Was he not now companion to his wife? And did she not, in an occasional moment of failure, address him as she had her husband? Yet when he shared his plans with Lady Marston she did not at all endorse them.

'Take the will for the deed, Cronin. Leave these people be.'

'But they are guilty. They may have killed Sir Giles.'

'They may have. And does it matter this way or that—to chop off a few dwindling years?'

Cronin saw no reason in her words. He pitied her, and hardened himself in his resolve.

'I am sorry to speak to you like this, Cronin,' Dankers said, 'but I cannot, you know, have you wandering about the house in this manner. There have been complaints from the guests. You have your room, with Lady Marston to talk with; why not keep more to the region we have set aside for you?'

'Yes, sir.'

'Of late, Cronin, you've become untidy in your appearance. You have a dishevelled look and often seem—well, frankly, Cronin, dirty. It's not good for business. Not good at all.'

The moon shall not be idle, Cronin thought. The moon shall be agog to see. The moon shall clear the sky of clouds that the stars may ponder on the pillows full of blood.

'Mr Dankers, sir, why is this place called the Idle Moon?'

Dankers laughed. 'A foible of my good wife's. She liked the sound of it. Quite telling, don't you think?'

'Yes, sir.' The moon shall like the sound of her. A shriek in a severed throat, a howl of pain.

'See to it, Cronin, eh?'

'Yes, sir.'

So Cronin kept to his room, descending the back stairs only for his food and Lady Marston's. The weeks passed, and more and more he sat entranced with the duty he had set himself. Sometimes, as though drunk with it, he found himself a little uncertain as to its exactitudes. That was when he felt tired; when he dropped off into a doze as he sat by his small window, staring at the sky and listening to the far-away hum from the house below.

Then one morning Cronin discovered that Lady Marston had died in her sleep. They carried her off, and he put away the pack of cards.

'It's a sad day for us all,' Dankers said, and in the distance Cronin could hear Mrs Dankers giving some brisk order to a servant. He returned to his room and for a moment there was an oddness in his mind and he imagined that it was Sir Giles who had said that the day was sad. Then he remembered that Sir Giles was dead too and that he was the only one left.

In the months that followed he spoke to no one but himself, for he was concentrating on the details of his plan. They kept slipping away, and increasingly he had a struggle to keep them straight.

When the razor was there the faces on the pillows were vague and empty, and he could not remember whose he had planned they should be. There was the pattern of moonlight, and the red stain on the bed-clothes, but Cronin could not often now see what any of it meant. It made him tired, thinking the trouble out. And when, in the end, the shreds of his plan came floating back to him he smiled in some astonishment, seeing only how absurd it had been that later in his life he should have imagined himself a match for the world and its conquerors.

XII

Miss Smith

ONE DAY MISS SMITH asked James what a baby horse was called and James couldn't remember. He blinked and shook his head. He knew, he explained, but he just couldn't remember. Miss Smith said:

'Well, well, James Machen doesn't know what a baby horse is called.'

She said it loudly so that everyone in the class-room heard. James became very confused. He blinked and said:

'Pony, Miss Smith?'

'Pony! James Machen says a baby horse is a pony! Hands up everyone who knows what a baby horse is.'

All the right arms in the room, except James's and Miss Smith's, shot upwards. Miss Smith smiled at James.

'Everyone knows,' she said. 'Everyone knows what a baby horse is called except James.'

James thought: I'll run away. I'll join the tinkers and live in a tent.

'What's a baby horse called?' Miss Smith asked the class and the class shouted:

'Foal, Miss Smith.'

'A foal, James,' Miss Smith repeated. 'A baby horse is a foal, James dear.'

'I knew, Miss Smith. I knew but—'

Miss Smith laughed and the class laughed, and afterwards nobody would play with James because he was so silly to think that a baby horse was a pony.

James was an optimist about Miss Smith. He thought it might be different when the class went on the summer picnic or sat tightly together at the Christmas party, eating cake and biscuits and having their mugs filled from big enamel jugs. But it never was different. James got left behind when everyone was racing across the fields at the picnic and Miss Smith had to wait impatiently, telling the class that James would have to have his legs stretched. And at the party she heaped his plate with seed-cake because she imagined, so she said, that he was the kind of child who enjoyed such fare.

Once James found himself alone with Miss Smith in the class-room. She was sitting at her desk correcting some home-work. James was staring in front of him, admiring a fountain pen that the day before his mother had bought for him. It was a small fountain pen, coloured purple and black and white. James believed it to be elegant.

It was very quiet in the class-room. Soundlessly Miss Smith's red pencil ticked and crossed and underlined. Without looking up, she said: 'Why don't you go out and play?'

'Yes, Miss Smith,' said James. He walked to the door, clipping his pen into his pocket. As he turned the handle he heard Miss Smith utter a sound of irritation. He turned and saw that the point of her pencil had broken. 'Miss Smith, you may borrow my pen. You can fill it with red ink. It's quite a good pen.'

James crossed the room and held out his pen. Miss Smith unscrewed the cap and prodded at the paper with the nib. 'What a funny pen, James!' she said. 'Look, it can't write.'

'There's no ink in it,' James explained. 'You've got to fill it with red ink, Miss Smith.'

But Miss Smith smiled and handed the pen back. 'What a silly boy you are to waste your money on such a poor pen!'

'But I didn't—'

'Come along now, James, aren't you going to lend me your pencil-sharpener?'

'I haven't got a pencil-sharpener, Miss Smith.'

'No pencil-sharpener? Oh James, James, you haven't got anything, have you?'

When Miss Smith married she stopped teaching, and James imagined he had escaped her for ever. But the town they lived in was a small one and they often met in the street or in a shop. And Miss Smith, who at first found marriage rather boring, visited the school quite regularly. 'How's James?' she would say, smiling alarmingly at him. 'How's my droopy old James?'

When Miss Smith had been married for about a year she gave birth to a son, which occupied her a bit. He was a fine child, eight pounds six ounces, with a good long head and blue eyes. Miss Smith was delighted with him, and her husband, a solicitor, complimented her sweetly and bought cigars and drinks for all his friends. In time, mother and son were seen daily taking the air: Miss Smith on her trim little legs and the baby in his frilly pram. James, meeting the two, said: 'Miss Smith, may I see the baby?' But Miss Smith laughed and said that she was not Miss Smith any more. She wheeled the pram rapidly away, as though the child within it might be affected by the proximity of the other.

'What a dreadful little boy that James Machen is,' Miss Smith reported to her husband. 'I feel so sorry for the parents.'

'Do I know him? What does the child look like?'

'Small, dear, like a weasel wearing glasses. He quite gives me the creeps.'

Almost without knowing it, James developed a compulsion about Miss Smith. At first it was quite a simple conpulsion: just that James had to talk to God about Miss Smith every night before he went to sleep, and try to find out from God what it was about him that Miss Smith so despised. Every night he lay in bed and had his conversation, and if once he forgot it James knew that the next time he met Miss Smith she would probably say something that might make him drop down dead.

After about a month of conversation with God James discovered he had found the solution. It was so simple that he marvelled he had never thought of it before. He began to get up very early in the morning and pick bunches of flowers. He would carry them down the street to Miss Smith's house and place them on a window-sill. He was careful not to be seen, by Miss Smith or by anyone else. He knew that if anyone saw him the plan couldn't work. When he had picked all the flowers in his own garden he started to pick them from other people's gardens. He became rather clever at moving silently through the gardens, picking flowers for Miss Smith.

Unfortunately, though, on the day that James carried his thirty-first bunch of blooms to the house of Miss Smith he was observed. He saw the curtains move as he reached up to lay the flowers on the window-sill. A moment later Miss Smith, in her dressing-gown, had caught him by the shoulder and pulled him into the house.

'James Machen! It would be James Machen, wouldn't it? Flowers from the creature, if you please! What are you up to, you dozy James?'

James said nothing. He looked at Miss Smith's dressing-gown and thought it was particularly pretty: blue and woolly, with an edging of silk.

'You've been trying to get us into trouble,' cried Miss Smith. 'You've been stealing flowers all over the town and putting them at our house. You're an underhand child, James.'

James stared at her and then ran away.

After that, James thought of Miss Smith almost all the time. He thought of her face when she had caught him with the flowers, and how she had afterwards told his father and nearly everyone else in the town. He thought of how his father had had to say he was sorry to Miss Smith, and how his mother and father had quarrelled about the affair. He counted up all the things Miss Smith had ever said to him, and all the things she had ever done to him, like giving him seed-cake at the Christmas party. He hadn't meant to harm Miss Smith as she said he had. Giving people flowers wasn't unkind; it was to show them you liked them and wanted them to like you.

'When somebody hurts you,' James said to the man who came to cut the grass, 'what do you do about it?'

'Well,' said the man, 'I suppose you hurt them back.'

'Supposing you can't,' James argued.

'Oh, but you always can. It's easy to hurt people.'

'It's not, really,' James said.

'Look,' said the man, 'all I've got to do is to reach out and give you a clip on the ear. That'd hurt you.'

'But I couldn't do that to you because you're too big. How d'you hurt someone who's bigger than you?'

'It's easier to hurt people who are weaker. People who are weaker are always the ones who get hurt.'

'Can't you hurt someone who is stronger?'

The grass-cutter thought for a time. 'You have to be cunning to do that. You've got to find the weak spot. Everyone has a weak spot.'

'Have you got a weak spot?'

'I suppose so.'

'Could I hurt you on your weak spot?'

'You don't want to hurt me, James.'

'No, but just could I?'

'Yes, I suppose you could.'

'Well then?'

'My little daughter's smaller than you. If you hurt her, you see, you'd be hurting me. It'd be the same, you see.'

'I see,' said James.

All was not well with Miss Smith. Life, which had been so happy when her baby was born, seemed now to be directed against her. Perhaps it was that the child was becoming difficult, going through a teething phase that was pleasant for no one; or perhaps it was that Miss Smith recognised in him some trait she disliked and knew that she would be obliged to watch it develop, powerless to intervene. Whatever the reason, she felt depressed. She often thought of her teaching days, of the big square school-room with the children's models on the shelves and the pictures of kings on the walls. Nostalgically, she recalled the feel of frosty air on her face as she rode her bicycle through the town, her mind already practising the first lesson of the day. She had loved those winter days: the children stamping their feet in the playground, the stove groaning and crackling, so red and so fierce that it had to be penned off for safety's sake. It had been good to feel tired, good to bicycle home, shopping a bit on the way, home to tea and the wireless and an evening of reading by the fire. It wasn't that she regretted anything; it was just that now and again, for a day or two, she felt she would like to return to the past.

'My dear,' Miss Smith's husband said, 'you really will have to be more careful.'

'But I am. Truly I am. I'm just as careful as anyone can be.'

'Of course you are. But it's a difficult age. Perhaps, you know, you need a holiday.'

'But I've had difficult ages to deal with for years—'

'Now now, my dear, it's not quite the same, teaching a class of kids.'

'But it shouldn't be as difficult. I don't know—'

'You're tired. Tied to a child all day long, every day of the week, it's no joke. We'll take an early holiday.'

Miss Smith did feel tired, but she knew that it wasn't tiredness that was really the trouble. Her baby was almost three, and for two years she knew she had been making mistakes with him. Yet somehow she felt that they weren't her mistakes: it was as though some other person occasionally possessed her: a negligent, worthless kind of person who was cruel, almost criminal, in her carelessness. Once she had discovered the child crawling on the pavement beside his pram: she had forgotten apparently to attach his harness to the pram hooks. Once there had been beads in his pram, hundreds of them, small and red and made of glass. A woman had drawn her attention to the danger, regarding curiously the supplier of so unsuitable a plaything. 'In his nose he was putting one, dear. And may have swallowed a dozen already. It could kill a mite, you know.' The beads were hers, but how the child had got them she could not fathom. Earlier, when he had been only a couple of months, she had come into his nursery to find an excited cat scratching at the clothes of his cot; and on another occasion she had found him eating a turnip. She wondered if she might be suffering from some kind of serious absent-mindedness, or blackouts. Her doctor told her, uncomfortingly, that she was a little run down.

'I'm a bad mother,' said Miss Smith to herself; and she cried as she looked at her child, warm and pretty in his sleep.

But her carelessness continued and people remarked that it was funny in a teacher. Her husband was upset and unhappy, and finally suggested that they should employ someone to look after the child. 'Someone else?' said Miss Smith. 'Someone *else*? Am I then incapable? Am I so wretched and stupid that I cannot look after my own child? You speak to me as though I were half crazy.' She felt confused and sick and miserable. The marriage teetered beneath the tension, and there was no question of further children.

Then there were two months without incident. Miss Smith began to feel better; she was getting the hang of things; once again she was in control of her daily life. Her child grew and flourished. He trotted nimbly beside her, he spoke his own language, he was wayward and irresponsible, and to Miss Smith and her husband he was intelligent and full of charm. Every day Miss Smith saved up the sayings and doings of this child and duly reported them to her husband. 'He is quite intrepid,' Miss Smith said, and she told her husband how the child would tumble about the room, trying to stand on his head. 'He has an aptitude for athletics,' her husband remarked. They laughed that they, so unathletic in their ways, should have produced so physically lively an offspring.

'And how has our little monster been today?' Miss Smith's husband asked, entering the house one evening at his usual time.

Miss Smith smiled, happy after a good, quiet day. 'Like gold,' she said.

Her husband smiled too, glad that the child had not been a nuisance to her and glad that his son, for his own sake, was capable of adequate behaviour. 'I'll just take a peep at him,' he announced, and he ambled off to the nursery.

He sighed with relief as he climbed the stairs, thankful that all was once again well in the house. He was still sighing when he opened the nursery door and smelt gas. It hissed insidiously from the unlit fire. The room was sweet with it. The child, sleeping, sucked it into his lungs.

The child's face was blue. They carried him from the room, both of them helpless and inadequate in the situation. And then they waited, without speaking, while his life was recovered, until the moment when the doctor, white-coated and stern, explained that it had been a nearer thing than he would wish again to handle.

'This is too serious,' Miss Smith's husband said. 'We cannot continue like this. Something must be done.'

'I cannot understand—'

'It happens too often. The strain is too much for me, dear.'

'I cannot understand it.'

Every precaution had been taken with the gas-fire in the nursery. The knob that controlled the gas pressure was a key and the key was removable. Certainly, the control point was within the child's reach but one turned it on or off, slipped the key out of its socket and placed it on the mantelpiece. That was the simple rule.

'You forgot to take out the key,' Miss Smith's husband said. In his mind an idea took on a shape that frightened him. He shied away, watching it advance, knowing that he possessed neither the emotional nor mental equipment to fight it.

'No, no, no,' Miss Smith said. 'I never forget it. I turned

the fire off and put the key on the mantelpiece. I remember distinctly.'

He stared at her, drilling his eyes into hers, hopelessly seeking the truth. When he spoke his voice was dry and weary.

'The facts speak for themselves. You cannot suggest there's another solution?'

'But it's absurd. It means he got out of his cot, turned the key, returned to bed and went to sleep.'

'Or that you turned off the fire and idly turned it on again.'

'I couldn't have; how could I?'

Miss Smith's husband didn't know. His imagination, like a pair of calipers, grasped the ugly thought and held it before him. The facts were on its side, he could not ignore them: his wife was deranged in her mind. Consciously or otherwise she was trying to kill their child.

'The window,' Miss Smith said. 'It was open when I left it. It always is, for air. Yet you found it closed.'

'The child certainly could not have done that. I cannot see what you are suggesting.'

'I don't know. I don't know what I am suggesting. Except that I don't understand.'

'He is too much for you, dear, and that's all there is to it. You must have help.'

'We can't afford it.'

'Be that as it may, we must. We have the child to think of, if not ourselves.'

'But one child! One child cannot be too much for anyone. Look, I'll be extra careful in future. After all, it is the first thing like this that has happened for ages.'

'I'm sorry, dear. We must advertise for a woman.'

'Please—'

'Darling, I'm sorry. It's no use talking. We have talked enough and it has got us nowhere. This is something to be sensible about.'

'Please let's try again.'

'And in the meanwhile? In the meanwhile our child's life must be casually risked day in, day out?'

'No, no.'

Miss Smith pleaded, but her husband said nothing further. He pulled hard on his pipe, biting it between his jaws, unhappy and confused in his mind.

Miss Smith's husband did indeed advertise for a woman to see to the needs of their child, but it was, in fact, unnecessary in the long run to employ one. Because on his third birthday, late in the afternoon, the child disappeared. Miss Smith had put him in the garden. It was a perfectly safe garden: he played there often. Yet when she called him for his tea he did not come; and when she looked for the reason she found that he was not there. The small gate that led to the fields at the back of the house was open. She had not opened it; she rarely used it. Distractedly, she thought he must have managed to release the catch himself. 'That is quite impossible,' her husband said. 'It's too high and too stiff.' He looked at her oddly, confirmed in his mind that she wished to be rid of her child. Together they tramped the fields with the police, but although they covered a great area and were out for most of the night they were unsuccessful.

When the search continued in the light of the morning it was a search without hope, and the hopelessness in time turned into the fear of what discovery would reveal. 'We must accept the facts,' Miss Smith's husband said, but she alone continued to hope. She dragged her legs over the wide countryside, seeking a miracle but finding neither trace nor word of her child's wanderings.

A small boy, so quiet she scarcely noticed him, stopped her once by a sawmill. He spoke some shy salutation, and when she blinked her eyes at his face she saw that he was James Machen. She passed him by, thinking only that she envied him his life, that for him to live and her child to die was proof indeed of a mocking Providence. She prayed to this

Providence, promising a score of resolutions if only all would be well.

But nothing was well, and Miss Smith brooded on the thought that her husband had not voiced. *I released the gate myself. For some reason I have not wanted this child. God knows I loved him, and surely it wasn't too weak a love? Is it that I've loved so many other children that I have none left that is real enough for my own?* Pathetic, baseless theories flooded into Miss Smith's mind. Her thoughts floundered and collapsed into wretched chaos.

'Miss Smith,' James said, 'would you like to see your baby?'

He stood at her kitchen door, and Miss Smith, hearing the words, was incapable immediately of grasping their meaning. The sun, reflected in the kitchen, was mirrored again in the child's glasses. He smiled at her, more confidently than she remembered, revealing a silvery wire stretched across his teeth.

'What did you say?' Miss Smith asked.

'I said, would you like to see your baby?'

Miss Smith had not slept for a long time. She was afraid to sleep because of the nightmares. Her hair hung lank about her shoulders, her eyes were dead and seemed to have fallen back deeper into her skull. She stood listening to this child, nodding her head up and down, very slowly, in a mechanical way. Her left hand moved gently back and forth on the smooth surface of her kitchen table.

'My baby?' Miss Smith said. 'My baby?'

'You have lost your baby,' James reminded her.

Miss Smith nodded a little faster.

'I will show you,' James said.

He caught her hand and led her from the house, through the garden and through the gate into the fields. Hand in hand they walked through the grass, over the canal bridge and across the warm, ripe meadows.

'I will pick you flowers,' James said and he ran to gather poppies and cowparsley and blue, beautiful corn-flowers.

'You give people flowers,' James said, 'because you like them and you want them to like you.'

She carried the flowers and James skipped and danced beside her, hurrying her along. She heard him laughing; she looked at him and saw his small weasel face twisted into a merriment that frightened her.

The sun was fierce on Miss Smith's neck and shoulders. Sweat gathered on her forehead and ran down her cheeks. She felt it on her body, tightening her clothes to her back and thighs. Only the child's hand was cool, and beneath her fingers she assessed its strength, wondering about its history. Again the child laughed.

On the heavy air his laughter rose and fell; it quivered through his body and twitched lightly in his hand. It came as a giggle, then a breathless spasm; it rose like a storm from him; it rippled to gentleness; and it pounded again like the firing of guns in her ear. It would not stop. She knew it would not stop. As they walked together on this summer's day the laughter would continue until they arrived at the horror, until the horror was complete.